Based in northern New South Wales, Australia, Brianna Rankin is a full-time primary school teacher with a passion for history. After living in the United Kingdom, her interest in the medieval period was further piqued by the genealogical discovery that traces her family back to The Plantagenets. *Rawdendale* is Brianna's debut novel.

To my family, with much love.

Brianna Rankin

RAWDENDALE

The Insatiable King

AUSTIN MACAULEY PUBLISHERS™

LONDON * CAMBRIDGE * NEW YORK * SHARJAH

A CIP catalogue record for this title is available from the British Library.

ISBN 9781398495029 (Paperback)
ISBN 9781398495036 (ePub e-book)

www.austinmacauley.com

First Published 2024
Austin Macauley Publishers Ltd®
1 Canada Square
Canary Wharf
London
E14 5AA

This book would not have been possible without the support of the following people:

My family; for always encouraging me to pursue my dreams and supporting my creative outlet.

Maximilian, my partner and talented artist. Working together, we encapsulated key elements of the story through a stunning cover design.

My cousin, Matthew, for your historical expertise. Your knowledge and insight on these times amaze me.

Sara; for her literary advice when my novel was in its infancy. Your editorial guidance was invaluable.

Thank you to everyone at Austin Macauley Publishers for allowing my story to be told.

And to you, the reader. Thank you for taking this journey with me. Continue turning the pages.

Chapter One

Saxon had a bad death.

Unprepared and unforgiven.

In the fifteenth year of King Ivanhoe's reign, he had fallen on the Rawdendale marshes, a great warrior buried amidst the rushes, reeds and salty pannes. His body weakened from a stomach wound, he had crawled across the sodden ground towards the wretched cries of men. His men. The men he had sworn to protect.

He reached them not.

Invading first his limbs and then his heart, a powerful toxin seeped through Saxon's body. It caused his muscles to weaken and his chest to tighten, his mouth to burn and his skin to tingle. As the cries for help faded, sorrowful tears fell from his eyes, and he lay his head upon the peat and there stayed he until next day did break.

It was then, as daylight warmed the grassy fringe, there came by a passing stranger who captured the glint of armour and hastened to his aid. But the aid was cast aside for prayers instead and so it was that this stranger knelt beside the dying knight to the very end.

It was an end he did not deserve.

For Saxon was a trusted leader. A gentle knight. A valiant servant. No greater man could be found.

With a chivalric heritage, long and most revered, he had the trust of the king and affection of his fellow men. Having fought in countless battles, he was strong in faith and courageous on the battle field. He led the patrol of the Rawdendale borders, exercising authority over those who would wish harm upon his king.

The funeral procession, therefore, was monumental.

Honoured first in the chapel with prayers and hymns, he was taken then to the adjoining courtyard, to a burial plot lined with stone. Dressed in robes of black, priests carried painted crosses and vessels of holy water which they sprinkled liberally onto both body and plot.

Sombre were the words spoken as the trappings of the deceased: helm, sword and shield, were laid beside his grave. No longer would they sing.

Bells rung. Women wept. Monks chanted.

Amongst the mourners was Saxon's betrothed, Rosellene, her heart slowly crumbling.

Behind him, she had walked, as he was carried aloft on the reeds, his body now cold and wrapped in white shroud. Swollen eyes watched as the blue and white pall was withdrawn and they lowered his body into the earth.

She could not let him go.

Not yet. Not until she lay one final kiss upon his sweet lips. So, dropped she into the earthen hole, and leaned down to touch her lips to his.

Alas, he did not awaken. With silent screams, she was dragged from her love, hitting and kicking with what little strength remained.

'Leave her,' the queen waved her hand. 'Let her mourn for a time before the feast.'

Feast. Rosellene did not hunger for food nor wine, in fact, she did not hunger at all. Her mind clouded, she went not to the great hall following proceedings but towards a small wooden hut on the edge of the moat, her dubious chambermaid trailing behind.

'Please, my lady, do this not. The danger is high and should by chance you get caught…' Isabelle's hands shook, not merely from the cold. 'I dread to think what will become of you.'

If I am suspected of witchcraft, Rosellene thought, *they will search for abnormalities on my skin, a mark sufficient to indicate my association with the devil. I will be pricked with the sharpest of implements until I bleed not or tortured until a confession is given. Following my trial, merciless and unjust, I will be hanged, pressed or drowned.*

'They took me to the chapel.' Rosellene threw a satchel upon her shoulder. It smelt strongly of herbs. 'But I did not want to be consoled by God. He had hurt me and I resent him. Can what they say be true? God is opposed to magic. Is he punishing me for using it?'

'Best it be God and not another,' Isabelle suggested. 'Your life may be taken.'

A chill burrowed its way beneath the thick layers of Rosellene's clothing onto her pale skin. She shivered. She was a princess. Her life had already been taken.

'It will not be long before I am called to take another.' Rosellene cupped her hands around Isabelle's, hoping they did not betray her racing heart. 'I would rather die than marry a man I do not love. My fate, nay, the fate of Rawdendale depends on it.'

'My lady, is this not hasty?' Isabelle paused. 'Lord Bannock may be an honourable man.'

Honourable? Rosellene all but choked.

John Bannock was the lord of McLean Manor, a rich estate on the Rawdendale borders. For a man of money, John was quite slovenly, eating too much and often sleeping in the stable with his horses. He wore ill-fitting clothes, taut around his stodgy stomach and his thick beard was wild and unruly, absorbing all manner of food when he ate.

John was quite obsessed with gaining Rosellene's affections. Rosellene, however, thought him quite repulsive, thwarting his advances.

'The man is an evil, greedy boar. I would like nothing better than to have his head mounted on the wall in my chamber.'

Perhaps not in my chamber, Rosellene reconsidered. *For then, I would have to lay eyes upon his wretched face day after day.*

'It is a sin, of this I know yet I see no other way forward,' Rosellene lamented. 'Once this spell is cast, I do declare, I shall turn to magic no more.'

Isabelle dropped her head. 'Very well, my lady.'

With the hood of her mantle pulled over dark, velvety hair, Rosellene unleashed a vessel from its rope moorings and guided it gently into the moat across to the forest on the other side. Through the thickets of briars and moss-covered pathways crept she, until the ancient ruins of what was once the original castle of Rawdendale was reached. It was here, on an altar of stone, her spell was cast.

With the spell nine times repeated and her belongings collected, Rosellene furtively moved back through the forest, quite bedraggled, angered that she had resorted to the use of magic.

When the door to the hut swung open sometime later, Isabelle was found pacing back and forth across the dirt floor, a shallow furrow developing beneath her.

'I feared you dead!' Isabelle exclaimed. She looked upon Rosellene's tattered clothes. 'Pray tell me what happened?'

'Much, dear Isabelle, but I dare not speak it now, for fear we are already late. We shall not want to be later still.'

With much haste, they returned to the castle. Entering the keep via the well, they moved through the enclosed passageway from kitchen to great hall and began their ascent up the spiral staircase to Rosellene's chamber. By now, the dampness of Rosellene's clothing was making her uncomfortable and she shivered inside the castle's stone walls.

Should her father see the state of the dress, he would be most oppressed. Spending a small fortune on fine cloths sourced from all over the country, the king had oft been heard to say that Rosellene would be better off wearing a suit of armour.

With the thought of a warm hearth on Rosellene's mind, the two were stopped only a few feet from the chamber door.

The queen stepped from the shadows into the corridor. 'Dare I ask?'

'It is better that you do not,' Rosellene admitted, trying to cover her battered dress with her mantle.

'Your absence did not go unnoticed.'

'There is no place for joy at this time,' Rosellene told her mother. 'I wanted not to feign happiness when all I feel is sorrow.'

The queen's expression remained indifferent.

'One could conclude you do not like the privileged life you lead. Perhaps it is you whom should be punished for your reckless behaviour and not your chambermaid?'

Rosellene fell to her knees. 'Please, I beg you.'

The queen tutted; her tone harsh. 'Away with you then, quickly, before your father finds you.'

But with the door handle in reach, Rosellene faltered yet again as her father, the king, stepped from his chamber. Having just written an important letter to be sent to McLean Manor, the king handed the sealed envelope to a courier waiting outside his chamber, then turned to his daughter.

'It appears you wrestled a lion and Isabelle did not?' His deep and guttural voice echoed through the corridor. Standing at over six-feet tall, his broad shoulders were intensified further by the fur-trimmed cloak that covered them. Rosellene feared him not. Despite his harsh exterior, there was a softness within.

'No, Father,' said Rosellene, quickly contriving an excuse. 'I fell into a briar and Isabelle helped me free.'

The king looked down upon his daughter's garment. His brown eyes softened.

'This briar must have been grand,' he said, at war with a smile that threatened his face. 'that it tore your dress to such threads and took you near on a day to escape.'

'Extensive, Father,' said Rosellene, gesturing as to the size of the briar with her hands.

The king nodded unconvincingly. 'I should like to hear more about it sometime.'

'And you shall, dear Father,' said Rosellene, reaching again for the handle of her chamber door. 'On the morrow, I promise.'

The king's neatly groomed moustache rose slightly, his mouth hinting at a smile. With hands clasped behind his back, he turned and strolled back along the corridor.

Next morning, Rosellene was awoken, not by the sun streaming onto her face, but by Isabelle's shriek as she drew back the window's thick drapes.

'My lady, how quickly does your spell work?'

Rosellene sat up in bed. 'Forthwith. Why ask you this?'

Isabelle turned her worried face to Rosellene. 'A visitor is nigh.'

'At this early hour?' Rolling back the layers of sheets, Rosellene stepped from her bed and hastened to the window. 'Heavens, no!'

The curtains were drawn abruptly.

'Alas, magic has failed me,' Rosellene drew in a short breath. 'I shall depend on it no more.'

'Perhaps he is here on other business?' Isabelle whispered.

'Let us be sure.' Rosellene swiftly dropped a narrow-fitting dress with a V-shaped waist over her smock and ran from the room.

The cabinet, a private meeting space for the king, was positioned on the keep's upper floor. Elaborately styled and furnished with books, it adjoined both the king's chamber and the solar. It was here, beneath a wall hanging in the solar, that a small crack in the mortar had appeared.

Not large enough to peer through, it was however, useful for eaves dropping on interesting conversations. While Rosellene did just that, taking in all that was said between her father and Lord Bannock, Isabelle kept watch by the door.

'As you know, I am a man of wealth,' Bannock began. 'I have in my possession land, property and the services of some fifteen vassals. While the death of Sir Saxon was certainly a great loss, it does however, leave your daughter without a suiter. I may not display the prowess of Saxon in battle, yet the virtues I have are high and I assure you I can provide for your daughter most generously.'

There came a screech upon the stone floor, followed by the sound of footsteps clinking back and forth across the room. Rosellene could tell her father was mulling the thought over in his mind, his hands, most likely, clasped behind his back, rolling the many gold rings upon his fingers. 'That you could.'

Threads loosened from the tapestry now gripped tightly in Rosellene's hand. Her chest felt constricted, as though it were caught in a vice. Voices and sounds seemed to grow distant as a feeling of light-headedness swept over Rosellene.

Her brain deprived of oxygen, she stumbled momentarily then would have collapsed if not for Isabelle, who having seen the tapestry tear from the wall, hastened to Rosellene's aid. For a time, she could see nothing but a veil of white before her eyes. Then, slowly the veil shattered into smaller fragments until fading entirely.

'Thank you, Lord Bannock.'

But what was said? Rosellene thought. An exhalation, long and loud, escaped her dry lips. *Am I to marry Lord Bannock? Did father agree to his terms?*

'I am endowed with an extensive estate,' added Lord Bannock. 'I can support a wife.'

'I will put your offer forward and consider it in due course.'

'God's blessing to you then.' Bannock bowed to the king.

'And to you.'

Back in her chamber, slumped in the folding armchair, Rosellene gazed absently at the wall. *Why is my identity dependent upon my father and in turn, my husband, should one be taken? Am I simply expected to be a child bearer, humble and most obedient?*

'If I am to marry, it shall not be to a short, hefty man who cannot bear the weight of his own longsword but to a man most handsome. He shall be tall and strong with every quality of a knight.'

'You are very specific, my lady,' Isabelle noted. She feared, after Saxon, there may not be another so suited.

'I know what I want. Marriage should be a union of love and not one of convenience for one's family.'

'While a man may possess many of those qualities, it is rare that he possesses them all.'

'Then I shall not marry.'

Of course, she knew this not to be true. With no male heirs, the lands of Rawdendale would only be passed to Rosellene on condition of marriage.

Isabelle paused. Her long hair had loosened and now she brushed back several golden-brown waves that hung over her shoulder. 'Would you not regret that, my lady?'

But there were other more pressing thoughts invading Rosellene's mind.

'Let us not think on marriage now,' she said, standing by the window, watching Bannock squeeze his way into the saddle. 'I must leave, before the throbbing in my head becomes unbearable.' She closed her eyes to block out the view.

'To get some air, my lady?' Isabelle hoped. 'To clear your mind?'

'Leave Rawdendale.'

Isabelle gasped. 'You cannot leave, my lady. You are the princess.'

'And that, dear Isabelle, is exactly why I must leave.'

Chapter Two

Rawdendale Castle was once an imposing figure. Set on a rocky pinnacle on the small island of Anu, its outer defence walls stood strong amidst four towers and a gatehouse. Of late, however, it bore the scars of battles lost.

Decorative windows that had adorned the main building lay shattered on the stone floor. Elaborate garden beds of roses and mazes were now overgrown by weeds, and sections of the surrounding moat, fed by the river, were near dry.

Ivanhoe was Rawdendale's king, a generous and noble man whose mildness had sadly brought upon his demise. Now at war with neighbouring King Tyrone, a hardened, greedy man who had killed his own son on claims of treachery, Ivanhoe sought to strengthen his brethren, and in doing so, pull his kingdom free from misery. A bid was made for the services of a young knight, renowned for his valour in combat. His name, Caprion of Green Mere.

Caprion was the son of Addison, a knight in the royal household of Beaumont, whom had been killed whilst defending the queen during a staged kidnapping. At the time Caprion had been a squire, merely fourteen years old. He had accompanied his father escorting the queen to her summer palace in Angelmoss and borne witness to the horrendous murder that befell him.

With nothing more than quilted armour and a belt knife, he had taken charge of the carriage horses and led the queen to safety. For this act of bravery, he had been dubbed a knight and earned a place within the royal household.

Now it was on this day in late June, a bitter wind in the air, that Caprion made his way to Rawdendale Castle. Through field, forest and valleys did he ride on a warhorse dark as the night sky, until he came upon a marsh on the outskirts of the castle. Here, struggling waist deep in the foul-smelling mud, he found a young lady alongside a white mare. With a heel to his horse's flanks, Caprion hastened to the lady's aid.

'Take my hand,' he offered, bounding from his horse in a single movement. 'I will pull you free.' But the lady waved him away.

'My lady,' Caprion took a pace back. 'Do you not seek aid?'

The lady, whose beauty Caprion had not seen matched elsewhere despite the brown speckles, took from the ground a handful of mud and through ruby-red lips so oft to pout said, 'On the contrary, it is good for the skin.'

Thick and oozing, the mud was smeared across her forehead.

Caprion's concerned eyes soon began to chuckle. He bowed his head and stepped backwards towards the horse. 'I bid you farewell then.'

But the mud bound her legs then seized her waist and would not let go.

It seemed to be swallowing her piece by piece and the more she tried to wriggle free, the deeper she became entrenched until at last, with deepest regret, she found herself calling for the knight's help.

'Please, leave not.'

Caprion leaned closer. 'You seek aid, my lady?'

Lips pursed. Blood simmered. 'Do not make me say it again. I will not beg.'

Caprion could tell by her voice that she was not pleased to accept his help, yet he edged nearer still and extended his hand once again. 'Surely your horse did not stray this far from the path.'

Without an upwards glance, the young lady replied, 'It has been said that the marsh cannot be ridden across.'

'Now you are satisfied it is so?'

'On the contrary,' the lady moved across to her mare and stepping into the saddle said, 'Now I am even more determined.'

With that, the young lady rode off towards the castle, hopeful never to see the arrogant man again.

Caprion slipped his soft leather boots into the enclosed stirrups. 'So, I shall see you on the morrow.'

King Ivanhoe was waiting for Caprion's arrival when he entered the castle gates. Dressed in emerald green, Queen Sophia stood by his side along with an entourage of no fewer than seven knights, three squires and a footman.

'Your arrival brings much joy, Caprion of Green Mere,' said the king.

Caprion made to curtsy before king and queen. 'It pleases me also to be in your service.'

Caprion stood. Catching sight of the mud on his cloak, he was most abashed. 'You must forgive my attire. On my coming, I passed a young lady caught in the marsh. She seemed quite determined to ride across it.'

On hearing this, the queen put a hand to her mouth and gasped. 'The sign of a true knight. I am certain the young lady was obliged by your kindness, dear Caprion.'

Caprion shook his head. 'I do believe I may have hampered her aims, my lady.'

'Stubbornness,' was the queen's reply.

'Indeed,' Caprion agreed.

The king looped his thumbs into the braided belt upon his hips. 'A quality sadly shared by our daughter.'

It was at this time that the king spied his daughter near the stables and beckoned her nearer. The king's daughter, however, pretended not to hear her father's call and continued inside the stable, to which her father beseeched her company louder still.

'Come hither, daughter.'

Head lowered, the king's daughter came nearer. 'I feel it best that I stay where I am.'

The king, at this point, was beginning to tire of his daughter's objections. 'First you offend our guest by your absence, then you distance yourself!'

'But, Father…' At the sight of two raised eyebrows the king's daughter moved towards her parents. 'I will come, Father, but not alone.'

For the entourage, the stench of mud was quite unbearable. They edged away. In unison, the king and queen sighed.

'I fear you may have already met our daughter.' The king lowered his head. 'Caprion of Green Mere, I give you Princess Rosellene.'

With breath held slightly, Caprion took Rosellene's hand and gently kissed it.

'Look now,' scolded the king. 'You have soiled his face. Be gone, child. Wash yourself clean of the stench.'

'I hear it is good for the skin,' remarked Caprion, sharing a smile with Rosellene before she hurried off to wash.

Once in her chamber Rosellene made to remove her soiled dress and set about washing herself clean. The stench, however, seemed not to offend Isabelle. In fact, she was accustomed to it by now.

For you see, it had been months since Rosellene learned of the impossibility of riding across the marsh. This of course she took as a challenge and had since that day been attempting to prove the naysayer wrong.

At arm's length, Isabelle held the soiled dress. Carefully, it was dropped into a bucket of water to soak. 'Success, my lady?'

'Had it not been for a certain interfering knight, it may have been so,' snapped Rosellene. She looked at Isabelle's raised eyebrows then continued. 'Like everyone else, he does not believe the marsh can be ridden across.'

Isabelle nodded then turned her face away, a cheeky grin beginning to tiptoe onto her lips.

'You are amused?'

Isabelle stared at the floor. 'No, my lady.'

'I refuse to be told what to do. It is not fair that our lives be dictated by whether we are man or woman.'

Standing now in her whalebone corset, laced together at the back and joined with a series of eyelets to her petticoat, Rosellene threw her hands on her hips. 'I will not sit in one's parlour embroidering whilst the men hold secret meetings. What knowledge of war tactics can be gained through needle work?'

'None, my lady.' Isabelle let a clean dress fall onto Rosellene's delicate figure and fastened the garment at the neck.

'I am intrigued by this knight though, *Caprion of Green Mere*.' She spoke his name as though it were the title of a grand novel then pondered on it for some time. 'He is tainted by arrogance however, certainly an undesirable quality.'

'What of this knight, my lady?' Isabelle asked. 'Do you believe he is the one to save Rawdendale from ruin?'

Rosellene moved to the padded stool so that Isabelle could comb her hair. Although there was a mirror affixed to the dresser, she stared not at Isabelle but at the flounces in her dress, plucking at a few loose threads. 'Time will tell. He is after all just a knight like all the others.'

'What does he look like, my lady?' Isabelle asked. Rosellene glanced up. 'In case I come across him and need to make an address. It would be impolite not to know his features.'

Rosellene looked again upon her dress. 'Tall. Slender. His hair is short yet full of golden curls and his eyes are brown like those of my father's.'

Isabelle tried not to smile. Caprion sounded most handsome.

Chapter Three

In his chamber, a room grander than any he had seen before, Caprion rested a hand upon one of the six-foot-high bedposts draped with rich cloth. He was about to sit upon the fine satin covers when the chamber door opened and in walked a maid. Caprion watched her stack blocks of wood in the kindling box by the hearth, then move to roll down the bed's thick quilting.

The maid's gaze fell upon the small travel roll on the floor. 'You have more luggage to come, my lord?'

Caprion shook his head. Armour, clothing, bedding. He had no need for more. He believed that the more one possessed, the more could be taken.

'You have something to wear to the ball, do you not?' The maid's large eyes grew wider still when Caprion merely glanced down at the clothes he wore. There were still a few mud splashes here and there but it was the finest tunic he owned.

'Heavens above, this will never do.' The maid hurried out of the room mumbling to herself. Some moments later, a tuft of grey hair peered back around the door. 'Red or blue, my lord?'

Caprion turned to the maid, his forehead creased. 'Red or blue?'

'The colour of your tunic.' There was an excited look in her eyes. 'Do you wish it red or blue?'

'I have a choice?' Caprion was most alarmed. He could make decisions on the battlefield, yet when it came to fashion, he was not at all skilled.

The maid just shook her head and said, 'Blue it is.'

Caprion had barely turned once around the room when the maid returned to the chamber, arms laden with an assortment of pins, needles, tape and the finest of blue cloth.

'Arms out.' But when Caprion failed to move, she pulled the measuring tape from her shoulders and extended it. 'So that I may measure you up.'

Although he did as he was asked, Caprion was most pleased when the measuring tape was again around the maid's shoulders and the whistling subsided. *She seemed to enjoy the process far more than one should,* he thought.

The maid smiled discretely. It was true. She need not have measured him at all, for she was in fact a fine seamstress, and could tell simply by looking at him what size the tunic should be.

Caprion reached for his money pouch but the maid held up her hand. 'Put away your coins.'

Caprion loosened the leather drawstring on the pouch. 'I pay my way.'

'You are a guest of King Ivanhoe. He would not take kindly to the thought of you paying for your garments,' she remarked then ushered him out the door. 'Away with you now. I will call when it is ready.'

Choosing to wander the tower, Caprion had made his way to the first of three State Rooms. It was here that Rosellene found him, gazing at a large oil painting. The painting was a portrait of an elderly man, a golden crown resting upon his head.

In his right hand, he held a longsword with a cross-guard hilt, the polished metal engraved with some form of lettering, too small to distinguish. He was seated upon a highly decorated throne, coronets carved into the wood. The expression on his face was grim. His skin was thick and leathery, his beard long and wiry, and he scowled as if someone had stolen something important.

'That is King Simon,' said Rosellene. She walked down the stone steps to join Caprion by the painting. 'Certainly not a well-liked man.'

Caprion turned to Rosellene who now stood beside one of the eight pillars in the room. 'Few men in position of nobility are.'

'Are you familiar with the story of The Insatiable King?'

Caprion shook his head. 'I am not.'

Rosellene led him across to the seat beneath the grand stained window and told to him the story of her ancestry.

'While there are many tales of The Insatiable King, few know the truth about how his wealth was won and lost. Over the years, the castle overflowed with gold, silver and more jewels than there were stars in the sky. But there was one jewel that shone brighter than them all. One jewel that the king kept hidden away.

Inside the castle there were three chambers, each closed by a different coloured door. On the left was found a red door, to the right a blue door and in the centre, a door of solid bronze.

The key to the red door hung on a chain around the guard. The key to the bronze door sat on the ledge above the very door. But the key to the blue door was found on a thick, gold chain around the king's neck, for it was here beyond the blue door, in a solid marble crypt that a ruby lay.

It weighed more than a small child, or so it was told, as no one but the king had laid eyes on the ruby. But there were those who had heard of the stone and planned to trick the king into bringing it to them.

One morning, whilst out for a ride, a peddler said to the king, "Why is it you keep that ruby hidden away? Would it not be the envy of all those in the land? Why not have me carve part of it into a fine ring so that all may see it on your finger and marvel at its beauty. What remains of the stone could then be returned to the chamber from whence it came".

So the king thought on it for a time. How he would like a ruby ring to place on his hand beside the rings of emerald and sapphire. He wondered what price a ring such as this would fetch. So the king asked the peddler, "What price would a ring such as this be?"

"I am but a poor peddler your majesty. I ask for nothing more than sufficient money for lodging, to purchase a horse and some seed so that I may have food".'

Captivated by Rosellene's melodic voice Caprion nodded, and although he was listening, his thoughts were not on the story being told.

'The king agreed to the peddler's demands and returned home to collect his prized ruby and three bags of gold. He then set out to find the peddler who had said he could be found by passing over the three stone bridges that lead to the village of Tableton. However, the peddler had failed to advise the king that while the three stone bridges led to the village of Tableton, they were narrow and old and there were miles and miles of valleys beneath each bridge.

And so it was that the peddler had tricked the poor king. With his horse already in the deep ravine, the king clung to the mountainside as the peddler watched on. He claimed that the king was far too heavy and begged him to throw up a bag of gold.

The king did just that and the peddler reached out for the king's hand and tried to pull him from the mountainside but again he claimed the king too heavy. This time the king threw up two bags of gold. But alas, the peddler could not rescue the king.

"Perhaps," said the peddler with a glint in his eye. "If you pass me the ruby, the weight will be less."

At this, the king became red with rage for he realised he had been tricked and that the peddler had planned to take the ruby all along. Delving into his saddlebag, the king pulled the ruby free with one hand. "The ruby belongs to me". And then the king released his grasp on the mountain and fell to his death, the ruby shattering into millions of tiny pieces.'

Her story complete, Rosellene leaned against the window. Caprion had not shifted the entire time. Not a muscle.

Had Father Michael's congregation been thus well behaved during the Latin teachings of mass, he would have been pleased, she thought.

'And should we all understand the moral of the story,' said Caprion. 'the world would truly be a better place.'

Heart in her throat, Rosellene diverted her eyes then said, 'I could not agree more.'

'Walk with me,' said Caprion, gesturing towards the entrance. 'I would like to know some more of Rawdendale. I hear the grounds are quite spectacular.'

There came a wrinkle to Rosellene's nose and she paused. She could not tell him it was all a facade. That beyond the manicured lawns, velvet to the touch, there lay a forest overgrown. Cast in shadows and crawling with infestation, the secrets held within were many.

'They were spectacular,' corrected Rosellene. 'When The Insatiable King fell, he took not only the ruby but also the key to the chamber. It was not long before Rawdendale began to suffer from the absence of this wealth.'

Casting his gaze upon the symmetrical garden beds before him, Caprion thought on the chamber. *Without a key, sheer force would allow entry to most chambers.* 'The door could not be unlocked without the key?'

'Since that day no one has laid eyes upon the door. We are not even sure if it exists.'

Caprion smiled. To him, wealth was more than sparkling trinkets and oversized crystals. Already he had seen Rawdendale's treasure. He would protect her with his life.

'Come,' said Caprion, extending his arm. 'Show me your home.'

With quickening heart, Rosellene interlaced her slender arm with his and together they walked from the arched room outside. Instantly they were bathed in sunlight, the strong smell of orange blossoms ingested.

'Surely that beyond the castle wall is greater than what we offer here.'

'You have warmth, protection, security,' said Caprion. 'Out there, you fend for yourself.'

For a moment, Rosellene was lost in her own thoughts. It was rare that she was able to venture far beyond the castle grounds and never alone. She had visions of such splendour and longed to hear more. She also wondered what truth lay in the songs of the bards, whose lyrics depicted Caprion as a wise and generous knight who travelled to far off lands to fight in great wars.

'Tell me of your adventures, Sir Caprion. I would truly like to hear about them.' But Caprion was most humble and did not like to talk of himself at length.

'Let me not bore you with such tales.'

Rosellene tightened her grip on his arm. 'It would not be a bore, I assure you,' she said, a slight twinkle in her blue eyes. 'Little happens in these walls to excite, at least nothing that bards would consider suitable for poetry. Tell me how you fought off a dozen men with your bare hands and gallantly led your men to victory at Bresingdon.'

A deep chuckle erupted from Caprion's belly. He had heard many far-fetched tales of his heroism but still they never ceased to amuse him. 'You forgot that I also slayed a dragon and rescued a maiden from the clouds themselves.'

Caprion watched as the twinkle in Rosellene's eyes seemed to fade. Her naivety was rare indeed. 'My life is devoted to the service of my king and my God. There is little sleep, minimal comfort and I can have no dreams of my own until those of the king are fulfilled. A glamorous lifestyle it is not.'

Rosellene sat now beneath the arbour upon a hardened bench. 'Then why a knight, Sir Caprion? Why not a blacksmith or a fletcher?'

'My father was a knight in the royal household of Beaumont. He was a most humble and honourable man. It was all I longed to be. Like him, I wanted to protect those who could not protect themselves.'

'Like your mother?'

Rosellene turned away. She had not meant her words to be spoken aloud. It was knowledge she should not have. 'I had heard she was taken from you after the death of your father.'

Caprion looked towards the clear, cloudless sky. He could almost smell the hollyhocks his mother used to pick, weaved into a garland and worn upon her auburn hair.

'I lost both my father and my mother within days of each other.'

Rosellene knew of his mother and the place she dwelled. She had seen it all when Caprion reached for her hand and pulled her free from the mud. With just a touch of his hand, she had touched his soul. She would not tell him so though.

Women should not be seeing the future, nor the past. They were to be ladies and doting wives, forever doing what they were told.

If I ruled, thought Rosellene, *of which I long not to, it shall be my orders people obey.*

Chapter Four

In the inner ward, below the king's chamber, stood the great hall. Emblazoned on the whitewashed walls hung painted cloths of blue and white, tapestries and shields depicting the royal household coat of arms. Often the sleeping quarters for servants, tonight, the great hall was to be the focus of a grand and elegant celebration.

Written on the finest of parchment and sealed with the king's crest, invitations had been sent to all the dukes, counts and barons in the kingdom, calling them forth to join in the celebration for the coming of Caprion.

Outside, in the small orchard, provisions were being gathered for a glorious menu of five removes. The recipes called for an array of oranges, apples, lemons and pomegranates, which were all picked and carried inside in wicker baskets to the kitchen cooks. Likewise, in the kitchen garden, onions, leeks, beetroot, carrots and garlic were being selected for their use.

Inside the great hall, servants busied themselves ensuring that the hall was not only clean but appealing to the senses. The long wooden trestle tables were covered with white linen and positioned around the edge of the large room with space made in the centre for entertainment and dancing.

The bare stone floors were strewn with mint, lavender and sweet-smelling rose-petals, their fresh aroma masking the foul smell that lingered well after the dogs had left. The fireplace (the largest in the castle) was laid and fifty beeswax candles were placed on the circular holders that hung from the loft ceiling.

Isabelle added a decorative jewelled headpiece to a hairstyle that had taken close to two hours to complete. Parted down the centre then plaited with interwoven ribbon and coiled over the ears, Rosellene's dark hair was dressed with pearls and covered with a fine gold hairnet. Coated lightly with powder, her face gleamed in the light from the hearth.

Dressed in fine silk material, crimped from sleeve to ankle, Rosellene was helped into a highly decorated corsage that was slipped over the gown and fastened. Upon her narrow hips was placed a belt made from goat hide. As she made her way down the spiral staircase to the great hall, she could hear the merriment of one hundred and eleven guests as they drank the fine ale that had been laid out for them.

She paused at the arched doorway, a frown upon her face. How she hated these affairs. What a chore it was having to smile, be polite and watch while good men turned into wild animals over the course of an evening.

Nonetheless, she instructed Isabelle to draw the heavy drapes and walked into the great hall, head held high, hoping that Caprion might provide a reprise from such boring proceedings. As the herald announced her arrival, silence fell on the crowd. Heads bowed. The guests stood and waited for Rosellene to move across the dais to her seat at the top table.

Caprion too was standing, his head gently bowed. The navy tunic fitted him well.

With raised tankard, the king stood and proclaimed, 'Let the feast begin!'

From the kitchen, a sea of servants came, arms held high with stuffed chickens, veal, hare and steaming pies, all served on the finest of wooden platters. With a centrepiece of roasted peacock, adorned with its own beautiful blue plumage and jellies fancifully shaped as lions, swans and dragons, there was little room left on the tables.

When the last of the sugared plums had been plucked from the king's plate and eaten, he wiped his mouth clean with a cloth napkin and stood, quietening the hall.

'Good ladies and gents. I thank you all for joining me in what has so far been a most splendid evening. I would like to welcome Caprion to the Rawdendale household, and pray that God bless and protect him during his time here.'

'Hosar!' cried the crowd, mugs raised.

But while most were comforted by Caprion's arrival and the thought that one day soon their kingdom would return to its rightful state, one-man scorned Caprion's presence at Rawdendale, his gaze barely shifting from the head table. This had not gone unnoticed. On several occasions throughout the evening, Caprion had caught sight of Lord Bannock's penetrating gaze and wondered had they met sometime in battle?

His face was not recalled but the look upon it was unforgettable, and although Bannock smiled as he tipped his mug, Caprion feared he was much disliked.

'Why is it that this man is revered like none other?' Bannock asked, taking a long sip of ale. 'Am I not a fine knight?'

Seated beside him Eric, a member of the royal guards, nodded. 'Indeed you are, my lord. You would rival any here in the kingdom.'

'Why then, Eric, do I sit with the paupers of this kingdom instead of being dignified with a seat at the head table?' Bannock thrust the bench backwards across the stone floor and stood, mug in hand. 'A toast.'

The room fell silent. 'To Caprion!'

Mugs were raised. Ale sipped.

Caprion nodded in appreciation then turned to Rosellene. 'A most true and virtuous man.'

'Some would disagree,' admitted Rosellene and she fidgeted with her jewelled coronet. How she wished she had concealed a thrusting knife within.

Bannock was neither true nor virtuous. He was, moreover, sly, cunning and most deceitful. During a great battle fought on enemy grounds in which Rawdendale had been victorious, Eldon (the current leader of the guards) had been unaccounted for. Finding him deep in combat with the enemy, Bannock watched on as a bloody fight erupted. With his right hand severed, Eldon fought bravely, using his left hand to deliver a most powerful strike that brought his opponent to the ground. Then, with one swift movement, he raised his sword and thrust it between steel collar and cuirass, deep into his opponent's neck, killing him instantly. Himself wounded, Eldon crumbled to the ground, a mass of blood and dented armour.

Comforted in the arms of Bannock, he handed his sword over asking that it be given to his son, Oliver. But as Eldon slipped away and a group of men descended upon the scene, Bannock took the sword and retained it for his own, claiming that he had overthrown the enemy trying to save Eldon's life. For this act of bravery, Eldon had given him the sword, asking that Bannock take his position as commander.

With the final dishes tabled and servants dismissed, the queen bade the players fetch instruments and the dancing began. Despite such gaiety in the room, Rosellene still seemed forlorn, her gaze fixed on the three small finches confined to the cage in front of her. She watched as they flitted from one perch to the next, barely able to stretch their wings.

'You seem troubled, my lady,' Caprion observed. 'And I fear it is not the birds in this cage that have your mind perplexed.'

'It is true,' Rosellene sighed, turning her eyes to Caprion. 'The birds remind me of my life. How like a cage this castle is to me.'

'There are much worse than fine clothes, food and company outside the castle walls. Think not of these walls as your cage but a place you can return to after having spread your wings.'

'You are blessed though,' Rosellene paused, the candlelight hitting the rouge on her high cheekbones. 'You can move from place to place at will. I, however, have a chain around my ankle that tugs sternly when I stray too far.'

Caprion moved nearer Rosellene, his almond-coloured eyes full of mystery. 'Should you ever want to stray that little bit farther, I am certain I could convince the king.'

Rosellene could hardly breathe with excitement, her heart all a flutter. 'You believe it could be so?'

'All you have to do is open the door.' With that, Caprion released the clasp on the cage and the birds flew out into the great hall.

'Would you care to dance, my lady?' Caprion asked, standing.

Well trained in the art of dance, Caprion took Rosellene in his right hand and led her to the floor. Here they joined seven other couples and danced in procession to music played on flute, fiddle and lute. For several hours, they danced to the pleasant melodies, repeating combinations of pivots, hops and jumps and weaving intricate patterns with ribbons, which they skilfully unravelled. On their toes, they moved stately and dignified and each time the music ceased, the women curtseyed and the men bowed.

To end the evening a minstrel, who whilst playing a harp, told a tale of a chivalrous knight who could not be beaten in combat. So feared and rivalled by his enemy that he was called to fight a duel on the river Dale which sadly brought his death.

The king turned to Caprion to gauge his response. He was surprised when no applause was given.

'Pray, Caprion, did you not enjoy the story?'

'It was a fine story indeed, your highness. I only question the knight's death.'

With a hand to his bearded chin, the king said, 'You believe it should have ended differently?'

'Indeed,' Caprion walked towards the minstrel. 'The way I heard it, the hero was told of a jousting match on the river Dale. When he arrived on the bridge, mounted wearing full armour, his opponent was not on horseback but on boat.

Despite being unprepared for such an event, the hero moved forth to the riverbed and stepped into a long boat.

Equipped with two men, he paddled towards his opponent into the deepest part of the river. Once there, the men cast their oars into the water and then dived in themselves. As the hero's opponent approached at tremendous speed, the boat he was in began to take on water through a hole deliberately made.

While trying to plug the hole, the hero was hit directly in the helmet. The dent so severe that try as he may, the helmet could not be removed. The boat sank, as did the hero, to the bottom of the river, drowned or so his opponent believed, for how, wearing such heavy armour and a helmet so damaged that its removal was impossible, could he survive?'

All was quiet in the great hall. Then, a chuckle echoed.

'Only fools joust on water.' Bannock took a swig of cider then stood. He turned to Caprion and said, 'I do not rely on stories to defend my reputation.'

'And yet your reputation relies on just that. A story.' Caprion paused. 'If the sword were a wordsmith, would it write a different story?'

Bannocks eyes narrowed and his skin looked pale green.

'I proclaim a tournament be run,' he cried, stepping up onto the table top. 'Let us determine the better man.'

So it was to be, two months hence, that the king announced a tournament.

Chapter Five

Word soon spread of the proclaimed jousting tournament taking place in the grounds of Rawdendale Castle. Notified by heralds, nobles far and wide sought their finest knights and bade them prepare for the event. From Dew Fortress, Lord Elliot sent Sir Drake; a fair-haired man of twenty-three, known for his gallantry during battle. From Marburg Court came Sir Griffin, Lord Marburg's son, a true champion in all manner of combat, despite being short in stature. Two brothers came from Dawson Keep, Sir Casper and Sir Constantine. Standing around six-foot-tall, these robust men had both tremendous strength and stamina. Mounted on horses specifically bred to carry the weight of man and armour, the brothers were fierce contenders.

To the west, from McLean Manor came John Bannock himself, clad in a newly made suit of armour. Crafted from the wood of a poplar tree and covered in red leather, Lord Bannock's shield was fashioned with a white boar.

The tournament also attracted many mercenary soldiers, of which in the lists there were at least fifty, who fought solely for the prizes. Then there were those from Rawdendale; Sir Franco the Brave, Sir Caprion of Green Mere and a newly dubbed knight, barely seventeen years of age named Sir Tristan of Dunnperry.

On the morning of the procession, Rosellene had woken early. Disturbed yet again by the same vivid dream, she had washed, dressed and taken the stairs to the observatory to seek the guidance of a very old friend.

Nicholas Cooper was a stargazer. An inventor who catalogued signs written in the cosmos. He had spent his life making connections between the stars and events on earth. Should one be looking for advice on sowing, harvesting or perhaps a glimpse into the future, then Nicholas could be of great assistance. For a fee of course. He was a jolly soul whom Rosellene had come to love and adore, tall and slender with a silvery beard which brushed the floor when he walked. His round spectacles were always dirty and seemed to be forever sliding down his pointed nose, and his appearance was as unkempt as his room.

As the thick wooden door heaved open, Nicholas' room seemed to come alive. Spiders danced across their webs, moths fluttered in large glass jars and metal contraptions creaked and chimed.

Nicholas, however, was nowhere to be seen.

Running her fingers across one of the many rows of books that lined the walls from floor to ceiling, Rosellene randomly pulled a title from the shelf. Holding the twisted spine in her hands, she let the pages drop open and watched the dust particles rise into the air.

'An interesting read,' said Nicholas, his head peering from behind a gigantic uncurled map. 'The one to its right may interest you more though.'

Angels and where to find them, the title read.

A grin crept upon Rosellene's face. Nicholas had always called her his little angel. He had even named a constellation of stars after her.

'My dear Rosellene.' The map was laid upon an already busy desk. Lines criss-crossed the parchment. 'I have just unravelled a mystery!'

'Mystery?' Rosellene questioned. It was then that she noticed Nicholas' bare feet. 'Nicholas, your shoes.'

Glancing above his streaky spectacles Nicholas said, 'Shoes?'

It was as though he had never heard the term "shoes" before. 'They are not on your feet.'

'No, they are not,' said Nicholas, his nose skimming across the parchment as he followed the straight ink lines. 'I have found a better use for them.'

'Better than protecting one's feet?'

Nicholas traced one particular line with his crooked finger. 'Much.'

'And that is?'

Nicholas pushed his spectacles onto the bridge of his nose. 'At this point in time, I cannot recall what that is.'

Rosellene allowed her eyes to sweep the room. It had changed. More strange contraptions had appeared. They creaked and chimed from different positions. Glancing at the writing desk Rosellene smiled.

'Ah yes,' said Nicholas, picking up a shoe from a stack of parchment, a large hole in the toe. 'Perfect to prevent one's parchment being blown off one's desk should the window be open.'

He took the shoe and placed it on one corner of the map.

'Nicholas,' said Rosellene. 'Last night, again was I tormented by a dream most strange.'

'Dreams are often strange, my little angel.'

'Pray tell me, do you know its meaning?'

'Yes, yes, of course.' He hurried over to a tall contraption with large copper cogs and tinkered away for several minutes with a sharp tool.

'Nicholas,' Rosellene said softly.

The sharp tool flew into the air and landed with a clatter on the floor. 'You are still here.'

Rosellene nodded. 'My dream.'

'Dream?' Nicholas said vaguely. He tugged at his beard which had become snared on a handle of the corner cupboard. 'Oh, insight. Now? You mean to say you would like the insight at this precise moment in time?'

'Please,' Rosellene continued. 'And perhaps while you are there you could confer with the stars and ask them whom or if I shall marry.'

His beard now free, apart from a thick chunk that remained attached to the metal handle, Nicholas proceeded to tinker some more. 'Predicting the future is condemned, child. We should not be meddling with God's path.'

Rosellene stepped nearer and whispered in his ear. He smelled of leather and candle wax. 'Please, Nicholas.'

She took off his spectacles and cleaned them with part of her dress. The light from the window hit Nicholas' bright blue eyes and Rosellene would have sworn she saw them twinkle.

'Just a little peek then.' He winked.

Rosellene hugged him tightly, his thick, unkept beard tickling her face.

'Telling the future is a talent of yours, is it not?' Nicholas asked, gesturing to a circular table by the window draped with red velvet cloth.

Magic. It served her no longer. She would call on it no more.

'Yes but when you do it, people pay you for your services,' said Rosellene, sitting at the small table opposite Nicholas. 'When I do it, I am likely to be burned at the stake for witchcraft.'

Nicholas fumbled through a pile of battered old cards. Upon them, the images depicted planets, stars, moons and the like. 'Tell me more about these dreams.'

So began Rosellene, 'Each night it is the same. A white falcon emerges from the sky, seizes me in its curved talons and carries me off.'

'The hour of your birth governs your every encounter,' said Nicholas as he lay three cards upon the red cloth. 'It is in the stars, my dear. Let us confer with them and…mmm, curious.'

Another card was tabled. And another. Nicholas scratched an ear then pulled on his beard. 'It cannot be prevented or avoided I am afraid. He is coming.'

Before another word could be spoken, Rosellene interrupted. 'I shall not lay with Bannock nor shall I have his children! Are women not useful for other things? Do they not possess intellect as well?'

Nicholas picked himself up from the floor. 'These are merely my astronomical observations. I cannot tell who this *he* may be. By all intentions, it may not be Bannock. I can give you guidance only. What you do with that guidance is ultimately up to you. There are choices to be made. Make them with this and not with this,' said Nicholas, pointing first to her heart and then her head. 'And you will live a life most content.'

'So it is wrong to wish the pox upon him then?' Rosellene asked.

The twinkle returned to Nicholas's eyes. 'Wishing and doing are two entirely different things.'

Church bells sounded in the distance, sadly marking the end of Rosellene's visit. Her heart plummeted to the pit of her stomach as she bade Nicholas a swift farewell.

She knew at once her stay had been lengthy and she hastened from the observatory. A procession was to take place this morn and she was expected to join her family on the balcony, watching while the tournament combatants rode two by two through the castle streets from gatehouse to tournament field.

She could not be late. Not again.

How her father must be fretting. And poor Isabelle. What would she do when she found the chamber empty, the silk dress she was to wear still hanging on the wooden divider?

Reaching the outer bailey, Rosellene could hear the spectators cheering and shouting in the streets. Coming nearer still she could see that many toted colourful banners and held fresh flowers ready to strew in the path of the combatants as they passed. She could also see the minstrels who led the procession playing lutes and beating small drums with the heel of their hand.

Relieved, Rosellene saw that the procession had not yet reached the balcony. It was here that her father stood, forehead knitted, hands clenched tightly around the balcony rail scouring the crowd, looking no doubt for his daughter. The queen stood beside him; her arm linked with his. She whispered something in his ear to which he nodded and stepped back slightly.

Entering the balcony from the inside (perhaps giving her time to step into her silk dress), Rosellene turned away from the crowd and the approaching procession into an alley. But she had not taken more than a few steps when quickly she turned back, eyes wide and curious.

Amongst the banners that danced gracefully in the wind, she had seen a white falcon.

On tiptoes, fighting with the congestion in the street, each and every banner was scrutinised. But when Rosellene could find no falcon, she began to doubt it had even been seen to begin with. Could it too be a dream? Perhaps it was a white lion she had seen or maybe a white dragon.

Still, she had to be certain. Was there indeed a falcon banner somewhere amongst the riders and if true, to whom did it belong? Could it be a knight from some distant land or someone she had met before? *Oh pray,* thought Rosellene. *Pray that they are nothing like Lord Bannock.*

Startled then by her father's bellowing voice, Rosellene slipped on the freshly strewn rushes that covered the street. She would have fallen, perhaps so to her death under a mass of trampling horses, had it not been for one particular knight who learnt from his horse and caught her in his arms. With both hands firmly around her waist, the knight pulled her from the street up into the saddle.

'My lady, thou art a flower to be thrown upon the street, and although you are as beautiful as a lily and as sweet as a rose, I do not believe your fate is to be trampled upon as though you were such.'

But Rosellene, still in shock, could say nothing in reply. Aimlessly, she stared into Caprion's eyes, lost in their warm chestnut colouring while he rode across to the steps beneath the balcony and lowered her from the horse.

'You are most pale, my lady.' Caprion watched Rosellene stand unsteadily on her feet. 'How fare thee?'

Rosellene took a moment to answer, the colour completely drained from her face. 'I am shaken it is so, yet it will soon pass.'

'So shall I see you anon?'

'You shall,' Rosellene smiled. 'I thank you, Caprion. You are most kind.'

After bidding the king and queen farewell, Caprion merged back into the procession, his green banner, emblazoned with a white falcon, trailing behind.

Chapter Six

On the edge of the tournament field, each combatant, along with their squire, blacksmith, cook and perchance a chirurgeon, was housed in pavilions; round and predominantly white. Although confined, inside the pavilions was quite orderly, with space reserved for eating, sleeping and storage. Woven rugs covered the earthen floor and some, such as Lord Bannock's, had fancy drapes which divided sections of the pavilion. Bannock's were decorated with a selection of his favoured artwork.

Inside, like most other competitors, Caprion was preparing for his first match, helped into his armour by Marcus, his young squire. For the past four years, Marcus had ensured Caprion's armour was in good working order, oiling and polishing it after every use. He was a dedicated worker and Caprion looked upon Marcus as a brother and confidant.

With legs dressed, Marcus assisted Caprion into his mail shirt, which fitted loosely over a quilted doublet, to which a breastplate was added. The armour then moved down the arms, from shoulder to wrist and finally to the hands which were covered by gauntlets that were tapered to each individual finger allowing for flexibility when gripping the lance. Caprion was then left alone, as was the routine prior to a match, to complete the final inspections.

Moving outside beyond the pavilion, Caprion checked each of the five heavy lances, ten foot in length and carved from ash, searching for any signs of cracks. He then spent a few moments with his horse who was dressed in full barding, speaking gently to the mare while inspecting the rivets in the criniere.

Assigned to tilt first against Sir Casper, a fine competitor who was rarely dismounted, Caprion sat quietly and considered his approach. He was familiar with Casper's style, having met him many times on the field and knew that scoring points could prove difficult. To be awarded the points, he would need to focus on striking the helmet or the centre of the shield and splintering a lance.

Soon the time came to parade before the tilt. As the nobles took their places in the newly erected berfrois, the knights assembled to one side of the field, forming a single file.

While all the ladies of the court were beautiful, there was none more so than Rosellene. Her beauty was truly breath-taking and it had captured many of the tournament's combatants. It was, therefore, not surprising that the knights were most disappointed when whilst parading, all except one rode on without receiving her favour.

But when Caprion approached, helmet cradled in his arm, Rosellene stood and moved down the berfrois steps. As he paused before her, a thin, cyan scarf was pulled free from her dark hair.

'May it bring you luck,' said Rosellene and she leaned forward to pass Caprion the scarf.

Caprion took the scarf and fastening it to his lance said, 'It shall, my lady.'

With announcements made (some more grand than others) and the crown saluted, a loud trumpet pronounced the tournament beginning. First to do battle were Sir Constantine and a mercenary soldier. Heeding the herald's call, the two knights rode onto opposite ends of the field, attended by their banner bearer and valets, who stood prepared at the edge of the field should their assistance be required.

With lances lowered, they rode towards each other, quickly gaining speed. A strike to the body was made and a lance shivered as Sir Constantine was awarded a point. Receiving a new lance from his squire, Sir Constantine prepared once more, galloping towards his opponent. Impact was simultaneous and the blow so great that both men were dismounted.

'This shall be interesting.'

Caprion lifted his head and watched Bannock enter the arena. Bannock raised a gauntlet to wave to the good crowd, then took up a lance. His polished harness gleamed.

'Five florins he does not stay on his horse,' said Marcus.

He slapped Caprion upon the back of the pauldron and hurried nearer the field. An early morning shower had turned the ground to a slippery, sodden mush.

Caprion raised his eyebrows. 'Ten says he does not even make it to the tilt.'

The lance was set. Visor dropped. Heels driven into flanks.

Caprion smiled. Marcus did not.

'I never agreed to the terms,' huffed Marcus. 'There is by far too much weight in that saddle. I would kick him off too, had I been the horse.'

Caprion was one of the final matches of the morning. Having discussed his approaches with Marcus, he proceeded onto the field, placing upon his head firstly an arming cap and then his great helm. With only a narrow eye slit, which faced upwards, his vision was truly compromised, seeing nothing but the clouds, brilliant white amidst a powdered blue sky.

It was only when leaning forward that he caught sight of his opponent at the opposite end of the field. Setting the lance in the rest, Caprion breathed deeply, the sound echoing within the helm. Barely able to hear the herald, Caprion's eyes focused on the flag bearer, watching and waiting until the flag dropped, indicating the charge.

Then, rather foolishly, his eyes scanned the berfrois, to find Rosellene, who stood, hands clenched tightly around Isabelle's. He looked next upon the scarf tied to his lance, then back to his opponent.

Sir Casper was on the move.

The flag had dropped and for the first time in his lifetime, he had missed the calling. Throwing his heels into the flank of his horse, Caprion surged forward, hoping that the slow pace of Sir Casper's horse would make amends for his late start. But Sir Casper's aim was good and the metal tip struck Caprion in the chest.

Coming to a halt, Caprion threw back the visor but looked not upon the berfrois, too ashamed of his error.

'What troubled you?' Marcus asked, hurrying to Caprion's aid. 'Helmet. Lance. Armour. Pray, what is it, Sir Caprion?'

'Neither,' said Caprion, shamefully. 'I heard not the call.'

Marcus raised his eyebrows and pointed to Rosellene's scarf, now slightly loosened from the ride. 'This needs to be removed,' he said, almost scolding as he tapped a finger against Caprion's helm. 'From your mind, at least, until after the tournament. You are most distracted, my lord.'

Caprion threw down the visor and turned his horse, leading it to the right side of the divider. 'An error that will not happen twice.'

And indeed it did not. Leaning forward in the saddle, Caprion angled the lance, successfully deflecting that of his opponent then striking him in the very same move. A cheer erupted from the crowd as Caprion was named victorious, with three points added to his score for unseating his opponent.

Eager to remove his armour and so too the gambeson beneath, Caprion headed for the pavilion, but not before glancing up at the berfrois to see a smiling Rosellene. Whether it was the scarf or talent, he had progressed to the morrow's match, somewhat bruised, yet humble, nonetheless.

Following a light supper of sturgeon and vinegar salad, Rosellene had retired to her bedchamber and now sat reading on the window ledge. Despite being in the room quite some time, she had not turned a single page, distracted most highly by a great raucous coming from the pavilions below. Finding it difficult to concentrate, she cast the book aside, took hold of the iron bar and forced open the glazed window.

Instantly, the sound of music filled her ears. She could make out the shrill sound of recorders and the low pitch from nakers, but above all else came the jovial sound of men as they sang songs which none but themselves knew the words.

So tempted by the merriment outside was she, that a shawl was thrown over her shoulders and she hastened from her chamber, down the secret stairwell to the gatehouse. A medley of smells wafted through the air as she moved across the courtyard to the field, meandering through the pavilions now ablaze with firelight.

Cooking pots hung over fires. Woven mats lay on the damp earth and banners charged with emblems or badges billowed in the wind.

Rosellene stopped. She stared at the green banner before her, a white falcon upon it.

I should not be here. I made a vow. It must be kept.

Outside the pavilion, a group of six men were seated on wooden stumps, talking loudly and drinking strongly spiced ale from clay tankards. A great fire blazed before them and over it, hung from what appeared to be an old jousting stick, a large hog roasted, its skin crackling in the heat.

One of the men, Angus, a robust man with thick, dark hair, greying slightly at the temples, moved towards the roast and using a sprig of rosemary, basted the meat with a thin layer of dripping. From a small, leather pouch, a handful of salt was taken, which he sprinkled onto the meat, before rubbing it in with his gloved hand.

'Ah, my lady,' he said loudly, noting Rosellene's presence at the campsite. 'I wondered whether you would be lured from the castle by the smell of my roasted pork!'

With the toe of his boot, Angus nudged Caprion, quite forcefully, hoping to wake him from his slumber.

Startled, Caprion's eyes shot open and he quickly rose to his feet, forgetting momentarily about his badly bruised chest.

'My lady.' Caprion started towards Rosellene but the throbbing pain of his chest held him back.

'He is just hungry, my lady. Some pork in his belly and he will be a different man entirely,' said Angus, trying to shield Caprion who grimaced as two of his ribs crossed over each other. But Rosellene had seen Caprion's exposed chest. Politely, she turned away.

'I came only to congratulate you on the day,' she feigned. 'I see now you are injured and my presence may be an intrusion. I shall take my leave.'

'Pray, it is not an intrusion,' Caprion reached for his plaid shirt and gingerly pulled it on. 'Your company would be most welcome.'

Rosellene hesitated then replied, 'If you are certain.' Nodding, Caprion led her to a vacant stool by the fire.

Angus took a step nearer the hog, sliced with his knife a thick slab of meat and held it towards Rosellene. 'Tell me this is not the best pork you have tasted, my lady.'

But before Rosellene could taste the meat, Caprion swiftly pushed the knife away.

'Where are your manners?' He said, rather appalled. 'Have we no forks or a plate to speak of?'

'Indeed we do,' smiled Angus, looking behind him. 'The fork holds that section of the pavilion to the post and the plate is currently a dog dish.'

'Thank you, Angus,' said Rosellene, reaching beyond Caprion to take up the knife. 'It does smell delicious.'

Angus held his breath as Rosellene tried the pork, his eyes scrutinising her expression. 'Your thoughts, my lady?'

'Indeed, it is the best pork I have tasted.'

Angus grinned like a child.

Rosellene then turned to Caprion, the glint of armour having caught her eye. Leg guards, beaver and helm lay neatly upon the table.

'How faired the armour?'

'Much is with the blacksmith as we speak,' said Caprion.

'And it shall be ready by the morning?'

Caprion nodded. 'It will have to be, my lady, as will I.'

'It does not have to be.' Rosellene spoke softly, her voice barely audible above the crackling of the fire.

'My lady?'

Rosellene turned away. 'It pains me to see you this way.'

Just like dents in armour, bruising was expected. Why did she care so much about how he fared? 'You need not worry.'

'Alas but I do,' Rosellene stared deeply into Caprion's dark eyes, her breath quickening. Gently she tilted his chin towards the light of the fire, then tucked a lock of hair behind his ear so as to inspect the deep gash across his forehead. 'Very well.'

She stood. Smiled. Moved inside the pavilion.

Caprion looked across at Angus, hoping for an explanation, but all he received was a shrug of the shoulders before another slab of meat was cut and thrown into his mouth. So Caprion waited, listening curiously as pots and furniture were disturbed inside the pavilion. Then Rosellene emerged, a small, clay pot in one hand, a bunch of rosemary, marigold and agrimony in the other.

'Would you mind if I used these?' She asked.

Angus swallowed down another mouthful then said, 'Not at all, my lady.'

From the shadows cast on the pavilion's canvas walls, Caprion could see that the leaves were broken from the stems and crushed in a small bowl with a pestle. Added to the bowl was what looked to be a few drops of water but the aroma hinted it may in fact have been an oil of some sort. With thoughts of childhood medicine forced regularly upon him by his mother, a liquid made from rosemary, sage and honey, Caprion moved uneasily to the pavilion opening.

Leaning against one of the poles, he watched as the herbal poultice was taken from the clay pot and spread onto a cloth bandage. In a separate bowl, an ointment of marigold petals had been prepared. It was mixed with chopped lemongrass, camphor and a decent amount of fat then set aside on the bench.

Rosellene gestured for Caprion to sit. 'If you insist on fighting on the morrow, which I am certain you shall, this should aid the inflammation.'

Caprion hesitated. 'Am I to drink this?'

'I would not suggest it.'

'I am much relieved,' said Caprion, moving inside to sit on the stool. Carefully, so as to cause as little pain as possible, Caprion's shirt was removed.

'It may be cool,' said Rosellene, taking up the bandage and applying it to Caprion's bruised chest. The ends of the bandage were wound once around his chest and then brought to the shoulder and tied. The marigold ointment was then carried from the bench. Crouching in front of Caprion, a small amount was taken from the pot and gently applied to the forehead wound.

'Allow it to dry and then wash it clean.'

As she stood, Caprion took her hand. 'Thank you, my lady. With you here, the pain has already subsided.'

Rosellene could feel the colour rush to her face as she returned the bowl to the bench. 'Should you need it on the morrow.'

With that, she bid the men good night and began her journey back through the maze of pavilions, rushing quickly past Bannock as he and a man she had not seen before worked on the crowns of several lances in preparation for the morrow. Rosellene jolted to a halt.

She had not seen such crowns before. These looked vicious enough to kill.

Chapter Seven

By dawn the next morning, Rosellene was already half way to the riverside, having learned that Caprion was attending a training session on the eastern bank. As she crossed the narrow bridge to the place where the men were training, the mist was just beginning to lift and nature was wide awake. Finches of red, yellow and blue flitted from reed to reed while curlews walked awkwardly on their long, thin legs. There were trees of variegated greens and vibrant purple wildflowers so tall that they tickled Rosellene's shoulders as she brushed past them. For some reason, everything seemed more beautiful than ever before.

Suddenly, she stopped.

Her pace had been quick. Unusually quick.

Why was she in such a hurry and what was the cause of this peculiar feeling in her stomach? She smiled. *Of course*, thought she, feeling much relieved. Believing it to be the absence of breakfast, she brushed the feeling aside and continued along the track.

Amid the clusters of flowering lilies, a quintain stood. Looking like a miniature knight equipped with helmet and breastplate, the mannequin held a shield and rotated when hit. Caprion, however, had forgotten that his task was to avoid the rotating arm and Marcus was displeased.

When the sand bag knocked Caprion to the ground for the fourth time this morning, Marcus could tell yesterday's distraction was still lingering. With the heel of his boot, he kicked Caprion into the water, claiming, 'Training is over!'

Rosellene met a furious Marcus along the trail. He mumbled something under his breath as he stormed past, and Rosellene wondered what had put him in such a bad mood.

Then she saw him, the peculiar feeling in her stomach growing more intense.

She faltered, eyes diverted and retreated up the bank, scolding herself from time to time for glancing not once but several times at Caprion's rippling body.

But in her striking dress of yellow, it was not long before Caprion set eyes upon her.

'My lady,' he called cheerfully, running callused fingers through his hair. 'Pray join me?'

'I must decline,' replied Rosellene, most annoyed that she had been seen. *Look away,* thought she, *look not upon his torso toned most delightfully.* 'I imagine the water is freezing.'

'I would call it refreshing,' Caprion rose from the water like an ancient God. 'You should join me.'

Rosellene's chin all but struck the ground as Caprion moved from the water to the bank, each and every muscle outlined by the trousers that he wore. She tried to steady her breathing as he moved further up the bank towards her. Despite longing to leave, she could go no farther, for in her haste the heel of her shoe had torn through the hem of her petticoat and pinned her to the bank.

'I am struck…stuck!' She cried. 'Stuck I mean to say. I am stuck in the mud.'

'Yet again,' Caprion smiled. 'What is the attraction?'

And before Rosellene could even contemplate an answer, she was lifted into the air and carried effortlessly down the bank.

Caprion felt Rosellene's fingers clench his biceps. 'Fear not. I shall not drop you.'

He rested her on a low-lying willow branch, extending her legs into the water where he first washed then dried both her unstockinged feet. The water was not refreshing. It was incredibly cold. He then vaulted up onto the branch beside her.

Rosellene removed the woollen shawl from her shoulders and extended it to Caprion. 'No, my lady, I could not.'

'You must,' insisted Rosellene. 'You will catch your death of cold.'

Caprion nodded. He wrapped the shawl around himself, taking in the scented oils that lingered on the tightly knitted garment.

Rosellene could barely think, let alone talk. She had completely forgotten her reason for meeting with Caprion and found herself trying to cover up her blushing cheeks with a few strands of hair. Finally, after several attempts, she managed to get a few words out, albeit muffled and spoken at an unusually fast pace.

'Marcus' temperament seemed strained. How does he fare?'

'Alas, I am to blame for his state,' admitted Caprion, resting an elbow on a nearby branch. 'It seems I am not performing my knightly role as I should.'

'Why thinks he that?'

'It would seem I have of late been distracted.'

If only you knew, thought he. *Knew how hard it was to breathe whenever you are near. How long your scent remains with me after you are gone.*

'Distracted?'

At the ball, jousting, on this very morn. 'On several occasions.'

'This has Marcus concerned?'

'Indeed, he fears that I will become weak.'

Like a poison, you enter my body, taking control of my extremities, making me dance like a puppet. I am indeed under your spell, fair maiden.

'I doubt you would ever be plagued by weakness,' said Rosellene, embarrassed that yet again she had glanced at Caprion's chest. Quickly, she thought on something else. 'How fare the injuries?'

How my heart aches for thee.

'I have many aches,' said Caprion, his voice soft and soothing. 'Yet they are not from tilting.'

Speak no more, Rosellene thought, her entire body numb. *Have I not suffered enough? I promise I will no longer be a distraction.*

'My lady!' Isabelle's cry was heard from a distance. In unison, both Rosellene and Caprion sighed.

Isabelle soon came into view, standing at the top of the bank, puffing as if she had run a great distance. She greeted first Caprion then turned to Rosellene. 'You must away, my lady.'

'What is the urgency?'

'A meeting with Lord Bannock. He waits for you in the gardens.'

Caprion jumped from the branch and carried Rosellene to drier ground. 'You must not keep him waiting,' he said gently.

Rosellene's head was spinning as she hastened towards the gardens. The small tear in her petticoat made by her heel had now become quite large as it caught on the spindly shrubs. Isabelle had little option but to rip the entire hem from her garment.

The king met them at the garden entrance. The wind tugged at his long opulent cape revealing woollen hose the colour of his reddening cheeks. He hid them not. Standing in the shadows his face seemed to have aged.

'Lord Bannock waits for your coming.'

The king hurried her away, gesturing to the pergola where, presently, Lord Bannock sat on a turf seat, biting most viciously at his nails.

Rosellene sighed deeply at the sight of the ghastly man and his nervous habit.

She would not love another. Had she not decided this? Perhaps, with Lord Bannock, her promise would be kept. She would never love him.

Her father sensed Rosellene's apprehension. 'He is a good and practical match. Be grateful and accept any token that he offers.'

Slowly, Rosellene meandered through the castle gardens, stopping from time to time to inspect first the gillyflowers and then the marigolds growing in one of the many raised garden beds. Finally, she arrived at the pergola where Lord Bannock, now standing, took her slender hand and kissed the back of it with his chubby lips.

As she curtseyed gracefully, Rosellene could see sweat dripping from his double chin and smelt an odour most unpleasant, wafting from beneath his cotehardie.

How can I accept a man who repulses me so?

How she would like to leave him amidst the maze, laughing as he got lost in the wattle fences, covered entirely by thick hedging.

Sitting close, yet not too close, Rosellene listened while Lord Bannock recited a flowery poem that spoke amongst other things of Rosellene's beauty and Bannock's undying love. Then, from behind his back, Bannock took a large token, two intertwining spoons carved from a single piece of lime wood.

Rosellene's heart sank. *Am I to accept such a grotesque ornament, a useless token to sit on one's shelf gathering layers of dust?*

'Accept this as a token of my love and commitment,' Lord Bannock's voice seemed higher than normal and Rosellene thought he was apt to cry. 'You may not love me yet but I pray in time your feelings will grow.'

Rosellene took up the spoons, and trying to smile, said, 'Thank you for the kind gesture, Lord Bannock. I will think on your offer.'

She watched him leave, the sleeve of his shirt used to pat his damp forehead, before she raced inside the castle.

'He angers me so!' Rosellene stormed into her chamber and cast something wooden at the wall. 'I detest him for making me feel this way.'

Isabelle ducked as the projectile hurtled towards her.

'Are they not the ugliest spoons you have set eyes upon?' Rosellene asked.

Isabelle took a closer look at the spoons. It was a wonder they were not broken, the haste with which they had been thrown. 'They are functional I suppose.'

'Take them. They are yours.'

'Lord Bannock's wooing was unsuccessful then, my lady?'

'It was enough to make one feel ill.'

In a huff, Rosellene collapsed onto the bed. 'I cannot get him out of my head. Why must he be so handsome?'

Isabelle was confused. Lord Bannock was not at all handsome. 'Handsome?'

'And strong. He could lift an ox with those arms. He made me weak, Isabelle. I was not in control.'

Isabelle tried to envision Lord Bannock lifting an ox. 'I am most concerned. Has something happened?'

'Something horrible, Isabelle,' Rosellene sat up, hands pressed upon her temples. 'Nay, I would call it disastrous.'

'Whatever can it be?' Isabelle asked, sitting beside her upon the bed. 'Pray tell me?'

'I have been hit with an arrow, most profoundly.'

Isabelle's eyes grew wide. 'Hit, my lady? With an arrow?'

'I am in love with Caprion,' said Rosellene. She flopped backwards onto the soft quilting and hid her head beneath the pillows. 'Or so I fear.'

Isabelle clapped her hands together. She had suspected the attraction long ago.

'Is that not most wonderful, my lady?' She asked, eager to hear more. 'He is a fine man.'

'Nay,' said Rosellene, sitting up abruptly. 'I shall not mourn another man.'

'But Caprion is not dead, my lady.'

'Not yet.'

'Then why would you mourn for him?' Isabelle shrugged.

Isabelle could see the heartache in Rosellene's eyes. She remembered all too well the loss of Saxon. How Rosellene had grieved. A month was the norm for mourning, yet a month had come and gone, then another and another. By the fifth month, Rosellene's black attire had begun to fade, as had her appetite, mood and will to live.

'I will just have to avoid him. Suppress my feelings until they are no more.'

Isabelle thought of her own family. She had a husband and two young sons. Love to her was more precious than gold and silver put together. 'You would deny him of love also?'

Rosellene turned. Frowned.

'Does he not deserve to love and be loved in return. Is it not cruel to take that from him?'

Rosellene moved to the window. 'He has no interest in myself. Knights do not get distracted with things such as love.'

Yet he was distracted, she thought. *On several occasions.*

No, it could not be. She was not in love, nor was Caprion.

'I feel you are mistaken,' said Isabelle boldly. 'When two hearts collide, it is best not to get between them.'

From the window, Rosellene saw Caprion below, collecting his armour from the blacksmith. Her urge to leave Rawdendale had faded. With reddening cheeks, she looked at Isabelle and smiled. 'The attraction is there but how I wish it was not.'

Suddenly, her thoughts became clear and she recalled an earlier conversation that was supposed to happen.

'The jousting points!' She cried. 'You must tell him. Go now and let him know.'

'Tell him what, my lady?' Isabelle asked, as she was jostled out the door. 'I know nothing of the points. Best if you go. Quickly, away with you before it is too late.'

Rosellene nodded. 'Indeed. I would never forgive myself if something should happen to him.' And away she ran to the blacksmith to inform Caprion of her concern.

Chapter Eight

Wearing spiced perfume and with her cheeks reddened, Rosellene joined her parents in the berfrois some hours later. The day was warm and Rosellene was thankful for her fan. She pitied the knights in their armour and wondered how many would suffer from the heat.

Her father shifted uncomfortably in the seat beside her, standing then sitting then moving between the two. Rosellene could tell he longed for the outcome of her meeting with Lord Bannock and it was not long before he enquired as to her favour.

'It is most grotesque.'

'So he has made his intentions known,' said the king, finally sitting still. 'That is good, is it not?' But no answer was given before the trumpet sounded and the heralds proclaimed the rules under which the knights would fight, reminding them that they had sworn an oath to fight not out of anger or desire to harm their opponent but to please and entertain the good crowd.

During this time, Lord Bannock entered the arena. Easily identified by his coat of arms (a white boar on a red field) which featured on shield, breastplate and horse cloth, he sat tall in the saddle, smiling smugly as he rode past the berfrois.

'Let her see my skill,' he said, cradling his helm. 'Let her be impressed by my valour and astounded when I defeat her beloved Caprion.'

By all accounts, Lord Bannock seemed confident that he would indeed be victorious in his tilt, so much so that he had made a wager of several silver pieces not only that he would beat his opponent but unseat them as well.

Two separate lists had been built for the occasion. It was whilst watching Caprion perform that the king received word that Lord Bannock had progressed to the next round.

'That should please you?' He said, informing his daughter of the news.

'My lord?' Rosellene had not taken her eyes from Caprion so was unaware of the king's message.

'Lord Bannock has progressed,' the king said, smiling. 'I admit I am surprised by his talent.'

'Indeed, my lord,' Rosellene knew at once that the progression was due not to talent. 'For what else could it be but talent?'

The king turned his questioning eyes on Rosellene. 'Do you know something that I do not?'

Rosellene watched a very smug Lord Bannock enter the tilt before them.

'The outcome is debatable,' she said. 'Let us see how far this talent takes him, shall we.'

The kings breathing deepened. 'Am I to halt proceedings?'

'Whatever for?' Rosellene relaxed into the chair's velour. 'The show is just beginning.'

It was not long before Bannock found himself sitting on the sandy ground having been thrown rather abruptly from his horse.

'Leave it!' Bannock demanded and Eric left his breastplate where it lay, distorted in two places, beside him.

'My lord?' On hearing Bannocks request, Eric was baffled. 'You cannot go into tilt without your breastplate. Let me get you another.'

Bannock remounted and dusted the straw and dung from his gambeson. 'There is no time,' he said. 'Besides, the conditions make it restricting.'

Eric noticed a ring of perspiration around the quilted neckline. Bannock was indeed saturated, yet there seemed no cause to risk his safety.

'My lord?' Eric questioned and he whispered then in his ear. 'Do you want to die?'

'I need it not.' And kicking his horse in the flanks, he continued on to the list, for Lord Bannock knew something that Eric did not.

Sir Constantine had already begun his charge, unaware that Bannock lacked the appropriate attire. By the time he realised, it was too late to pull back. His lance tip hit Bannocks shield and deflected the lance upon his chest. The blow knocked Bannock from his horse.

'Get me another breastplate!' Bannock insisted, doubled over in pain.

Eric wondered if perhaps there was more at stake. He had wagered silver on the last tilt. What had he gambled on this?

'My lord, you cannot continue.'

Bannock struggled to breathe. Several ribs were broken and had it not been for the extra flesh around his chest, the injury would have been far worse.

'A win is assured.'

Eric shook his head.

'No, no it is not,' he replied. 'The only thing you can be assured of is serious damage and perhaps an early visit to the grave.'

'It is assured,' repeated Bannock. 'Pass me my lance.'

'What is it you stand to lose? Money is not worth dying for?'

Bannock glared at Eric with a rare hint of fire in his eyes. 'My lance.'

Eric and Bannock had had their disagreements before but despite that, he bore Lord Bannock no ill will. He definitely did not long for him to die, so he held back the lance and refused to pass it over. Bannock reached out for the lance. There was a tussle and Bannock fell once more. He landed on top of the lance head, shattering the tip.

'I have been jaded!' Bannock inspected the lance, pulling the splintered wood from the head. 'These were to be steel, single and double-pronged spears.'

Alas, this was not the case. For unbeknown to Bannock, Caprion, after first hearing Rosellene's concerns, had gone to Bannock's camp. Here he had discovered that the blunt coronels of several lances had been replaced with a sharp point, the kind typically used for war. The heads were a mixture of single and double-pronged spears, some cleverly hidden beneath a clenched iron fist. All five lances had been replaced with blunted tips and so consequently, Bannock was misinformed of his skills.

Bannock watched Caprion ride towards the arena. Despite his injuries, Bannock stood tall. 'I will not let him take her from me.'

'And I thought you were playing for honour.'

'Get me on my horse,' Bannock demanded. He looked then upon Rosellene, who, like most others in the berfrois, was on her feet, fearful of the injuries Bannock had sustained. 'I will have her favour and win her heart.'

Bannock reached beneath the high pommel of his saddle and withdrew from it a fine, lace glove. He lifted it aloft and addressed the captured crowd. 'Let it be known that the princess has given her favour.'

There were murmurs from the crowd as speculation grew. Enraged, Rosellene descended upon the ring, halting the proceedings, noting that the glove, *her glove*, had been placed upon Bannock's shield in the barracks.

Bannock watched Rosellene approach. 'Such thoughtfulness, my lady, that you should come to check upon my health.'

The look upon her face told a different story.

'I am here to reclaim my glove,' pronounced Rosellene with open hand. 'It was not given in favour.'

'Yes, but to their eyes,' Bannock turned his glance upon the watchful crowd, 'your concern is undeniable. No other woman has ever stopped a tournament.'

Fighting the urge to flatten him with his own shield, she took a deep breath and said, 'You infuriate me, Lord Bannock,' before turning swiftly on her heels.

'Do you not want your glove?'

Rosellene paused. 'I should take it back only to strike you with it.'

It was then, while walking away, that she noticed Bannock's squire. It was not so much the squire himself but more so the flag that he toted, a red flag edged with gold trim. A mischievous glint crossed her eyes and before she knew it, she had pulled the trim from the flag.

Nine times it was knotted while an incantation was said, her spell thus cast. With the knots then untied, the trim left burning in the flames of a pit fire, she sat again in the berfrois and looked upon her father's ashen face.

'Fear not, Father,' she said. 'There is little to see.'

While the crowd jeered, amused by the entertainment, Lord Bannock hurried from the arena struggling to pull up the trousers that had fallen below his ankles.

Moments later, with the shield laced to his shoulder, Bannock rode up to the padded barrier and awaited his next opponent, furious at being made a fool. To his joy and Rosellene's misfortune, Caprion stood at the opposite end.

Bannock threw down the visor of his blackened great helm. 'Let thee be vanquished.'

He leaned forward in the high-backed saddle and charged.

Whether it was in anger or just through error, Bannock struck the harness on Caprion's horse and was thus disqualified, enraging him further still.

Caprion met Bannock by the tilt.

'I shall have your horse. You may keep the armour.' Caprion rode away then turned back. 'Perhaps you could give me some advice.'

Bannock had dismounted. It hurt to walk. 'On what matter do you speak?'

'Had we the opportunity to compete again, which lance would you prefer me to use?' Angus appeared beside them, cradling two lances with sharp steel heads. 'The single or double-pronged spear?'

Bannock had no words. He made to leave but Rosellene stood in his path. 'The king says I should be honoured to have your favour.'

'And you, Rosellene,' said Bannock, his voice tainted with bitterness. 'What say you?'

Rosellene caught sight of Caprion and tears welled in her eyes. Lord Bannock would bring advantages to the kingdom but little love. Caprion, however, would be a love for life.

'You are a man of wealth and position. Rawdendale would be pleased to have you as future king.'

Bannock laughed.

'You think me a fool? I see the way you look at him and he upon you.' Bannock stepped closer so that he now looked down upon Rosellene. In the shadows, his face reminded Rosellene of the gargoyles. Ugly and grotesque. 'But your happiness will be short lived.'

'We make our own future, Lord Bannock.'

Rosellene went to leave but Bannock caught her by the wrist, his grasp firm and deliberate.

'By all means, go to Caprion and be merry but take note. Men like him are broken, scarred from battle. Like a beautiful rose, they soon wither and die. You will be a lonely widow in a castle that crumbles around you. Within one month, you will be pining.'

Rosellene broke free of his grasp, tension on her face. 'So say you.'

Moments later, Bannock caught sight of Rosellene at camp, Caprion so near her that their hands appeared to be linked, entwined like the carved spoons. Rage filled his entire body, so much so that the tin button on the bottom of his cotehardie popped from the cotton threads that bound it. His jealous eyes watched the two of them closely as he contrived a plan, most devious.

Chapter Nine

Her beauty haunts me.

Teasing. Taunting. Tugging at my heart so severely that I want to scream. All night she lingered like the sweet perfume that she wears, dancing in and out of my mind. There was no escape and I was terrified.

But am I not a knight? There is no fear within me. I am here for one purpose, bound to defend the king. Nothing more. Yet how can I fulfil my duties whilst ever she is near?

Nay, I must be strong. Think only of the kingdom and my knightly duties. But how I would love to hold her in my arms and feel the softness of her skin.

A cry from beyond the tent and Caprion was alerted to the fact that daylight had snuck upon him. 'Leave me,' he called as he rolled over, staring vacantly through the sheer curtain wall.

'My lord, are you ill?' There was concern in Angus's voice.

I am sleep deprived, that much is true, yet am I ill? My stomach aches and the palpitations of my heart are like nothing ever felt before.

'I know not.'

The bed shuddered as Angus dropped himself down on the mattress, his thick arms crossed over his chest. 'Either you are sick or you are not. There is no knowing to it.'

The thin, cyan scarf twisted between Caprion's fingers.

'Ah,' Angus tutted. 'Worst sickness you can get, I am afraid.'

Caprion looked towards Angus, his bloodshot eyes burning. 'What am I to do?'

'No magical poultice for that kind of sickness.' Angus shrugged. 'You will probably die from it.'

'It can be nothing more than an idea.' said Caprion as his chest heaved. 'She is far too good for me?'

Angus simply agreed.

'There is nothing I have to offer her.'

Angus grunted. His gigantic head shook. 'Nay, nothing at all, my lord.'

'I should just let her be,' Caprion rolled onto his back, interlocking his fingers behind his head. 'Bannock is a far more suited match.'

'Yes, let her be. He is surely more competent and handsome than you, my lord.'

Caprion propped himself up on an elbow, an eyebrow cocked. 'And I call you a friend.'

'*Slightly* more handsome.' Angus smiled.

'Better.' Caprion sat up, rubbing dark eyes with the heel of his hands.

'She wants for nothing, my lord, but someone to love.'

Could I be that someone? Could I give her everything she needs? Love.

'She will only get hurt.' He was blunt but truthful. 'Knights fight and die. That is not for a princess.'

There was tension in Angus's face. The small, blue vein in his temple bounced and Caprion knew the conversation was coming to an end.

'You fight for a castle, an inanimate object. Why not fight for her? Is she not worth that?'

'He cares for her. He will make her happy.'

'And you will not?'

'What happiness can I offer?'

He should have seen it coming but he could not stop it. The bed was upended and Caprion found himself between floor and mattress.

'Get your arse up!'

Angus threw him over his shoulder and carried Caprion out into the cold. He was thankful for a time that only the biting winds were felt. Gone were the crazy thoughts that Rosellene would fall for a knight such as he.

'Act like a child and I will treat you as such.' Angus shook his head. His pace seemed to quicken as the stable came into view. 'Your father, God rest his soul, would have my head if he were here to see you now.'

Father. Childhood memories hit him like a crossbow bolt through the head.

Caprion flapped about on Angus's shoulder as the water trough loomed. 'You would not?'

'Oh, I would.' Angus grinned; his eyes locked on the trough. 'I seem to recall being here before. Dragging someone's sorry arse into the courtyard. Cleansing them of their foul temper and vile tongue. Your father would be rolling in his grave.'

Father. Angus had been the only father Caprion had known. After his own father was murdered, a crossbow bolt through the eye, Angus had been there to teach the boy right from wrong. The task at times was difficult. Very difficult. This would not be the first time Angus had hurled him into an ice-cold trough of water.

'You feel that pain?' Angus thundered, as the air was sucked from Caprion's lungs. 'Like knives through your chest. Being alone feels just the same. Painful.'

His entire body blue, Caprion exploded out of the trough. It was nothing like the last time. Last time he had been young. Angry. Bitter. The punishment deserved. His father had been taken from him and he had wanted everyone to feel his pain.

He had fought often and stolen much. Spoken harshly and cared little for his own life, taunting in fact, for someone to take his life from him. It was Angus who had given him a purpose. An understanding of consequences, morals and ethics. He had ensured he lived by honour and glory. If not, he had found no pillow beneath his head, but a sow, sleeping many nights in the pig pen. Angus had made his father a promise and aimed to keep it.

'So I say honour your knightly virtues, kiss some royal arses and plunder a few villages in the name of God, but you need a good woman to make you a better man. You cannot be a grumpy bastard and expect to be a decent knight.'

Caprion sat upon the base of the cold trough. His teeth shook. 'You are the exception then?'

Angus winked. 'Best be mindful of where you rest, laddie, and the length you wish to stay there.'

Shivering, Caprion hauled his body from the trough then looked around for something to warm his pimpled skin. Finding a horse blanket, he pulled it from the stable rail and threw it around his shoulders. 'There is something I dislike about Bannock.'

Angus laughed. 'There are many things I dislike about Bannock.'

Moving to the warmth of a fire, Caprion stripped the clothes from his quivering limbs. He dressed quickly then sat for a time gazing upon the orange flames that spat and hissed like a bickering couple. He had not known love could be so powerful. So intense. So debilitating.

Angus spoke the truth when he said it was a sickness. A sickness that invaded every cell in his body. A sickness that would only fester should Bannock take Rosellene for his own.

'The union would be a mistake.' The water had cleared Caprion's mind. 'You were right to question me. Rosellene may not want me, yet I feel I cannot allow Bannock to have her either.'

Chapter Ten

He needed money. Shillings. Pounds.

To pay for military expenses. To pay for allegiances. To pay off the Ormans. There was none.

Collected in cash or kind, the king's taxes were recorded by royal officials on great sheets of parchment, rolled and sealed in leather cylinders. Over the past ten years however, tax exemptions had increased and a significant amount of the revenue raised, had been given to the church. While the tithe paid in kind appeared in excess (grain and livestock stored in barns), little money had been seen.

Was a dower the answer? His daughter's betrothal for economic gains? Alliances must be made, but at the expense of his daughter?

Should she marry Bannock, land would be bestowed upon her. The income from these lands would be hers, and in turn, ours. Meanwhile, Bannock would gain property and title. A marriage of mutual benefit.

The king massaged his aching head. He had spent the evening in the cabinet looking through scrolls, checking the accounts, a chore usually delegated to his treasury and overseen by the Abbot. He was, however, no closer to finding a solution to raising revenue.

What he had was a deficit. What he needed was a horde of treasure.

As the ink on the scrolls blurred and his stomach begged for food, the cabinet door opened and the queen entered. She carried a wooden platter and on it lay bread, fish and wine.

After laying the platter before the king, the queen moved towards the window and stared upon the markets below.

'Rosellene and Caprion are becoming close,' she noted, as she watched the pair meander amongst the vendors.

Noisy, cramped, colourful and fragrant, peasants walked for miles each week to sell their produce at the castle markets. Wagons filled with barrels of onions, apples, potatoes and leeks, lined the cobbled streets. Flat breads, dusted with flour, were stacked in towers. Laying hens clucked in their cages and cloths of the finest quality were laid out before the buyer. Baskets, woven of wicker, could be purchased for storage and transportation. Carried on one's head, back or the side of a beast, these baskets were finely crafted.

'Are they?' The king's head remained imbedded in the words of his scroll as he chewed on a mouthful of dry bread. 'I had not noticed.'

The queen strolled towards her husband. Gently, she removed the scroll from the table. 'There are many things one can miss when one's head is constantly in paperwork.' The queen held out her hand. 'You have eyes, my love, but I fear at times, they see no better than someone who has lost their sight. Let me draw you away for a moment.'

Through the thick glass panes, the king gazed into the courtyard. The scene appeared like any other. People bartered. Exchanged goods. But in the centre near the large water feature, ringed by musicians playing lutes and small drums, a couple danced. Gracefully they turned and hopped, skipped and jumped, all done hand in hand.

The king's shoulders dropped. He had not seen his daughter this happy for the longest time.

'There was a time, not so long ago, when the sun shone not on her face.' The king looped his hands in his belt. Sighed.

'Have you asked her thoughts on Bannock and his proposal?'

'He is a good match,' said the king, defensively. 'It is what the kingdom needs.'

'That may be so, yet what does Rosellene need? Has she not already had her heart broken? Can we bring that upon her once more?'

'She is to be married. Furthermore, to a man of wealth. Why then would her heart break?'

The queen stared at Caprion through the yellowed panes. 'Given the choice of suiters, whom do you think she would favour?'

The king's tone changed. The veil was removed from his eyes. 'You believe she favours Caprion more than Bannock?'

'They have been seen together,' the queen replied. 'On several occasions.'

'Kamden,' grumbled the king. 'It is no place for a princess.'

The town of Kamden was cursed. The people outcast. A punishment, some believed, for those amongst them who practised the unholy act of witchcraft.

Infested with sickly inhabitants, the dilapidated shacks reeked of death. Red soil brought poor yields and livestock scrounged the terrain with their worn teeth.

'I forbade her to go there.'

'You forbade her to go alone,' corrected the queen. 'We must not forget those less fortunate than ourselves. It was charitable.'

'It was foolish on both their parts.' Despite his harsh words, the king had been comforted by the thought of Caprion by his daughter's side. 'The Ormans had not two days before raided what little they had.'

'Should that not be a reason for calling upon them? They are still our people.'

'Yes, yes,' the king agreed and he held aloft a piece of bread.

'And did Caprion not watch over our daughter, each time returning her safely home?' The queen watched her husband as he chewed laboriously on the piece of bread. 'Would it be so wrong a match?'

'She does need someone with strength.' The king sat. Stood. Then took to strolling around the room, his hands behind his back. 'He has virtues that are desirable. A strong reputation. A good status. He has been of great service to Rawdendale since his arrival, monitoring the borders and ensuring our safety from enemy attacks.'

The queen smiled inside. 'You make some excellent points.'

The king stopped. A frown lurked beneath his crown. 'If this is true, why then has she not voiced her feelings? She freely does so on many other subjects.'

'You are her father. Her king. She may be stubborn and completely independent yet she knows her role.' The queen took his hands. Looked into his eyes. 'She would follow you to your grave should you ask her.'

Salt water invaded the king's eyes. It was difficult to see. 'He is noble-hearted I suppose.'

'Let us look over the numbers once more.' The queen smiled. 'Perhaps we could increase the geld to two shillings. Pay off those wishing to raid our lands?'

The king tore off a section of bread, pushed it into his mouth and followed it with a long sip of wine.

'Perhaps,' he mumbled.

'A hearth tax?' The queen queried. 'I have heard it common on the northern islands.'

The king pondered the proposition, then replied, 'One shilling for each hearth or fire within a dwelling?'

The queen nodded, then gasped. The king was in tears.

'My love, what troubles you?'

'We have lost one daughter,' the king sobbed. 'Are we to lose a second because of my stupidity?'

'We will not let it come to that.'

'Pray that it be so.'

Chapter Eleven

To the castle's south, lay a barren and unforgiving ground. It was here, in a small hut nestled amongst the jagged rocks and sharp needlepoint pines, that a great and powerful sorceress lived. Her name was Grindella, young and alluring, yet frightfully dangerous.

To get to the hut, one had first to cross a wide river then climb one hundred steps to the top of the mountain peak. If one were not blown from the mountainside, one could then set about searching for the hut in Jules Forest. Few men had scaled the mountainside in search of Grindella. Those that had were either desperate, greedy or in search of revenge.

Lord Bannock was all of these.

In the early hours one cold winter morn, Lord Bannock set out for Grindella's hut. Tied to his belt was a small, leather pouch filled with gold and silver pieces. Should she want more, perchance, Bannock was willing to oblige, for if she fulfilled his desire the money would be well spent.

When he reached the forest edge, the sun was high in the sky. He scanned the trees and made his way towards those that bore the greenest leaves, for it had been told to him by an elderly gypsy that this was the path he should follow. The gypsy had also warned not to bargain with the sorceress, for he would get nothing but pain and despair for the rest of his lifetime, just as the gypsy himself had suffered.

Yet Bannock could not be deterred by the old man's fears. He would not suffer the same fate as the old man.

So it was, as the old man had implied, that the hut appeared, surrounded by a circle of dark green conifers, all of them bent and inclined towards the hut as if listening to the sorceress's secret spells.

He stepped up to the doorway, vines of ivy twisting uncomfortably at his ankles, and raised his hand to knock. But before his knuckles hit the wooden door, it creaked open and Bannock's gaze fell on the inside of the hut.

'So, Lord Bannock,' came a sharp voice from the depths of the hut. 'It is banishment you seek?'

The hut was so dark that Bannock could barely see three feet in front of himself, let alone Grindella. He dared not step a foot inside without being asked to do so first.

'There is a knight most unwelcome at Rawdendale,' said Bannock. 'I would be pleased to see him relocated.'

The same sharp voice spoke again. 'What will be given in return?'

Bannock unfastened the money belt from around his waist and pulled a handful of coins from it. 'I have gold and silver and more should you wish.'

The sorceress laughed.

'I have no need for that of which you speak!' Grindella's voice was loud and seemed to be nearer. 'Tell me more of this knight. Does he give his affections to another?'

'There is someone,' said Bannock, listening to approaching footsteps. Then, in the doorway, she appeared.

Bannock was taken momentarily by her beauty. Tall. Slender. Her skin like a child's. 'Go on,' said Grindella.

'The king's daughter, Rosellene.'

A sudden stiffness came over Grindella and the hair on her arms stood on end.

Bannock would have sworn the sorceress's eyes flashed red like flames in the hearth. 'Do you know princess Rosellene?'

'Her name is somewhat familiar,' said Grindella. 'And is this knight young, handsome and strong?'

'Indeed,' said Bannock. 'He is all three.'

The sorceress appeared to mull the idea over. Finally, after a long silence, she said, 'Come in.'

Stepping inside the darkened hut, Bannock felt most uneasy. He had never been one to scare easily but now, as he scanned the room for the sorceress, sweat leached profusely from his skin. He did not like the tone in her voice. She either planned to kill him or had considered an adequate payment.

'I am in need of a new companion,' said Grindella. The door slammed shut behind Bannock and he heard the lock slide across. 'As you can see, my last one has lost his tongue.'

With a single clap of her hands, Grindella brought light to a dozen candles, the inside of the hut now visible. She then turned her bright blue eyes to a chair in the corner. 'He ate something that did not agree with him.'

Thinking there was someone else in the room, Bannock turned quickly in the direction of the chair and there in the corner, propped up by a mill broom, a skeleton could be seen dressed in a man's shirt and trousers. Bannock guessed that it was not something he ate but more so what he did not eat.

Realising that he may be in a dilemma, Bannock moved swiftly towards the door, fumbling to grasp the dagger he had hidden beneath his shirt.

'Fear not, Bannock. It is not you I seek.' The sorceress joined him in the doorway, her long golden hair skimming across the floorboards as she walked. 'If this man is as handsome as you state, I shall banish him here and take him as my own. Does that please you?'

Bannock breathed a sigh of relief. 'Very much so.'

The sorceress then turned on her heels and approached a shelf lined with shapely glass bottles filled with things that were both dead, alive and partly in between. Reaching high to the top shelf, she retrieved a squat bottle, smothered with dust and cobwebs and containing what appeared to be a dead toad. With the lid removed, she took from it the toad and holding it by one slimy leg, dangled it over a cauldron of bubbling water.

As steam rose from the cauldron, the toad suddenly jerked, let out a pleading croak and was dropped into the water. When sufficiently cooked, the now floating toad was scooped from the surface, placed onto a wooden board and dissected.

'There is a key, hidden somewhere in the castle. I want you to find it and bring it to me.'

'A key?' Bannock asked, diverting his eyes from the wooden board.

With intestines strewn from corner to corner, intermingled with heart and lungs, the board now resembled a map.

Perspiring, Bannock stepped away from the cauldron. 'What does it unlock?'

'Your concern is not what it unlocks but its whereabouts.'

'And the details of this key?'

'Come closer and I will show you.' Grindella beckoned and she walked nearer the hearth.

'You understand there are many keys in the kingdom,' said Bannock, trying to sound brave. 'I shall not know where to begin.'

'This key is unique,' said Grindella with a smile that made Bannock uneasy. 'Hold out your hand.'

Without hesitation Bannock stretched out his right hand. Instantly, Grindella seized his hand, spun it sharply so that his palm faced the roof, then branded him on the wrist with a hot iron.

Bannock squealed in pain as the smell of burning flesh joined that of boiled toad. 'Find me this key and I will gladly banish your unwelcome knight.'

Whilst waving his wrist madly in the air, Bannock searched for something to supress the pain. Water. Sand. Dirt. Anything to stop the throbbing.

'Here.' Grindella thrust a wad of old rags and a live snail at Bannock. 'Now go. Begin first in the princess's chamber. Find me that key.'

Bannock nursed his injured wrist the entire trip back to Rawdendale. It had been a difficult ride, especially given the use of only one hand. Rockslides impeded the narrow mountain road and biting winds were determined to blow him from his horse.

He was, therefore, grateful when just on dusk the towers of Rawdendale Castle came into sight. As he rode across the bridge, he looked again upon his wrist. He had bandaged the now blistered skin with the rags he had been given.

Preoccupied with his injury, he did not hear the warning from the watchtower and was startled when Oliver appeared before him in the darkened foyer, sword unsheathed.

'Lord Bannock,' Oliver stowed his sword. 'My apologies. I had no word of your approach. I shall announce your arrival to the king.'

Parched from the long journey, Bannock's voice was harsh and broken. 'No need.'

'You are here to see the princess then?' Oliver asked. He walked alongside the horse and noticed a slight nod of Bannock's head. 'Does she know of your coming?'

'No,' said Bannock gruffly. 'It shall be a pleasant surprise.'

'Indeed,' said Oliver, under his breath.

He did not like Lord Bannock. He liked even less Bannock's affection for Rosellene. He and Rosellene had known each other since childhood. She was like a sister to him and, as such, he was very protective of her.

Oliver glanced at the watchtower then back at Bannock. He would not be gone long, he thought, just long enough to warn the princess of her intended guest. So while Bannock left his horse in the stables, he bounded up the internal stairwell. Isabelle met him in the corridor.

'Dear Isabelle, Lord Bannock is this very moment on his way to find Rosellene,' said Oliver, almost without a breath. 'Pray tell me where she is so that I may warn her of his approach.'

'That man is a beast,' snapped Isabelle. With a look of regret, she put a hand to her mouth. 'Forgive me, Oliver. I should have held my tongue!'

'May you speak openly in my presence.' Oliver lay a gentle hand upon her shoulder. 'It is true. He is a difficult man to like.'

'She is in the western tower,' said the chamber maid.

'I shall go now and warn her,' said Oliver, taking the hall towards the tower. 'Delay him if you are able.'

Isabelle had just finished plumping the third cushion on the chaise lounge by the time Lord Bannock burst into the hall, demanding that he see Rosellene. She had an urge to hurl the cushion at Bannock's fat belly but she controlled herself, curling her fingers around the soft, velvety fabric before setting it gently on the lounge.

'I am afraid Rosellene is occupied at present. Perhaps if you call again on the morrow.' She watched Bannock pace back and forth across the floor, tripping on the corner of the large tapestry mat. Isabelle stifled a laugh. *Such a clumsy man*, she thought.

'I shall wait upstairs then,' said Bannock and he made to leave.

Isabelle let out a disgruntled cry. 'If you are intent on waiting, I insist you wait for her here.' She shook her head as Lord Bannock began up the stairwell.

'Perhaps you did not hear me, Lord Bannock?'

While Bannock supported himself against the wall, drawing in a few deep breaths, Isabelle snuck beneath his arm.

'Perhaps you did not hear me!' Bannock said, pushing her out of the way. 'I shall wait for Rosellene in her chamber. You will be seeing more of me in the months to come. Best you become accustomed to it.'

Grudgingly, Isabelle followed Lord Bannock up the winding stairwell then let him in to the chamber. She was surprised to find that instead of resting when he entered the chamber, he moved towards the dresser then proceeded to open the drawers and pull the entire contents onto the wooden top. Isabelle was speechless. It was the strangest behaviour.

'Please,' she begged. 'Those are the princess's private belongings. She will not take kindly to you rifling through her drawers. Heavens! What are your intentions?'

Leaving the items scattered on the dresser he pulled back the lid of the trunk at the end of the bed, using both hands to pluck out the neatly folded dresses from within and throw them carelessly onto the floor. Isabelle raced to the trunk and tried to close the lid. It was then that she noticed the loose bandaging around his wrist.

'My lord,' Isabelle touched him softly on the arm. His skin was damp and clammy. 'Let me tend to your wrist.'

Lord Bannock pulled away. He stood up quickly, a little too much so, for he tottered a moment before steadying himself on one of the carved bedposts.

'You are not well, my lord,' said Isabelle, trying to guide him towards the window seat. She knew that she would have no hope of shifting him if he fell. Just as Bannock was easing himself down onto the padded seat, Rosellene appeared in the doorway, short of breath. Her eyes were wide and questioning as she rushed to kneel at Bannock's side.

'He is not well, my lady.'

'Nor is my room, at first glance.' Rosellene took a clean handkerchief from the floor and used it to mop the beads of sweat from Bannock's forehead. 'What is it you were searching for?'

'Sp…sp…spoons,' Bannock stammered. 'I wondered where you had set the spoons.'

Rosellene made a gesture with her eyebrows and Isabelle pulled out the wooden spoons from behind the window seat.

'Pride of place on the window ledge, my lord. Pride of place.'

'I am pleased,' said Bannock and with that his face turned pale and he crumpled forward onto the floor, the cloth bandaging unravelling from his wrist as he fell. The two women gazed at the strange markings on his wrist. Isabelle went to touch the blisters but Rosellene snatched her hand away.

'It could be contagious,' Rosellene picked up an old piece of fabric from the floor and covered up the weeping sores. 'We should keep it covered for fear of it spreading.'

'Shall I fetch the physician?'

'No,' Rosellene's shoulders tensed. She could hear the panic in her own voice. 'The markings are most strange. Best if we not mention it to anyone.'

'You are wise, my lady,' said Isabelle, nodding. 'How shall we treat it then?'

'I will need some snails from the garden. The slime will prevent further blistering and heal the skin. If not, some eggs, nightshade and clean linen cloth.'

With a nod, Isabelle left the room wondering how it was that Rosellene knew that snail slime was a treatment for burns. When the door finally clicked shut, a closer inspection was given to the wound, and although the skin appeared red and weeping, the shape of a key was clearly visible.

But there was something else beneath the key. Five distinct symbols. A script of swirling letters, read easily by Rosellene.

The witches' alphabet.

A shiver tracked her spine. 'What have you done?'

It was undoubtedly the work of a sorceress. The key was a sigil and Bannock was bound to her. But what was given in order to receive?

Chapter Twelve

In his plight to find the key, Bannock returned to the castle no less than eight times in the course of a month. While the king looked upon his frequent visits most highly, Rosellene could not disagree more. She quickly grew tired of his company and protested that he leave on account of his nose constantly being where it should not.

So after his failed search attempt to secure the key, Bannock trudged back up the mountain to re-evaluate the conditions of his contract. Stepping towards the ominous-looking hut, the vines of ivy moving like thin, green snakes, he was grateful when the door groaned open. Entering the hut, he found Grindella with her back to him, hunched over a book, her long fingernails running back and forth across the page.

Beside her, resting against the table, was a staff. Slender and twisting, like the ivy outside, it was thicker at the top and tapered at the bottom. Carved from hickory it was topped with a crystal rosebud, leaves curled around the unopen petals. Bannock had not noticed it before and was about to ask as to its origin, when the sorceress spoke.

'It was gifted to me by the nuns.'

It was a lie. Many years before, living under the nuns' protection, she had seen the crystal in the chapel, forged to the side of the altar. Instantly, she had wanted it. When they discovered she had defaced the house of God, the nuns had been furious and had had no option but to expel her from their care.

Grindella tapped her nails against the top of the staff. 'Do you have my key?'

'I have many keys,' Bannock threw open his cloak to reveal a range of keys of all shapes and sizes affixed to a large, metal ring. 'We shall try them all. Surely one will unlock…whatever it unlocks.'

Grindella's expression did not change. She simply continued tapping her nails, louder and with growing intensity.

Bannocks shoulders slumped. 'Could you not just say some magic words and have it appear?'

'Something like this?'

Grindella curled her fingers around the staff, muttering an incantation that brought a carving knife flying through the air. It hovered for a time so near Bannock's nose that it seemed to tickle the very end, before being driven into the floorboards.

'Indeed,' said Bannock, picking up the knife before it could be used again. 'That would be splendid.'

Grindella snorted loudly. She contemplated slitting Bannock's throat and feeding him to the pigs outside but did not want to clean up the mess.

'Were it that easy, I would have done so before.' She hustled over to the overflowing shelves and cast aside some bottles with the back of her hand. Reaching towards the darkened back wall, she pulled from the shelf a large, uneven-shaped bottle containing purple liquid.

The bottle was shaken gently and the colour quickly blended. 'The chamber was revealed to me in a vision.'

'Have no doubt, if it had been in Rosellene's chamber like you suggested, I surely would have found it.'

'Indeed,' said Grindella and she stepped closer to Bannock. 'Very well. It shall be done.'

Bannock took a step back. The burn on his wrist throbbed. 'What shall be done?'

'You want me to rid you of a certain knight so that you and the princess can be together, do you not?'

'Why of course,' said Bannock, stepping backwards until he could do so no more.

'Very well then,' Grindella twisted the lid from the curious bottle, drawing the liquid up into the fine needle point end. 'Open your mouth.'

But Bannock shook his head and closed his mouth.

'Do not make this difficult,' said Grindella, most annoyed.

She was a sorceress after all and had many ways of getting what she wanted.

'Make what difficult?' Bannock asked, through a small opening in the side of his mouth.

Grindella was in no mood for games. She swiftly raised her boot and brought it down heavily on Bannocks left foot. He let out an awful scream that allowed

Grindella to deposit three drops of the liquid onto Bannock's tongue. She then held his lips together and waited for him to swallow.

'Never have I tasted anything so vile!' Bannock spat, his stomach convulsing.

'Bat droppings are an acquired taste.' The lid was replaced and Grindella returned the bottle to the shelf. 'This is my way of ensuring you remain true to our contract for as long as I require.'

Bannock gave her a quizzical look.

'Should you decide not to continue searching for the key, you will die a very, very unpleasant death.'

Bannock went to speak but Grindella hushed him with a single wave of her hand. He shuffled against the wall and eased himself into a chair, never letting his eyes move from the sorceress. He watched as, with the point of a knife, she etched some symbols into a purple candle then spoke the names of absent people.

Next, she lit three candles, black, blue and purple, and laid them on a table with cloth of green before taking a sprig of mint and letting it burn in the flames. With one hand on her staff, she prayed first to the four elements, then made her intent clear.

Breathing deeply, she allowed her eyes to close and said, 'In two days' time, the king will hold a meeting. All the lords and barons of Rawdendale will be in attendance. You will go to him then with word that the Ormans have breached the northern shores, seeking to invade the kingdom in the dead of night.'

Grindella drew in a few short breaths, each one more restricted then the first. Her chest sounded full of fluid and Bannock feared that at any moment she might collapse to the floor, dead. 'When day becomes night, send Caprion to the water's edge.'

Grindella buckled at the knees, falling forwards onto the table, her eyes no longer blue but a cloudy white.

Bannock rushed forth to her aid but Grindella threw up a hand to stop him.

'Leave me now,' said she, and using the staff to support her weakened body she ushered Bannock from the hut.

And so it was, in two days' time that during the king's meeting Bannock burst into court to make an announcement. As foretold, the room was occupied by lords, barons and a great many knights of whom were holding a grave discussion on reuniting alliances with the nearby tribes, when conversations were halted by Bannock's untimely entrance.

The king lay his hands firmly on the table, alarmed by the intrusion. 'What manner is this in which you interrupt court?'

'Forgive me, your highness,' said Bannock, with a bow. 'But I have disturbing news that must be told.'

The king stood from his chair, his deep brown eyes filled with concern. 'Then pray tell us.'

'It is said that the Ormans are headed for our shores.'

Silence filled the court. Several of the knights stirred in their chairs, hands automatically resting on the hilts of their swords.

Caprion rose to his feet. 'And the source?'

'Reliable,' Bannock replied, trying to keep his focus steady as he lied.

The Ormans had been dormant for a good few months but the king had known all too well that this time would come.

'How long do we have?' The king asked, trying to remain calm amongst the room of anxious nobles.

'They will be here by night's end.'

All eyes turned to their king for instruction. There was no hesitation as he said, 'Then we shall ride out and welcome them at the shore.'

No words spoken amongst them, the knights left the hall for the armoury. Squires worked efficiently readying their knights for battle. Soon, the warhorses were mounted and the knights rode towards the gatehouse. All except Caprion, whose path took him towards the inner bailey in the opposite direction.

'Caprion?' Bannock questioned, spying the route by which Caprion was headed. 'Do you run?'

Caprion turned to Bannock, a bitterness in his mouth. 'I run to Rosellene. She has not yet heard the news.'

'There is no time!' Bannock said harshly. 'The shore of which we speak is half a day's ride. You must not delay.'

The queen, having acquired the news from her husband, hastened to farewell the men. Battles were not new to her. She had seen many dear friends lost during these times. And although, she did not condone them, she accepted their presence as part of life.

Unfastening a small, silver brooch from his surcoat, Caprion rode up to the queen. 'Might you give this to Rosellene?' The brooch was placed in the queen's hand. 'And tell her that the marsh's east rides well today.'

'I will.' The queen cupped the brooch in her palm then said, 'God bless you, dear Caprion, and may the winds bring you safely back to these walls.'

The men had travelled not yet a mile when Rosellene caught whispers of the attack. From her chamber window, the riding party could be seen making their way along the ridge, their bodies thickly dressed with armour that reflected the morning's light. Praying all the while that the whispers were simply tainted rumours, Rosellene rushed to the gatehouse to confront her father who stood beneath the great stone arch alongside his queen. 'Why did you send him?'

The king looked down upon his beautiful daughter and cursed his position. Once before he had sent his best knight and a small company to scan the borders of Rawdendale. There had been little to suggest foul play, yet when the company had not returned by nightfall, fear had begun to escalate.

Rosellene had no knowledge of the king's orders that day, yet her skin crawled. Blood froze. Hands shook, as she took up the mortar and pestle, grinding ginger and garlic with a drop of elderberry. But as she ground, she knew he was fading.

So, a healing had been sent, wrapped in the smoke of an incense bundle. Crystals positioned. Intentions spoken. Spells cast.

But it had been in vain. Before the sun reflected the tears on her face the following day, Saxon was dead.

'Rosellene, understand that this is his duty.'

'Duty? It is not his duty, Father.' Rosellene could feel her eyes filling with tears. *I was never given the chance to say goodbye. I never told him how much I loved him.* She turned away from her father, wiped her eyes clear then turned back once more. 'Fifty men against how many? The more men you send out, the fewer return. The Ormans are too strong, Father, and I fear that it is not duty, it is murderous.'

'Rosellene, wait,' the queen called after her daughter, who had begun down the cobbled pathway. 'He bid I tell you something. He spoke of the marsh.'

Rosellene faltered. Slowly, she turned, tears rolling freely down her cheeks.

Raising her full skirt a few inches from the ground, Rosellene moved towards her mother. 'What of the marsh?'

'He said the east rides well.' The queen's eyes were weeping, yet she stayed composed holding out her hand. 'Oliver minds your horse.'

'Bless you, Mother.'

A kiss was laid upon her mother's cheek before Rosellene took the silver brooch from her mother's palm, fastened it to her shawl and rushed forth to where she found Oliver waiting with her saddled horse.

Chapter Thirteen

Twas not long before the marsh was reached, the war party a mere speck on the outskirts of the village. Without a shift in momentum, Rosellene urged her horse towards the eastern section of the marsh, her heart weighing heavy in her chest. She wondered if this would be the last time she saw Caprion alive.

She knew far too well of the Ormans, despising the battle tactics of these ruthless savages who hacked their opponents to pieces with long-handled axes. In battle, few were left with their lives and those that were spared suffered both emotional and physical torture long into old age. Killing was a sport to the Ormans and neither age nor gender impacted on their rules of fair play.

The eastern section of the marsh spread almost to the ridge along which the war party had just ridden. Rosellene's approach did not go unnoticed.

'Do my eyes play tricks?' One of the knights queried, slowing his horse to a walking gait. 'What do you call this, madness?'

Several other men reined in their horses to capture the strange sight on the marsh. As they watched, their heads shaking in disbelief, Giles, the veteran amongst the riders, moved past these men to the back of the group to gain Caprion's attention. Soon, the entire party paused momentarily and gazed upon the marsh, for this was a sight to be seen.

Never before had the marsh been ridden across. Nor had it had, in sections, the water drained away so that a series of small islands protruded above the surface, making a path for a lone rider.

'Come back to me,' Rosellene pleaded, jumping from her horse into Caprion's arms for an embrace both wished not to retreat from. While her tears marked the lining of his hood, she used her index finger to draw a symbol of protection gently upon his back.

'I would be a fool not to,' said Caprion, caressing Rosellene's small, soft hands in his. Suddenly, the strangest sensation washed over his body and for a fleeting moment he was inclined to stay. It was not apprehension about what he might face; it was more a fear of what might happen if he left. 'I see you have my brooch.'

An image flashed before Rosellene's eyes and she felt compelled to remove her heart-shaped ring, passed down through the generations, said to protect the wearer from all manner of evil. 'And you shall have my heart.'

Far too small to fit any of Caprion's fingers, Rosellene slid the ring onto her necklace, put her arms around Caprion's neck and fastened the clasp. It slipped beneath the padded undercoat and fell onto the strong muscles of his chest. And with a kiss on a tear-drenched cheek, Caprion bid his love farewell.

A scout, on hands and knees, crawled along the damp ground and peered down upon the northern shore. His eyes grew wide as he gazed upon a dozen boats, all fashioned with a highly curved stern. Backing away from the cliff edge, he tumbled and turned most terribly as he returned to the base of the cliff where the riding party waited.

The men congregated around the scout, waiting while he found his breath. 'What news, Nathaniel?' Giles enquired. 'Do the Ormans approach the shore?'

'Nay,' Nathaniel loosened the gambeson around his neck. 'They have already made shore; some twelve boats now rest on the sand.'

Giles shook his head, quickly calculating the number of Ormans they were to face. He kissed an amulet strapped around his neck, praying for strength as he turned to the men. 'It seems the Ormans are already upon us. Take courage this day and…'

Giles was cut mid-sentence by the scout.

'I could not be certain that they have in fact breeched the shore. In this weather, tracks, had there been any, would have surely vanished.'

'You imply that they may still be on the boats?' Giles paced silently as he mulled the situation over. Twenty men at least would have boarded each boat and from the stunned look in the eyes of his men, he could tell they too, had considered their plight. 'We wait till nightfall.'

So the men waited on the cliffs edge, lying on the cold, wet ground, watching the boats for any sign of movement. But when the hours passed with nothing more seen than the movement of the Ormans flag, as it flapped unnervingly in the wind, Caprion grew restless.

'Let us be gone. I fear we have waited long enough. Perhaps they have made for the castle. What say you, Giles?'

Giles rubbed his tired eyes. They were not the same eyes that had helped him hunt when he was young, now they blurred and were out of focus. 'A point duly noted.'

'The night has yet to fall,' Bannock's voice seemed panicked. He faced the veteran leader and added. 'It could be an ambush.'

Caprion slapped a hand to Bannock's back then started down the bank, onwards to the shore. 'If you are as skilled with that bow as you claim to be, then I have nothing to fear.'

As he watched the small group of men descend the bank, Bannock looked to the sky and then to the shore. How was Grindella to reach the boats if not under the cover of darkness? Surely, she could not have done so before now with the men keeping watch like they did.

Standing closely together with their shields raised, the men edged nearer the boats, stepping cautiously, their ears and eyes open. But when they were close enough to touch the boats and see the damage of rough seas, they were struck by such a powerful odour, a rank smell of organs, blood and faeces, that many of the men backed away, emptying the linings of their stomach on the sand.

'Dead! All of them dead!' Caprion climbed on board one of the boats and walked amongst the carcasses. 'What has befallen them I cannot say.'

Removing the cloth from his mouth and nose, Giles spoke quietly to Caprion. 'Do you surmise it was their own doing, Orman against Orman, or is there another evil at play?'

'Either way it would not be wise to linger.' Caprion looked to his leader for a response but Giles seemed lost for words, his face a ghostly white.

When asked what it was that had scared him so, Giles could only point to a menacing cloud forming over the ocean. Quickly building in size and deepening in colour, the cloud moved towards the men bringing with it much rain, wind and lightning. In the centre of the cloud, dressed all in black, a woman floated in mid-air, her long, golden hair whipping across her face in the wind.

Fearing the worst, the men got to their knees, praying that their lives be spared, but the woman did not shift her gaze from Caprion, extending her arms towards him as she rode the dark cloud.

Having nothing but sword and shield to protect himself, Caprion raised them both, staring the woman down as he said, 'Do your worst, devil woman!'

So tried she, casting spell after spell, but all attempts to seize him failed, the spells ricocheting from Caprion's sword and shield back to the water in which she stood. Then finally, when Caprion stumbled, the necklace with heart-shaped ring falling outside his surcoat, Grindella understood.

Scornfully, she retreated beneath the surface only to reappear beside Bannock on the hilltop. 'You told me not of the ruby!' Grindella said, enraged.

Bannock was taken aback by the sorceress' presence. 'I know nothing of a ruby.'

'Caprion wears a protective ruby around his neck. He cannot be touched whilst ever it is worn.'

'Then I shall cut it from his chest and he is yours,' said Bannock, pulling his sword free.

'The protection will still hold. It must be given willingly.' Grindella's eyes narrowed as she watched Caprion below. He had not yet risen from his knees, too stunned by the event just passed. Then, she smiled most wickedly.

'What is it?' Bannock asked, looking at the scene below. 'What pleases you?'

Grindella turned her piercing eyes towards the sea. 'The sword is double edged.'

'Your riddles are lost on me.'

'We may have a problem, yet now we also have a solution.'

Bannock shrugged then went to sit down but Grindella seized his arm and pulled him back to his feet. 'The necklace not only holds a ruby…it also holds a key.'

Bannock was quiet, seemingly still confused.

'Are you truly that daft?' Grindella shook her head in disbelief. 'The key for which we search is worn around Caprion's neck!'

Bannock frowned. 'And that is good news?'

'For you,' said Grindella and she quickly understood how Caprion came to possess the ring and the repercussions for doing so. 'Think now of Rosellene, for without the ring, she is unprotected.'

Chapter Fourteen

Sunlight streamed through the tower's arched window onto the fine, silk material that hugged Rosellene's figure. Three women, all of them skilled in the art of dressmaking, pleated, puckered and poked pins into the material so that it was soon shaped into sleeves, bodice and full skirt as yellow as the sun itself.

For a time Rosellene stood perfectly still, waiting patiently while the women made her turn this way and that, ensuring the length was even, but as she stared out the window at the crowd of people congregating in the market square below, her thoughts quickly turned to the riding party and her stillness faltered. With her nose pressed so near the panels of the window that fog formed, there came a sudden knock upon the door.

'Pray, you may enter.'

Rosellene turned and the door swung open, her eyes lighting up at the sight of her uncle's face. Elated, she jumped from the stool she had been standing on to embrace him.

'Apologies for the intrusion, my lady,' said Giles. His eyes met those of one of the seamstresses, a sleeve torn from the dress held in her arm.

'What word of the party? Does Caprion return?'

'He does, my lady,' Giles looked at the women and stepped nearer the door, his voice lowered. 'Something occurred whilst on the shore.'

'To Caprion?' Rosellene's voice was panicked. 'Injured, pray tell me not?'

Giles shook his head. 'Physically, nay.'

Rosellene's forehead encroached her eyes. 'He is plagued then, an illness?'

'In a sense,' said Giles, tentatively. 'A sight most strange was seen on the northern shore.'

Rosellene tilted her head. 'Strange, my lord?'

'Most strange,' Giles continued. 'And since that time not a word has Caprion uttered. Not one word and it is feared that his voice may be stolen.'

Rosellene gasped, a hand upon her heart. She knew of a young boy whose voice had been taken from him. After witnessing the murder of both his parents and two older siblings, it was months before the boy's voice returned, and although he could again speak, he forever jumped at shadows and found sleep most difficult. It was thought that the lack of sleep drove him to distraction, for in the end he took his own life, leaping from the chapel's highest steeple.

'What a sight this must have been for it to take a man's voice,' Rosellene paused in thought. 'Stolen? I pray that it is only hidden.'

'It has affected us all in different ways,' explained Giles. 'Some of the men have taken to drink. Some have returned to their faith. Myself, I have tried both but neither provides relief nor answers to the many questions I have.'

'Take me to him,' Rosellene begged, clutching Giles by the hands. 'I would very much like to comfort him if I am able.'

News of Caprion's heroism spread quickly throughout the kingdom, nay, throughout the land. Whispers of sorcery circulated and depending on whom was telling the tale, Caprion had either defeated a three-headed dragon or a water serpent, tearing it to pieces with his bare hands.

Regardless of who or what had been defeated, the king was most pleased. He quickly called forth his chief advisor, having him draw up a contract that saw that Caprion now owned a section of the king's finest land, along with one hundred shillings (a year's wages for many).

When the king called for Caprion so that he might extend his congratulations and hand over the contract, Caprion was found in the chapel, kneeling before a painting of the Lord, praying, as he had done so for the past few hours, that some sense would come of this.

'Caprion, the king bids you join him in the great hall.' Genuflecting on the way in, Marcus moved along the chapels slate floor towards Caprion and laid a gentle hand upon his shoulder. 'Sir Caprion, the king calls for you.'

With his eyes still set on the painting, Caprion stood, nodded at Marcus, then accompanied him from the chapel to the great hall. The king was seated at a large writing desk when they arrived, marking a sheet of parchment with first his signature and then the kingdoms seal.

Noticing Caprion in the doorway, the king stood, threw open his arms and said, 'Dear Caprion.'

But before the king could say another word a flash of yellow caught his eye and Rosellene stood before him in her half-made dress.

Speaking in a whisper, she said, 'Treat him gently, Father, for he is most troubled.'

The king looked scornfully upon the unlaced dress with its absence of sleeve and said, 'It is I who am troubled.'

He turned to Isabelle, who near but fell into the room.

'Sorry, your grace,' Isabelle bowed her head most regretfully. 'She could not be stopped!'

Giles hurried across to the king, and speaking in a hushed tone, said, 'Rosellene speaks the truth. Caprion is not himself. The northern shore has affected him. Rendered him speechless.'

Suddenly, a great thud was heard as Caprion crumpled to the floor.

Giles rushed to his aid, supporting him under the arms while Rosellene tended to a gash upon his eyebrow. Yellow satin made for a good bandage.

'Rosellene, fetch the physician.' The king's order echoed through the room. Rosellene sighed. She wanted not to leave.

'As you wish,' said Rosellene and reluctantly she made to leave. But when she stood, a weak and pale hand, clasped her wrist.

'Pray, may she stay?' Caprion asked, his gaze upon the king.

The king looked to Giles, who stood with mouth agape. He nodded and as Giles rested Caprion's limp body against his own, the king spoke to his daughter.

'Listen, should he decide to speak so that we may ease his state of mind.' Rosellene looked upon her father's aging face. Was there concern within his eyes?

'That I will, Father, but only if he desires to speak. I shall not force him into conversation.'

When someone was mad in mind, it was practice to take a bath of steam. The use of hot rocks was said to restore a man's health if done oft enough. This, along with sustenance, was the physician's first call of action.

'Isabelle,' said Rosellene, after the physician had treated Caprion's gash with a strong-smelling ointment. 'Prepare a bath for Sir Caprion and see to it that he has clean clothes.'

'That I will, my lady,' Isabelle hurried off to heat the small boiler.

'Have you eaten?' Rosellene asked of Caprion.

It was obvious from the hollowness in his face that he had not, yet Rosellene asked still. 'Not for days,' came Caprion's reply.

'Breakfast will be ready upon your return then,' said Rosellene with a hand gesture. 'The bathhouse is that way.'

'My lady, you are most kind.' Caprion nodded then headed down the hall to the bathhouse.

With tub, basin and pipes of gold, the bathhouse was elaborate. Fresh herbs, hollyhock, mallow and camomile, sprinkled delicately in the water, could be smelt even before the heavy drapes were stepped through. Steam thick and warm struck Caprion's face, shifting day old grime in an instant.

His clothes resting on a stool, Caprion gingerly stepped into the water, immersing his body in the herb-strewn bath. Accustomed to washing in streams or oft not at all, the sensation of being cooked like meat in a stew took some time to get used to. As instructed, he washed, rinsing his face and neck in rose water taken from a large, ceramic basin, then submerged all but his head.

Water tickled the hair at the base of his neck and that on his head, particularly around the temples, curled in the heat. He was beginning to relax, body and mind. His eyes slowly closed, the drapes, steam, bath, disappearing into the blackness of his eyelids. Peace was coming.

Then she appeared.

Eyes of red. Hair of gold. Skin so black it looked burnt.

Water cascaded over the rim of the tub as Caprion sat up in fright. Even at rest, he could not escape the devil woman.

On her way to the great hall, Rosellene heard the splash from the bathhouse. She had been to the kitchen and was returning with a tray full of fresh fruit, plums, apricots and cherries, a bowl of figs and sliced bread that had been toasted. Alarmed by the sound, she tilted the tray, a plum falling to the floor and rolling beneath a wall hanging.

What if he is drowning? She thought. *Is it even possible to drown in a bath? And what of murderous deeds? Could someone have stolen into the castle and thrust a knife into Caprion's chest whilst he bathed? But who would gain from Caprion's death?*

Rosellene tried to shake the thoughts from her mind. Did she need the bath of steam more than he?

Spying Isabelle in the alcove, she beckoned her near and asked, 'Would you call upon Caprion?'

'Call, my lady?' A pink hue crept into Isabelle's cheeks. 'What if he is unclothed?'

Rosellene smiled to herself. She hoped Caprion would be unclothed if bathing. A vision from the riverbed returned, a stomach of toned muscles, skin bronzed from the sun.

Isabelle lay a gentle hand upon Rosellene's shoulder. 'My lady.'

The vision faded and Rosellene turned her head away. She too felt the colour rising to her cheeks. 'Call by means of checking that he fares well, call to him.'

'Very well, my lady.' Isabelle smiled. It was not a secret between the two that Rosellene found Caprion most appealing.

Isabelle moved towards the plain, red drapes of the bathroom, Rosellene two steps behind her, both looking yet trying not to see through the steam.

'Caprion,' Isabelle called when she stood in reaching distance of the drapes. 'How fare thee?' They waited for a reply. None came.

'Perhaps he has drowned?' Rosellene nudged Isabelle urging her forwards. 'Call again.'

'Caprion, how fare thee?' Isabelle called again, a hand to the drapes.

The ladies jumped and together let out a cry as Caprion appeared behind them, fully clothed (to their disappointment).

'I am most refreshed, thank you, ladies.' Caprion stated and then he smiled.

There was something about his smile. Teeth that, despite many battles, remained straight and quite unmarred. Rosellene liked his smile. Indeed she liked his eyes, his square jawline and his hair, to which at present she was staring.

Rosellene reached out and pulled away a piece of hollyhock caught on a damp curl. Caprion smelled good. Not of stew but of the garden in springtime, fresh flowers. He was most attractive.

'We are pleased that the bath was to your liking,' Rosellene spoke quickly and walked away even quicker, colliding firstly with a large column that seemed to appear from nowhere and then the tray of food as she moved into the doorway. 'Shall we eat?'

So Caprion ate all that had been on the tray and drank thick ale, listening as Rosellene spoke of all manner of things, from her new dress to tales of her youth. While Caprion was grateful for the distraction, he knew in time past events would be mentioned, so best if he broached the subject.

'You have not asked after the northern shore?'

'Nor shall I ask,' said Rosellene, removing the tray. 'I am sure that whatever you saw has been relived a thousand times.'

'My mind is most troubled,' Caprion began. 'It has been days since I slept and my eyes grow weary. But I dare not close them for fear of seeing that woman.'

'Then you must change this thought,' Rosellene suggested. 'Change the situation. The outcome.'

Caprion stood and paced, hands joined behind his head. 'Is that a possibility? Can it be done?'

'It is your mind, Caprion. Anything is possible.' Rosellene replied, hoping that she sounded convincing. Wise women in the village had cured many men of their ailments. Those that could not be cured had either been bled or burned to remove the devil.

'Think of all that man has achieved. The ideas. The visions. Did they not begin first in the mind? Indeed, the torment must be great and though I know not why she sought you, I do know that you are safe whilst in my father's home. Pray that you lay your head down, and should, perchance, your eyes grow heavy and close, allow them to remain so and take comfort, while you dream most pleasantly, that I will be here when you awake.'

So lay Caprion down and allowed his eyes to close, his head upon a cushion. In an instant, with a fury most intense, the devil woman appeared. But slowly, little by little, he willed her to change.

Eyes once red, now blue. Hair once long and unruly, now contained in a plait along her spine. Skin once dark as charcoal, now soft and pale. And with the devil woman gone, Caprion fell asleep, feeling the gentle grooming of Rosellene's fingers through his head of curls.

Chapter Fifteen

In the corner of a darkened chamber, she sat, eyes fixated on the golden candle arbour in front of her, the glow from its single flame the only light in the room. But it was not like before.

Something was wrong.

The rounded mirror sitting on the dresser next to the arbour had moved quite easily, its long handle leading the way as it almost glided across the top of the dresser. So too had the circular hairpiece and also the pewter comb, somewhat easier than them all. All three had been moved in no time at all but the arbour would not budge.

Why is it so difficult? *the young girl thought.*

So stared the young girl until her head began to ache and her eyes watered, her thoughts on nothing else but the candle arbour and her intent that it move. How it moved was of little concern. A shift to the right would please her equally as a shift to the left; even an extinguished flame would be something.

It was not until sometime later, when her body shook and the items on the dresser were no more than an orange blur, that it happened. Quite unexpectantly her focus became unsteady and she voiced her intention. But it was not the candle arbour that moved. No, it remained quite stationary in the centre of the dresser, the flame merely heightened by the sudden shift in the room.

Instead, it was a small, leather-bound book that rested beside the arbour that moved. One could have thought that it simply fell of its own accord from the dresser to the ground but that would not explain how firstly it rose from the dresser, hovered for a time, then landed with a thump on the ground. Of course, the book would have hovered longer had it not been for a shriek in the hallway that made the young girl turn her eyes away from the book and onto the queen who now stood, ashen faced, in the bedroom.

'Mother.' The young girl moved towards the queen. 'Whatever is the matter?'

'This has to stop!' The queen said, entering the room. 'Did you learn nothing from your grandmother?'

'Come, sit a while,' the young girl directed her mother to the window seat. 'You look ill.'

The queen hesitated, then allowed her daughter to lead her to the padded window cushion where she then sat. Small beads of sweat had formed on her forehead and she felt compelled to open the window for some air.

'I tried to ignore it. I did not want it to be true. How could I bear to lose another? But I see now that it is in you, just like it was with your grandmother.'

'I will fetch the physician,' said the young girl, now patting with a handkerchief the queen's moist forehead. 'I fear you are not yourself on this day, Mother.'

'It is you that needs the physician I fear, not I.' The queen stood, steadying herself on the stone window frame. 'Why did you feed this darkness within?'

'Please, Mother,' said the young girl, trying to sit her mother back down. 'Wait here and I will get some help.'

'No!' The queen demanded. 'I have to go. I must tell the king.'

'Tell the king what, Mother?'

A single tear left the queen's eye. 'That our daughter has succumbed to the same sickness as her grandmother. She too, must be banished.'

The young girl twisted a few strands of her long, blonde hair between her fingers.

'Oh, Mother. Grandmother was not sick,' said the girl. By now, the queen was edging her way closer to the hall, towards the door and the way out. 'And you should not worry, for nor am I.'

'I saw you…with the book,' said the queen, heart racing as she felt the curved edge of the doorframe. 'We will get you the help you need and this will not happen again. A few months in the abbey and you shall be cleansed. There will be no more magic.'

'Grindella! Are you ill?'

When Bannock arrived at the hut, he found the sorceress lying on the floor, shaking and perspiring as though sick from fever. With rigid limbs, she arched her back and mumbled something about the castle and stared through unseeing eyes.

'The time has come,' she said.

Awoken from her trance, Grindella looked most unwell. Using the staff for support, she stumbled across to the large, oak table in the room's centre, sifting through the assortment of items on it. She then cast a leather satchel at Bannock.

'Make yourself useful,' she snapped.

When, after a moment, Bannock had not yet moved, she beckoned him nearer with a single finger. 'What is it we are doing?' Bannock asked, sorry he had not left sooner.

'Packing provisions,' said Grindella as she slipped several thin bottles into the folds of the satchel.

'Provisions?' Bannock questioned, peering into her glassy eyes.

She appeared not to see him. When he packed provisions, it was the bare essentials, necessities to keep one fed, warm and protected. He wondered what journey lay ahead when all Grindella packed were candles, charcoal, herbs, oils and a knife with curved blade.

'Do you need that?' Bannock asked, his voice suddenly a high-pitched squeal as a live snake was nestled into the bag. 'What is that for?'

But Grindella did not respond, leaving Bannock to contend with a very lively reptile. 'Are we not kidnapping the princess?'

'We are,' said Grindella, her eyes only just returning to their normal blue hue.

'Rosellene?' Bannock confirmed.

'Do not speak her name!' Grindella roared.

Bannock jumped, his hands thrown in the air. 'My apologies, only it seems you are expecting the task to be, how shall I put it, difficult?'

A scornful look was cast in Bannock's direction. 'How little you know.'

'The castle is well protected, of that I am certain.' said Bannock. 'What is it you are expecting?'

'It is not the protection you can see that has me concerned,' Grindella threw a mantel upon her shoulders before stepping outside. 'It is what you *cannot* see that will cause us most grief.'

Chapter Sixteen

In a small hut by the edge of the sea, a little, old woman woke from slumber in a lather of sweat. Jumping quickly from the bed, a shawl was thrown over her shoulders as she fumbled in the darkness trying to light a small lantern. Once lit, she held the lantern high as she rummaged through a cluttered shelf and into a basket placed a strange assortment of items. Amongst the items was a small, wooden box. Taking a cape from a hook behind the door, the old woman left the hut and trudged up the steep bank to where a horse was tethered to the branch of an oak tree. Putting the cape on, the thick hood covering her wild, grey hair, the old woman rode off towards Rawdendale Castle, the basket now full, held tightly in the crook of her arm.

When she arrived at the castle's main gate, a good time later, the old woman rode up to the guard, and speaking sternly, said, 'You must let me in to see the king.'

But when the guard stepped nearer the rider, the light from his lantern shining upon her face, he saw skin that appeared both wrinkled and unclean, and thought at first that the old woman was merely a beggar come here to ask the king for money. So asked he, 'And why at such a late hour should I allow this?'

To this the old woman replied, 'The king's daughter is in danger.'

The guard flashed a set of yellowing teeth. Rawdendale Castle contained two curtain walls, both with a height of thirty feet. Built with ashlar stones and filled with a rubble core, the fifteen-foot-thick walls were strong and could not be breached or undermined by any man.

There were one hundred and eighty arrow loops, a watchtower and a quarter mile of wall walk that stretched between ten open backed towers set at regular intervals, patrolled at present, by twenty men. The king's daughter was not in any danger.

'Unless you have an invitation or the king's personal seal, I fear I cannot allow you passage into the grounds.' The guard took hold of the reins and turned the old woman's horse around. 'I suggest you return from whence you came and know that the princess is very well protected.'

Growing impatient with the guard's unwelcoming reception, the old woman reached into her basket and pulled from it the small, wooden box which contained a gold ring. 'As I said, you must let me pass.'

The guard took the ring which had been thrust into his face and authenticating that it was in fact marked with the king's seal, he opened the gates with a bow, allowing the old woman into the castle grounds.

It had been many years since the old woman had walked through the courtyard, yet despite the years, little had changed. The chapel, with its detailed masonry columns, still stood on the far-east wall, the small presbytery beside it. Three ancillary buildings were found adjacent to the chapel, along with a wheat-filled granary, a dwelling belonging to the cobbler and nearest the kitchen garden, a large mew housing twelve white gyrfalcons.

The old woman moved swiftly across the uneven courtyard, pausing briefly at the mews to tut at the birds (an excessive expense in her opinion), then moved inside the keep. In the feeble light, the old woman negotiated the spiral stairwell that led to the bedchambers, stumbling much on the worn stone steps.

The old woman was most alarmed when, after opening the heavy, wooden door to the bedchamber, Rosellene was not in the room. Looking first upon the high-post bed down to tussled sheets and then stepping towards the fireplace with embers burning still, the old woman turned back towards the door and said, 'You need not the weapons, child.'

When the light touched the old woman's silvery hair, the water jug in Rosellene's hand fell to the floor, shattering into pieces. 'Grandmother?'

The old woman smiled. 'I dare say you can do without the knife as well.'

Rosellene looked down upon the thin, needle-like knife clutched in the palm of her hand, then stowed it carefully within the folds of her nightwear.

She shook. 'Surely I am dreaming?'

Her feet touched the floor, yet it felt like she was floating above it, looking down on herself from afar.

Sabine cupped Rosellene's hands in her own. 'No, my love.'

Rosellene threw her arms around the woman she had mourned, not knowing whether to rejoice or cry. 'They told me you had died.'

'In a sense, I did,' admitted Sabine. She brushed back Rosellene's hair with her rough hands. 'Not being able to see the ones I loved was a death in itself.'

'Why could you see us not?'

'They thought it best if I stayed away for a time.'

'They told you to stay away?' Rosellene's eyes grew wide. 'You were banished?'

Sabine nodded. 'It was better than the alternative.'

'But father is the king, your son.'

'I am here now,' Sabine said gently. 'Let us not dwell on the past. He did what had to be done. I will not condemn him for his decision. He allowed me to live when others wanted me dead.'

How dare he cast her aside? Rosellene thought. *And lie about grandmother's existence? Despite the harsh words and cruel names thrust upon her, she cured ailments and flushed out toxins. She was a healer, nothing more. How many died because of her absence?*

'I am sorry to come at such a late hour but I have concerns for your safety.'

'Concerns? Rawdendale is heavily guarded, no man could…' Rosellene looked into her grandmother's eyes which seemed to twinkle. 'Yet here you are, not man but woman.'

Sabine turned her faded emerald eyes upon the window. Rushing forth, she leant on the sill, looking beyond the glass at the darkness fast filling the sky. A storm had settled over the castle, cold rain and bitter winds that shook the wooden shutters.

'We are too late,' Sabine spoke solemnly. 'She approaches.'

Rosellene felt her heart sink to the depths of her stomach. 'Who approaches?'

Changed now from her bedclothes, Rosellene looked to her grandmother for an answer, but instead Sabine turned to Isabelle, who had appeared in the hallway, a new determination upon her wrinkled face.

'Go forth to the kitchen and gather as much salt as you can muster.' Sabine could sense Isabelle's confusion and with no time to broach the subject carefully, she added. 'Salt will ward off evil spirits. Make haste, child!'

Rosellene's body trembled.

'I am beginning to take fright.' She watched as her grandmother bound some herbs in cloth and set them alight. 'Pray answer me, who approaches?'

Moving from corner to corner, Sabine shook the smoking bundle, mumbling words that Rosellene recognised as a spell for protection. With the room now filled with a sour smelling smoke, a mixture of sage and myrrh, Sabine set about unloading her basket, positioning candles of black, white and red in precise

90

places around the room, lighting the wax wicks. The candles flickered and hissed.

'A sorceress, more powerful than I.'

Rosellene rushed to the window. A feeling of helplessness weighed heavy on her heart. Since Saxon's death, she had shunned magic. It had let her down in a time of need. Why then would she waste her time memorising charms or creating potions? There had been no room for magic in her life.

Until now.

'Why has she come? What does she seek?'

But Rosellene received nothing more than mumbling as, after pouring hot wax from a candle into the water basin, Sabine peered at the hardened shapes now floating on the water's surface in an almost trance like state. It was not until Rosellene shook her quite forcefully that the pupils in her eyes returned to their rightful size and Sabine looked once more upon her granddaughter.

'While the room is well protected, having been so for many years, I fear it may not be enough. These past few moons her strength has grown.'

The window shutter was pulled closed and secured with a leather tie.

'When you speak of protection, you speak of Giles?'

Sabine shook her head and gestured towards the chamber door.

In the doorway, a single floor stone was shifted, eased free with the tip of a letter opener. Beneath it lay an iron knife wrapped in a piece of white linen. There were more protective symbols etched on the walls, above the many arched windows and upon the paving on the floor, strange circular markings neither of beast nor written word, yet a combination of both.

Gently, Sabine touched Rosellene's hand. 'Now that you have lost your protection, you are most vulnerable. Lost?' Sabine squinted as she searched for answers within Rosellene's eyes. 'Nay, given to another. His plight was greater than your own. You have a kind heart, child.'

Rosellene touched her naked fingers. She had been eight when her grandmother had given her the heart-shaped ring and she had sworn to wear it always, despite it being too large for any of her fingers bar her thumb.

'You speak of the ring?' Rosellene dropped her head. 'I did not know.'

'How could you if you were not told?' Sabine spoke gently. 'It may be to our advantage that the ring is not here.'

'Am I the one she seeks?'

Her grandmother's face fell. 'Do not alarm yourself, though. She shall not harm you.'

A sudden wave of panic crashed upon her stomach and Rosellene felt she had fallen from the steeple. 'Why? What is it I have done? Have I offended her in some way or form? Or father? Does she use me for revenge against him? I do not understand.'

'There is little time so I shall be brief in what I say,' Sabine spoke quickly. 'Magic has always been within us but you possess something more. A power not yet harnessed. A power that in the wrong hands would lead to devastation.'

Rosellene's legs wobbled. She sat before she collapsed. 'Power?'

'You will be a great leader one day but Grindella wants to tap into this power, claiming it for herself. She has not the mind to control it.'

But should I not want to lead? Rosellene thought. *And power. It leads only to misery and pain. I want it not.*

'How am I different? My mind may choose the same path.'

'Nay,' Sabine grabbed her granddaughter's hands. 'Your heart is pure. Your love is true. Your path is just.'

Isabelle soon returned; arms laden with bags of salt. Slicing the hessian open with a knife, Sabine took one of the bags and scattered the salt along the window ledge and beneath the door, in an unbroken line.

When the bag had been drained, she turned to Isabelle. 'Continue with the remaining bags as I have done, ensuring no gap is left.'

Isabelle nodded.

Then, from the sky, came a mighty roar and a blinding flash of light. The candles flickered madly then went out in unison. The three women stood in darkness.

Chapter Seventeen

'Whilst ever you remain in this room, she cannot harm you.'

Between the flashes of lightning, Sabine managed to find Rosellene, embracing her one last time before moving through the doorway. 'Lock the door behind me and do not leave this room.'

A crushing sensation took hold of Rosellene's heart. It squeezed. It squashed and threatened to shatter her heart entirely.

'No,' Rosellene caught Sabine by the wrist. 'I will not let you go.'

I should be the one to go. It should be me.

But it was too late. Magic had failed her, and as such, the knowledge required to defeat a sorceress was buried deep in the cortex.

'I love you far too much not to go.' And with Rosellene's fingers peeled one by one from her wrist, Sabine slipped from the room.

Without the light from the candles, Isabelle could not be certain that her line of salt was unbroken. So using flame from the hearth, she set about lighting the wicks. No sooner had the wicks been lit then a breeze crept through the window and blew them out once more. If the protection of the chamber failed, how was she to keep the princess safe?

'My lady, has the sorceress set eyes upon your face?'

Even though her face was shrouded in darkness, Isabelle could almost feel Rosellene's frown, a bad habit that too oft crept upon her brow.

'Sorceresses can take many shapes. I cannot be certain,' Rosellene paused. 'Why ask you, Isabelle?'

But there came no answer.

'Isabelle. Pray answer me,' Rosellene's voice trembled. 'Dare not do something foolish.'

Still, no reply was given. She was beginning to think that Isabelle had left the room when all of a sudden two hands held her by the shoulders and forced her back towards the eastern wall that was covered almost entirely by a large tapestry.

'I am sorry, my lady,' Isabelle lifted the tapestry from the bottom and thrust Rosellene into the hidden chamber behind it, the heavy, stone door firmly locked. 'I could not forgive myself if any harm came to you.'

Rosellene blinked in the darkness.

'Isabelle, I admire your bravery, but this is foolhardy. I command you unlock this door!' But Isabelle would not listen to reason; her mind was made up.

Fighting back tears, she said, 'When the voices in the room are long gone, turn the lever near your left hip. It has been a pleasure serving you, my lady.'

'Isabelle! Pray do not leave this room unless we do so together! Isabelle!'

For what seemed an eternity, Rosellene pounded her fists against the hard, stone door until her knuckles grew red. Slumped on the floor, she listened for any sign that Isabelle remained still in the room. Nothing was heard.

Then the hairs on her arms awoke as a shrill voice echoed in the distant hallway. 'Come forth, Rosellene, or I shall cut the old woman's throat.'

Not wanting anyone's blood on her hands, Isabelle stepped nearer the doorway, her palms cold and clammy. Sabine lay on the floor, a bunch of her grey hair caught between Grindella's fingers. Her thick cape was reduced to threads, as if she had been dragged a great distance across the stone floor, and her left foot appeared to jut out beneath her skirt at a strange angle.

With a knife pressed firmly against the thin skin of her neck, Sabine carefully lifted her chin. She prayed that her expression did not give Grindella any indication that it was not Rosellene dressed in the pale blue evening gown.

A single tear meandered down Sabine's wrinkled face. 'Stand your ground, child.' The grip on Sabine's hair tightened and the knife tip pierced the skin.

'Do so and she dies,' Grindella cackled. 'Come forth and she shall live.'

A series of alternative outcomes swirled within Isabelle's mind, the majority of them ending with the old woman's blood drained on the floor.

'I shall move only when you do,' Isabelle's voice was slow and deliberate. 'With each step we take in the direction of that suit of armour, grandmother takes one towards this door.'

Grindella cackled once more but agreed to Isabelle's terms. One pace at a time, she moved nearer the suit of armour, watching in delight as Isabelle stepped beyond both the silver dagger and the salt line out into the hallway. While Sabine, whose ankle was indeed broken, pulled herself along the floor with her hands into the safety of the chamber, Isabelle was seized and dragged down the hallway. Screams echoed off the hard walls.

Bannock met them at the top of the spiral stairwell, his rounded boots bespattered with mud. 'Come, let us away,' Grindella scowled, barely slowing her pace as she began down the stone steps. 'I have what I came for.'

Bannock did not follow, his eyes set on the figure in the pale, blue dress. 'You came for the princess, did you not?'

Grindella stopped abruptly, her voice raised. 'Is this not she?'

'Nay,' Bannock admitted, watching Grindella's eyes grow wide. 'That is her chambermaid.'

Grindella screamed. The thick panes of glass in the alcove window shook.

'You dare waste my time, chambermaid?' The veins in Grindella's head thickened with rushing blood. A hand was raised.

Isabelle's body tensed. Trembling hands covered her face but nothing could stop the wrath of a sorceress. A bolt of fire struck her chest and Isabelle was thrown backwards, flames leaping from her dress. They burned through fabric and flesh. They stopped her heart.

'She must be in the room still,' Grindella's hands curled into fists. She turned her eyes to the guards who had appeared at the top of the stairwell, then looked back at Bannock. 'Go! Seek her out.'

Bannock could see little past two feet in front of him as he searched the darkened chamber. As he moved to open the window shutters, hoping for the aid of light, he felt something soft crunch beneath his feet. When the light filtered into the room, he looked down below the windowsill at a figure slumped against the wall, the shattered fingers of a hand cradled in her lap.

'Where is she, witch?'

'See for yourself,' Sabine said through shallow breaths. 'She is not here.'

With his sword pulled from its scabbard ready to take the old woman's life, he caught sight of a smear of blood leading to a large tapestry hung on the wall.

'Yet, she was here.'

Pulled from the wall and cast aside, the three-hundred-year-old tapestry rested on the chamber floor as Bannock tried unsuccessfully to open the stone door. Knowing that Rosellene would surely evade him if he took the stairwell, Bannock instead ripped the fine, satin sheets from the bed, twisted them most profusely, tied an end to the window frame then proceeded, somewhat awkwardly, to scale the outside of the castle.

While Bannock descended, so too did Rosellene. Anxiously, she had waited in the small closet, hand upon the metal lever, listening as the voices faded. But then a voice had returned.

At first, it had been soft. A female voice, elderly and in pain. Then, it had grown louder and more distinct as Sabine had approached the door, imparting a message of how to reach her hut and instructing her not to return to Rawdendale, unless she was sent for. Footsteps were heard. More voices and her grandmother's firm instructions to go. So the lever at her left hip had been pulled and a chute, released.

She was falling. Quickly. The rough, stone wall scraping through first cloth then several layers of skin. With no shoes upon her feet, she could not slow her descent. Below her, a glimpse of light. Larger and larger it grew until she landed on the soft grass of the courtyard.

Darkness.

A hood was pulled over her head and she was thrown carelessly into the back of a wagon, shackled as if she were a pig on the way to market.

Chapter Eighteen

Long before the men awoke and prepared themselves for battle, Caprion, having heard the sky's unrest and seen the strange transition of lanterns from chamber to chamber, was at the watchtower searching for answers. When he climbed the enclosed tower to the platform on the fifth floor, he wondered not at the fact that the guard who met him in the darkness tried to take his head before discovering he was an ally.

'Forgive me, Sir Caprion,' said Oliver meekly, his sword resheathed. 'I am most uneasy on this night.'

With a nod, Caprion moved to the platforms edge and leaned on one of the many merlons that surrounded the watchtower. From this height, it was the norm to see for miles, yet on this night, as the rain extinguished the last of the fire sticks, Caprion could see nothing of the courtyard between lightning strikes.

'You have reason to be, as you say, uneasy. I, too, feel a presence that brings a shiver to my very core.'

As the rain strengthened, Oliver took shelter beneath the roof, the thin, woven cape affixed to his armour pulled tight across his chest. 'The old woman is to blame. Trouble began the moment she entered the gates.'

They took the spiral staircase down to the third floor, moving across the scuffed, wooden floor to the fireplace. Taking up a poker, Oliver stoked the fading embers and soon the flames danced once more in the hearth. It was in this growing light that Caprion noticed several deep gashes upon Oliver's face, scars attributed to many years of battle he guessed. Yet Oliver was a young man.

'Old woman, you say?' Caprion tried not to stare at the poorly treated wounds. 'What business does she have at Rawdendale?'

'A warning for the king,' Oliver shook his head, moisture dropping from his russet-coloured moustache. 'I fear it now a ploy that may cost me my life.'

'I shall take my leave then and see to it that no harm befalls the king.'

But as Caprion stepped towards the stairwell, Oliver's mail-covered arm reached out to stop him. 'Nay, it is not the king's life in danger,' Oliver spoke loudly so as to be heard above the heavy fall of rain. 'It is Rosellene's.'

A flash of lightning filled the sky and Caprion fell upon his knees.

'My lord, were you struck?' Oliver looked down at Caprion whose face was a ghostly white. 'My lord?'

For a time, Caprion was still, frozen, in a sense, like the moat below. He could not hear the words spoken by Oliver nor feel his touch as he tried aimlessly to raise him from the floor. His eyes were transfixed on Rosellene's chamber and the devil woman that stared back at him.

There came then a noise from the base of the keep, a sound as though something, or in fact someone, had fallen from a great height.

'Oliver, the lantern!' said Caprion, now on his feet. 'Quickly, make haste!'

But although their pace was swift, it did not allow them to reach Rosellene before she was thrown into a covered wagon and driven away.

Rosellene's muffled screams could be heard in the distance as Caprion hurried towards the livery stable. The rain had melted the snow, making the ground hazardous under foot, and with Oliver gone, the lantern with him, Caprion moved quickly, yet cautiously.

How has this happened? Caprion thought. *Yet again, I have failed to protect those closest to me. Why did I not hear something sooner? Perhaps I am no longer fit to be a knight, for what else is the responsibility of a knight but to protect? I must find her. There will be no more excuses. I will not lose another from my life.*

'Mine was the only one saddled,' Oliver led his mare from the stable and handed the reins to Caprion. 'Trust that she will go the distance.'

Caprion threw himself into the saddle. It was worn and had no fur for comfort. Still, it would have taken time to ready his own horse and time was something he did not have.

'I will treat her kindly, as is the favour you have shown.'

'Go. Bring Rosellene safely home,' said Oliver and Caprion dug his heels into the mare's flanks. 'I will raise the alarm. Alert the king.'

As Caprion rode off in pursuit of the wagon, Oliver hurried towards the church and the large brass bell that hung from the tower.

Arms raised above his head, Oliver pulled through the rope and let the bell ring out long, sharp and clear. A continual chime that sent panic to the guardhouse and the sentries within.

'My lord,' Marcus stepped from the guardhouse, rubbing his temple. The alarm had been sudden, unexpected, and evidently, he and a wooden rafter had clashed. 'What has happened?'

Leather straps were pulled and the mare turned. Caprion's face was pained. 'They have taken Rosellene.'

Marcus tightened the belt around his knee length mail shirt. 'Whom, lord?'

'I cannot say,' admitted Caprion. 'But when I find them, they shall go to hell on the end of my sword.'

Angus stepped from the shadows, his game of dice interrupted by the tolling of church bells. 'Assemble at the western tower,' his voice rang out. He watched his men leave then turned to Caprion. 'You fear it a trap, my lord?'

Hooves stamped in the mounds of snow that were quickly being eaten away by the falling rain. Nostrils flared. 'Even so, I must give chase.'

Angus grunted. 'We ride with you then.'

'I need you here. The castle cannot be unprotected. Defend the king and queen.'

'From whom, lord?'

'The devil herself.' Caprion's eyes shifted to the chamber. Angus shuddered.

'You should stay,' he suggested. 'She likes you. I shall rescue the princess.' The bell chimed again. Intermittently.

Marcus turned. Nodded. 'She moves to the eastern tower.'

Caprion paused. He had not the strength to match the sorceress again. But dare he leave the men to face her alone?

'Go, lord,' Angus slapped the horse's rump. 'We will do what we can here. Go. You are needed elsewhere.'

Men fell into the bailey. Helmets were slammed upon their heads, swords and shields at their side as they made for the eastern tower. When they reached the defensive structure some of the men faltered.

They could see no army before them. No enemy to fight. No one except a woman.

'Shield wall!'

Angus' orders echoed through the night as he joined the men in front of the tower. No one moved.

Angus turned disgruntled eyes upon his men. 'You will obey me.'

'It is a woman, lord,' one man stammered. 'A woman. Why do we bear arms?'

Angus pushed through the men, the tinkering of rain on his shield. 'She is no woman.'

A long, black cape was draped around Grindella's foreboding figure. The heavy hood, dampened by the rain, rested upon her golden locks. She crossed her hands against her stomach then rested them upon her hips. Tilted her chin to the heavens.

Shields were lowered. Glances exchanged. Orders should not be disobeyed of this they knew, yet they wondered how much defence a single woman required.

'Pick up your shields!' Angus roared.

'She is but one woman.' A voice said. 'Who appears unarmed.'

'Do not be fooled,' the king called from the left flank where he joined his men. Dressed in plate armour, he was prepared for battle. 'Let us not forget it was she we faced upon the northern shore. She has the strength of an army behind her.'

It was then that the wind howled. A long and sorrowful cry that resonated through the courtyard.

The sorceress, her fingers twitching, reached into the leather pouch affixed to her belt and from it withdrew some pebbles to which were cast onto the ground. Her eyes closed, she took her hands to the air and appeared to paint upon an invisible canvas, lines that were straight, curved and interlocking. Flags tore from their banners and drifted upwards beyond the curtain wall. Weapons wavered, slipped from the hand that held them. Soldiers, with no control over their own feet, stumbled and fell on the icy ground.

Grindella dropped her hands and the wind fell silent.

Angus threw down his visor. 'I say again, shield wall!'

This time the men listened. They took up the leather straps at the back of their shields and raised them, trudging slowly across the bailey closer to the eastern tower. The sorceress could exit nowhere but through the wooden door at the base of the tower. This had been barred from the inside and presently twenty bodkins were locked on her. And so it seemed, Grindella was trapped.

'We shall be merciful,' the king commanded. 'Come forth and you shall not be harmed.' The sorceress took note of the archers above her then looked to the king.

'I have seen your merciful actions.' She edged towards the shields and the wash of blue and white that coated them. 'They are no more so than I am God fearing.'

'I will honour that which I have said.' The king thrust his sword into the earth. 'No harm will befall you.'

'Forgive me if I do not believe your lies,' the sorceress mocked. 'Too easily do they slip from your tongue. While you have lowered your weapon, many more have not. Your men are anxious. I hear their thoughts. I shall not be staying. I have what I came for.'

The king glanced to the archers above. To the trembling fingers that rested on a drawn bow. The unblinking eyes. The muscles that flexed. One word and he could bring the sorceress down.

He hesitated. Grindella did not and one by one those archers fell from the curtain wall into the courtyard below, a bodkin nestled in their skull.

The king hung his head as the tower's wooden door skidded across the ground and landed at his feet.

And just like that, she was gone.

'Out of my way,' came a shout. 'I must speak with the king.'

Heads turned towards the keep as something took out the right flank, flattening a half dozen men, who kissed the earth with their bevors. They scrambled to make rank again and rid themselves of the delicate fabric that clung to their armour like mist.

Although, covered by his basinet, the scowl on the king's face was undeniable. 'What is this, Bannock?'

Bannock shook off the last of the satin sheets caught upon his armour then said, 'Caprion, lord king. I fear he has again lost his mind. He has taken the princess.'

'No.' The king tried to brush Bannock aside. 'I do not believe it to be true.' Bannock did not move.

'Best sit down,' Angus suggested. He pressed his hairy face against Bannock's ear. 'You are talking through your arse.'

Bannock caught sight of Oliver, clutched his mail shirt and drew him nearer.

'Believe it, your highness.' Bannock declared as Oliver now stood before the king. 'This boy saw it with his own eyes.'

The scars on Oliver's face seemed to twitch. He knew from past experience that Bannock did not bluff. Threatened, he gave a feeble nod then cast his eyes at the ground.

The king scanned the boy carefully. 'Now is not the time for accusations.'

The king's voice broke off as Isabelle's body was carried along the foyer. Draped in linen cloth, it did little to hide the damage cast upon her. The king's shoulders slumped. This was indeed a sad day.

Angus too felt the loss. The pain of death. The agony of war. The anger of sheer incompetence.

'You imbecile!' Angus hurled himself at Bannock. 'This was your doing, you daft piece of shit!' Marcus struggled to hold Angus back.

'Inside,' the king demanded. 'All of you.'

Back in the great hall, the queen fidgeted nervously with her rings.

'What an absurd notion,' she said after being informed that Caprion had been involved in the kidnapping. 'That sorceress is behind all this.'

'That may be so,' Bannock bowed his head more than once. 'Yet Caprion is surely possessed by her doing. The madness is taking control.'

'I want not to believe you.' Suddenly feeling dizzy, the king eased himself onto his throne. 'Yet I fear the repercussions if we do not at the very least find Caprion, if only to clear his name.'

Bannocks chest broadened. Angus exploded with rage.

'He told me himself that the princess was taken!' Angus roared, a great, purple mass swelling at his temple. 'I swear it, lord king. He is maddened not, nor is the princess in harm's way by his making.'

The king curled his fingers around the throne's arms.

'You are a friend of Caprion.' The king paused. 'Bannock, see that my daughter is returned.'

'It would be my honour, your grace.' The smirk on Bannock's face was not hidden. 'I shall organise a riding party this very moment and lead them myself in search of the princess. Worry not.' Angus could do little but clench his fists.

While panic settled in the king's veins, the queen however, was feeling a different emotion. She did not like the way Oliver clung close to Bannock, nor the way Bannock smiled most contentedly when he strode from the hall.

So called she after him, 'Oliver, how fare thee?'

'He is simply overwhelmed, my lady,' Bannock chimed. 'The night's events have stunned us all.' But the queen would not be satisfied with the response. 'I wish to hear from him myself.'

Released from Bannocks grasp, Oliver trembled. 'It is true, I am most overwhelmed. But I shall rest easy, my lady, knowing that Rosellene is protected by the angels above.'

Protected by the angels above.

For an instant, the queen's breath was taken. She had not heard that expression since Rosellene was a child. Used as a warning signal when in danger, those words had been drilled into them as children.

'We must keep watch on Bannock,' she whispered to Angus in the shadows of the corridor. 'Better still, let us seek Nicholas for guidance. I am most suspicious.'

Chapter Nineteen

It was late afternoon when Rosellene finally awoke, the shrill sound of seagulls echoing around her. On the bridge of a grand castle, she found herself chained to a mooring post, her lips so blistered she was barely able to speak. Trying to escape the harsh sun, she moved nearer the open drawbridge, seeking refuge in the shadow cast by a large dragon statue.

With its wings spread wide, the dragon sat back on its hind legs, watching over the ocean, which at present was at low tide. Each and every scale was etched deeply into the stone, from its head to its tail, which wrapped itself down a stone pillar and into the underground forest of kelp below. Here, amongst the shiny, brown weed, birds feasted on the exposed limpets, wrenching them off the rocks then pecking open the conical-shaped shell to eat the muscular foot inside.

Harvested at low tide and added to dishes like broths and stews, kelp had once been a staple food for the villagers of Rawdendale. Limpets too had been used oft, and on some occasions, eaten raw.

It was while reaching for a limpet to do just that, stretching the chain links attached to her ankles as far as they could, that there came a series of tremors. The drawbridge lowered and there appeared on the wooden deck a most ugly looking creature; man or beast, Rosellene could not be certain.

Barely clothed and with rounded shoulders, it crossed over the moat, its long arms hanging close to the ground. What little hair sprouted from its head was long and greasy, and its skin was marked with knife slits which crisscrossed their way across his flesh.

Now hovering between bridge and sea, Rosellene wondered if she should play dead in the hopes the ogre would leave her be. But as the ogre raised his nose to the air and sniffed through the smell of salt, she felt a hand upon her head and was dragged up onto the bridge by her hair.

'Stay,' commanded the ogre, his breath so repulsive it made Rosellene's stomach churn. 'He comes.'

'Who?' Rosellene asked, her voice strained. 'Who comes?'

'He comes.' the ogre repeated.

Rosellene slumped to the ground. Whoever *he* was, it did not matter, for without food and water, she would be dead before he arrived. She watched as the ogre lumbered back across the deck and from beneath the spiked portcullis picked up a large, wooden barrel and rested it upon his shoulder. In his other hand, he took up a goatskin bottle, and returning to Rosellene, he dumped them both at her feet. He then sat down with a thud and waited.

'Good,' he said, and with a single hand, pushed the barrel nearer Rosellene.

Nervously, Rosellene pulled herself up from the ground and peered into the barrel. She was much relieved to find it filled with bright, red apples. And so she took one from off the top. Biting into it, she thought it the tastiest apple she had ever eaten.

Then she picked up the goatskin bottle, and removing the clay stopper, put the spout to her lips and let the sour ale trickle down her dry throat. Taking a second apple from the barrel, she looked across at the ogre.

'Thank you,' she said gratefully, to which he grunted in reply. But the second apple was not tasted.

Barely had it reached shoulder height when a pointed boot kicked it from her hand and it tumbled from the bridge, landing softly amongst the weed.

'Let us not waste our precious apples on Rawdendale filth.'

The ogre stiffened as the same pointed boot connected with his ribs.

Rosellene held a hand to her forehead, trying to block out the sun as she stared at the slender figure before her. Squinting, she watched helplessly as the ogre was knocked to the ground and a woman, with hair of gold, sat upon his bulging belly.

'The years have treated you well.'

Rosellene looked upon the golden-haired woman. *How can someone so beautiful be so cruel?*

'You speak as if you know me or have done so in the past.'

'As children, we once played.' The woman watched as Rosellene's face turned ashen then added, 'Yes, I, too, spent time at Rawdendale.'

Rosellene's body twitched involuntarily. Her eyes glanced upwards and her breath quickened.

'Ah,' said the woman. 'You do remember.'

Rosellene shook her head. 'I recall nothing of you from my childhood.'

The woman blinked several times, her lengthy lashes almost tickling her eyebrows. 'And your sister? Tell me what you recall of her?'

Rosellene looked away. 'I have no sister.'

'Yet you did.' The woman crouched beside Rosellene, the scent of rosemary strong. 'Until she was driven from the castle.'

'You speak of lies.'

'I speak of memories deep within your mind. Memories that haunt you still.'

Rosellene's head ached. Her eyes burned and she thought she glimpsed something on the surface of the water. The images soon strengthened. A child appeared, in a white linen dress, running through the buttercups. Behind her an older child, perhaps twelve years old, her long, blonde hair pulled into a plait down her back. *Mirium?*

'I murdered that man for you. I saved your life, yet I was punished,' said Grindella. 'So think you on your past while you wait for your saviour. Pray that Lord Bannock will not be far away. The tide is fast approaching.'

'Lord Bannock? You are mistaken,' Rosellene shook her head. 'Sir Caprion will come to my aid.'

'Yet that is not the plan.' The woman pulled hard on the chains tied to Rosellene's wrists so that the metal cut deeper into her skin. 'You will be rescued by Lord Bannock and live happily ever after. For a time, that is. You have something valuable that I desire. When I reclaim what is rightfully mine from Rawdendale, I will come and find you. Together, our destinies lie. But first, I shall have some fun with your knight. It seems he too, has something I want.'

The chain was released abruptly and Grindella stepped away, her eyes almost eating into Rosellene's flesh. And as she stared, her hand fell into the depths of a satin pouch affixed to her belt and from it she pulled some rosemary sprigs, which were crushed between her fingers. As the leaves dropped to the ground, the scent remaining upon her skin, she pressed her hands to Rosellene's temples and closed her eyes.

'You will remember me yet.'

Try as she might, Rosellene had not the strength to stop the memories as they seeped into her mind, a mass of heat and pain. Drowsiness overcame her and as she struggled to support her lolling head, she heard the sorceress and the ogre speaking.

'No one is to take the princess, you hear me, beast, unless they are Lord Bannock. You will know the man when you see him for he is big and slovenly,'

Grindella paused. 'Much like yourself. You will ask him the riddle, to which he must answer: a tanner, a fletcher, a blacksmith, in that order.'

There came upon Rosellene's head, a hand which with nails, long and curved, brushed through her hair. 'Sleep well, Rosellene. Sleep well.'

And when Grindella stepped upon the shore, the ogre took the now dreaming Rosellene, placed something soft beneath her head and covered her from the heat. He was not as repugnant as he looked. He came from a peaceful tribe in the Shattered Mountains and missed his family.

Dragged from the arms of his mother when just a child, Grindella had claimed him as payment for damages when a runaway cart had almost knocked her down. Magic, of course, had released the chock that held the cart and Grindella had every intention of returning with an ogre. Sadly, Hermes was that ogre.

Chapter Twenty

The full moon looked in upon the astronomy tower and frowned.

Nicholas Cooper did not sleep. Nay, he was wide awake.

'Curses and crucibles!'

Tired eyes skimmed yet another scroll. They blinked and yawned under the light of a dimming lantern.

'Why so cryptic?' Thin, bony fingers held down the parchment that was marred in several places. Round spectacles were adjusted. 'Perhaps it reads graynes and not scruples as first thought.'

A flask exploded behind him. The fifth for the evening. His old body rattled. 'If only I could remember,' he moaned. 'My mind is not as it once was.'

Worn shoes shuffled slowly across to a desk where books, piled dangerously high, had been read and re-read. Finding a particularly thick spell book, marked in several places with gold ribbon, Nicholas took hold of the laced spine and carefully wiggled it free from the pile. 'Let us try another potion,' He thumbed through the pages, thick with dust. *'Finding someone who is lost…*perfect.'

A mouse scuttled across the desk's embossed, leather top. It peered up at Nicholas with beady, brown eyes.

'Do not look at me like that,' Nicholas narrowed his eyes. 'I am trying. Truly, I am.' The mouse continued to stare.

'No, I have not! The nerve of you even asking such a question.' Nicholas turned on his heels. Familiars could be testing at times. 'You know all too well what happens when I use that crystal. Nothing good I tell you, nothing good.'

The mouse twitched its whiskers. Nicholas watched as it leapt from the desk and scurried across the floor, disappearing beneath a tall oak cupboard.

'I know where the ball lies,' said Nicholas gruffly. 'You do not need to show me.'

The muscles in Nicholas's face tensed. His breathing quickened. *Perhaps it is time,* he pondered. *No council can be sought from the cards.*

He strolled across the room, fingers steepled.

But nay, high is the danger of scrying.

Hands were thrust into the pockets of his robe, the lining crushed between fists. *Yet I must know Rosellene's whereabouts.*

And with his mind torn, he opened the cupboards bottom drawer and pulled from it a small wooden chest. 'I shall have but a brief peep.'

Set upon the desk, the lid was carefully raised. The smell of myrrh ascended into the room as wrinkled hands reached inside and took out first a bronze stand with wire fastenings. Setting the stand upon the desktop, again the wrinkled hands reached into the deep chest, pulling out next a bundle covered with silken cloth.

Nicholas hesitated.

Disturbing were his visions of late. Armoured men. Flying beasts. Snow not white but red. Dare he be haunted again by such evil?

Alas, it must be so.

Trembling, the cloth of black silk was unfolded, one corner at a time. And there before him, a crystal ball lay.

Nicholas eased himself into the high-backed chair, his breathing fast and irregular. With fingertips pressed lightly against the clear, quartz crystal, he closed his eyes and allowed his rational mind to be suspended. Many moons had passed since their last union and Nicholas wondered how long it would take before the connection was made.

Then it happened. As quickly as that.

Nicholas bolted forward, his eyes wide like crucibles.

The subconscious surrendered and he slipped into a deep, meditative trance.

A mist swirled. Thick, wispy fingers that danced for a time within the sphere. Then it disappeared.

'Heavens above!'

He wanted to scream. He wanted to scrawl ink across the parchment before the visions were lost but that would only break the connection and so he sat, quiet and still, as more and more images passed before him.

Bannock. Rosellene. Grindella. Caprion. Bannock and Grindella.

Eventually, the images dissipated.

Nicholas let his fingers slip from the crystal. 'No more. I have seen enough.'

In an instant, the crystal was covered, replaced in the chest and returned to the cupboard. The salt water cleanse would have to wait.

Nicholas paced across the stone floor, shaking his fingers. How they ached. 'What to do…what to do.'

Spying a half-filled mug of ale, he threw it down his parched throat then carried on pacing. His head pounded so much that it was difficult to think.

'Ahh!' He caught his reflection in the full-length mirror and threw it back. It did not look right. His beard was not white but blue. He moved in for a closer inspection. 'Ink…but how could I? Why is there?'

He looked towards the desk and the spilled ink well. *Stranger things had happened during meditation*, he thought.

From below, the sound of a rooster crowing was heard. Night had ended.

'I must inform the queen before it is too late!' Nicholas twisted his beard tightly then tucked it into the front of his navy gown as he hurried from the tower, onwards to the keep. Far too often, he had tripped on his beard.

'Yet what do I tell her majesty? Surely not the truth. Nay, not all of it. She is, however, suspicious of him. How would the information be received? It cannot be planned. My tongue is apt to disobey me regardless of the script. So let us speak to the queen and share the secrets we have uncovered.'

'Secrets?'

Nicholas faltered.

'My lord.' He steadied himself, a hand upon the stairwell's cold wall. 'You are yet to leave?'

'At first light,' Bannock locked his eyes on Nicholas. 'Why the haste? A change in the stars perchance?'

Nicholas noted Bannock's tone. He had never been fond of the sciences. 'The stars are ever changing, my lord.'

'You are far from the confines of your tower. What brings you to the keep? A council with the queen?'

Nicholas hesitated. His heart pounded against his blue beard.

'Nay, foolish really. I seem to have taken a wrong turn. The joys of old age, I am afraid.' Nicholas made to leave but could not. A chubby hand reached for his robe.

'You have lived your entire life in this castle. I do not believe you are lost.' The robe tightened in Bannocks hand. 'You come to share some kind of secret. It is not for me to keep you from the queen. I am headed that way myself. Let us go together.'

Nicholas dropped his head. 'As you wish, my lord.'

The walk to the queen's chamber seemed longer than usual. What now would he say to the queen in the presence of Bannock? Would he lie? Invent a different vision or somehow try to alert the queen of Bannock's intention.

But matter, it did not. The queen's chamber was never reached.

'You should not meddle with royal affairs.' Bannock pushed closed the iron door. 'You will only get hurt. Best you stay here, in this cell. Rosellene will be safe with me. I can assure you of that.'

Nicholas stiffened. A hand slipped into his pocket. 'I do not meddle.'

'You do many things, old man, and I will feel safer knowing you are confined.'

A metal candle arbour was used to secure the door. Nicholas wrapped his frail hands around the iron bars. 'Confinement will not stop what is coming your way.'

Bannock threw back his head and sneered. 'I do not need your council, old man. Fare thee well.'

A hand was withdrawn. Unfurled. 'God speed, my lord.'

And with a gentle breath, fine particles drifted into the air.

'You fool!' said Bannock, frantically trying to brush the powder from his clothes. 'What spell is this you have cast upon me?'

Nicholas stepped back. 'Protection, my lord. Merely protection for your journey.'

'Pray you are not here when I return.' Bannock waved a fat finger towards Nicholas and then fled down the stairwell into the darkness.

'You need not worry.' said Nicholas with a smile.

As soon as Bannock's footsteps faded, the legs of a wooden stool were pushed beneath the door and used to lift the door off its hinges. Now freed from the cell, Nicholas hastened up the stairwell and burst into the royal chamber, relaying his visions to king and queen without invitation.

'I had my suspicions.' A frown marred the queen's beauty as she looked to her husband for advice. 'My love, what are we to do?'

The king stared out the window, hands clasped behind his back. Glassy were his eyes.

'If Nicholas speaks the truth, a battle is upon us. A battle like no other that has come before it.'

'So we do nothing to save our daughter?' The queen questioned. 'Is that your wish?'

'I wish she had never been taken to begin with.'

The queen erupted into tears. 'We cannot leave her to fend for herself.'

'She is not alone. Caprion is in close pursuit. He will watch over her.'

'And if he does not? What then?'

Nicholas had said nothing since delivering his vision to king and queen. Feeling awkward, he had drifted closer and closer to the door, hoping to simply slip away back to the astronomy tower so he might think more on the prophecies seen. But he had been struck by a thought.

'Your majesties,' he said meekly. 'There is someone who can help.'

Chapter Twenty-One

The first thing I noticed were her eyes. Mirium had such strength but for the first time, I saw fear in her eyes. It took me a moment to comprehend the situation. Why my sister's hands were bound with rope, her mouth silenced by a piece of dirty linen.

It was not until they had hauled her into the back of a wagon, a cover of hessian pulled down upon her face, that my mother sat down with me and explained my sister had to go away. She had been sent to the nunnery to help cure the aches that invaded her head. Pain so bad that it was making her do things. Unusual things. Things that none of the other twelve-year-old girls in the kingdom were doing.

Perhaps that was why she killed father's friend, the one that kept whispering things in her ear. The pain in her head must have made her do that.

The day it happened, she was very upset. She came running into my chamber and made me hide behind the drapes. 'Stay there,' she instructed. 'No matter what happens. No matter what you hear.'

And I did, for a time. Then my father's friend came into the room. He started shouting at my sister. Threatening her. Threatening to harm me if she did not do as he asked. Then came a sound like feet being dragged across stone.

Furniture fell and the drapes were pulled from the wall. That was when the blood hit me. Warm and thick across my face. My father's friend turned to face me, blood squirting from a slit in his throat. He tried to stem it with his hands but the red liquid simply oozed through his fingers.

He stumbled forward towards me, reaching out a hand, his eyes wide as if begging me to save him. Then, he was in the air. His feet were off the ground and he flew backwards, hitting the wall and collapsing in a heap on the ground, a tangled mess of drapes, blood and man.

My sister ran to me and turned my head away, then covered his body with a corner of the drapes. She did not want me to watch the man die and neither did

113

I. We heard him, though. Coughing, spluttering, then heaving one last sigh before death claimed him.

As my sister wiped the congealed blood from my face, I began to cry. Her magic had been getting stronger. Stronger, and at times, brutal. We practised levitation together in the fields, far from the castle. It began firstly with rocks.

When we had mastered the rocks, we moved next to fruit and eventually small animals, like mice and toads. But I had never seen her lift a man before and move him with such force. I was in awe of her strength, yet it also terrified me.

'They will come for you.'

We were different and they would punish us for it if they found out.

'Yes,' Mirium slumped to the floor. She was shaking. 'They will.'

'Then we must leave. Head into the forest where no one will find us.'

'No,' said Mirium, staring blankly, her head in her hands. 'You have done nothing wrong.'

'Neither have you.' I tried to pull her to her feet but she would not budge. 'I will tell them what he said.'

Her hands wrapped now around her legs, Mirium rocked back and forth. 'I killed a man. I slit his throat. I ran the letter opener across his jugular.'

'We will hide the body then,' I moved over to the drapes. By now, the green material was stained with red and had affixed itself to the man's body. 'No one has to know.'

'How will we move the…' Mirium stopped, suddenly aware of her irony. She almost allowed the sides of her mouth to turn upwards. 'There is no place for magic in our world.'

'Please, Mirium, let us away.' I could hear the panic in my voice. It would not be long before father's friend would be pronounced missing. We could not afford to linger.

'They will find us. They always do. They will hunt us like wild animals and treat us just the same.' Our hearts sank as our father, the king, entered the chamber.

'What has been done?' He looked upon the stained drapes then straight at Mirium. 'If that is indeed the body of Lord Chancer, you, child, are condemned.'

It was midnight. The tide had come and gone and Rosellene, still tied to the mooring post, was weak and delusional. Already she had seen fairies flit across the surface of the water, their wings flecks of golden light, and memories of a lost childhood were returning like lightning bolts, jolting her body in and out of consciousness.

Then, the stillness of the night was broken by something on the shore. In the moonlight, Rosellene could just make out a rider approaching. From the distance, she could not define the rider until they stepped into the boat and took it safely across to the castle.

Desperately, she tried again to release the bindings from her hands and feet but, as it was before, the magic held strong. She looked then to her right, to the ogre whose chest rose and fell heavily as he slept. So called she to Hermes in the hopes that he would wake, and despite being told to release her to the slovenly man, save her from Lord Bannock.

'Wake up! Please, Hermes, wake up!' Panic set in as she saw the boat edging nearer the bridge. Then, feeling something beneath her shoe, she picked it up and threw it at the ogre. 'Wake up!'

There came a short, sharp breath. Then nothing.

Rosellene peered at the ogre, fearing that he had swallowed the stone she had cast and was choked. But then came a cough and a ping, as the stone catapulted from the ogre's mouth up into the air, where it landed then upon the bridge.

When next she looked towards the boat, it had stopped. Rosellene shook her head. Heroes were meant to be fit and strong and should never tire in their attempts to aid the fair maiden.

Nevertheless, it allowed her more time to think of an escape.

'Rosellene,' said Bannock, as he tapped upon the wood. 'Fear not. I am here.'

Evidently, her escape was poor. She had been found and although she clung tight to the top of the lid, Bannock managed to pull it from the barrel then set about releasing her chains.

'What is it you seek to do?' Rosellene asked, still slumped inside the wooden barrel.

'Set you free,' said Bannock. He watched the bright red apples bob upon the water's surface then strangely, smouldering, they disappeared. 'Is that not obvious?'

Rosellene could not agree. A life with Bannock would be a life condemned.

If only he had become lost along the way or been eaten by a bear, she thought. *He would be a fine meal for a bear. Quite a large helping.*

'Uhh!' Bannock screeched, as the ogre stepped forth. 'That is close enough, beast.'

Arms folded across his expansive chest, Hermes made his stance wide. From nostrils flared, came several looming breaths. Bannock grimaced.

'I am here to rescue the princess. Ask me your riddle so that I may get on with my task.' Bannock listened while the ogre thundered out his riddle.

'Now, what was it I had to say,' he pondered, tapping his forehead. Rosellene sighed. 'Ah yes. A tanner, a fletcher, a blacksmith.'

Hermes grunted and reluctantly reached a hand into his loincloth and handed over a key that appeared small in his large hands.

Bannock cursed, then in silk handkerchief, took up the brass key and inserted it into the first of two locks.

'What is your motivation?'

'I love thee, Rosellene.' Bannock moved next to the second lock which bound her wrist. 'That is my motivation.'

With sincerity, Rosellene pulled his hands away from the shackles and looked into his russet-coloured eyes. 'But it is unrequited. I do not love you, Bannock.'

'I have money, land and possessions,' Bannock did not take his eyes from the lock. 'You were kind to me in our youth. You will be so again. I will make sure of it.'

It was true. When other children had bullied Bannock in their youth (teasing and taunting him because of his weight), Rosellene had shown him kindness, momentarily tying knots in the boys' tongues so that their cruel words could not be spoken.

'Love makes you a fool. You think not, speak not, breathe not and walk as if one is floating in the clouds. I do not love you, Bannock, yet there is someone out there that does. I pray that someday you find her.'

Still, Bannock said nothing save to curse at his fat fingers and the small key that would not, try as he might, unlock the bands.

'Stop!'

This time her cries brought Hermes to her aid. With a growl that shook the ground, the ogre trudged towards Bannock. Before he knew what was upon him, the ogre had swung a gigantic arm and Bannock was propelled across the bridge.

'You stupid fool!' Bannock said, nursing his injured ribs.

Hermes looked at Bannock then turned his small eyes to Rosellene. Without her even speaking a word, he knew how she felt. He had taken a liking to the princess and despite being told by Grindella to release her to Bannock, he had intentions to refuse.

'Mine,' said the ogre, stepping in front of Rosellene, his nostrils flared.

'Well, no, I disagree. She is not yours. So if you would kindly step aside.'

Bannock continued walking, hoping the ogre would move. He did not. Bannock bounced off his bulging stomach and fell backwards onto the hard ground, the key falling from his hand.

The ogre then took from a hook, an old fishing net, threw it over Bannock, bound him with some rope, set him in the boat, then pushed him back towards the shore.

'Good riddance,' said Rosellene and she saw the ogre smile. 'Come, let us find another boat so that we may leave this place.'

But Hermes remained where he was. 'No.'

'You want not to come or nay there is no other boat?'

'No boat.'

Bannock's departure had rippled the water and now small waves tapped at the castle walls. Rosellene was struck by an idea. 'We shall swim then. It cannot be that deep.'

And she moved forth towards the stairs that led into the water. Just shy of the last step, she was stopped however, by a very powerful bicep and a roar that shook her every muscle. 'No!'

'No?' Rosellene questioned. 'We must reach the shore. Why is it that we cannot swim?'

A scrap of material (the remains of an old flag) was cast into the water. There came a hiss as the cotton fibres quickly charred. White smoke spiralled into the air and a smell like burnt leaves remained. The lake was enchanted.

Rosellene hugged the ogre. 'We will wait until the tide goes out.'

Chapter Twenty-Two

Grindella, although a powerful sorceress, could do nothing, try as she may, to harm Caprion whilst ever he wore the protective ruby ring around his neck. It was her intent, therefore, as she set out in search of Caprion, to somehow persuade the young knight to hand over the ring.

Caprion had been travelling two days straight, searching forest, mountain, hillside and every dwelling that he came upon. By now, his thirst and hunger had grown strong and he set forth for the nearest village to drink and eat. But before the village was in sight, there came before him a wagon. On a hollow stump, an old man sat cooking by an open fire all sorts of good-smelling foods and sipping wine from a carved, wooden mug.

Taking a bag of coins from his saddlebag, Caprion asked the old man for a share in his food, offering the coins in exchange.

'Indeed,' said the old man. 'You shall have a share, for the food is far too great for any one man.' So Caprion joined the old man by the fire and ate and drank his fill.

With his stomach and thirst quenched, Caprion set out again. He took a narrow trail that led him through a thicket and into a clearing. It was here that he came upon a woman sobbing over the body of a child.

'Please, Sir, I am a poor woman and have not the money to pay for my son's burial. I should like to bury him properly before the birds and beasts pull him apart and he is no more than bone.'

Caprion took pity on the woman.

'Had I the time I would bury your son myself but alas, I have not,' said Caprion and he pulled a bone handled knife from a loop in his belt. 'So you shall have my knife and pray that it be used as payment for the burial.'

A while later, he was passing by a vast lake when he saw an old woman wading through the water. She appeared to be searching for something.

'What is it that you seek?'

'Oh, alas, alas!' The old woman cried. 'I was cleaning the ring that was to be given to my daughter as a wedding band when it slipped from my hands into the depths of the lake. What now will my daughter have?'

Caprion looked first upon his left hand, at the worn silver ring he wore. Then, a hand to his chest, he felt the chain of the necklace and the delicate ring upon it.

Yes, yes, thought Grindella, cleverly changed into the form of an old woman. *Hand over the ring.*

But instead Caprion loosened the silver ring from his index finger, and with the ring nestled tightly in the woman's hand, he continued on his way.

The hours passed and soon Caprion arrived at a village where he was greeted by a young woman selling baskets of fresh produce.

'Pray, if I had money enough to purchase your goods I would indeed do so, but nay I have not. Perhaps, though, you could be so kind as to tell me if a lady, much like yourself, has passed by this way? She would be dressed in fine clothes and would not be alone, accompanied most likely by a golden-haired woman.'

The young woman stood and pointed to a distant mountain range, cloaked in swirling grey mist. 'Do you see the fortress?'

Caprion nodded. 'Indeed I do.'

'It is known as the Floating Fortress, for it would appear at times that it is floating amongst the clouds.' The woman paused, a frown upon her pretty face. 'I am afraid the lady of whom you speak is in there.'

'Take me there, kind woman, and in return I will give you this horse.'

'A horse such as that would plough a field in no time,' The woman thought on the proposition awhile then said. 'Very well, I shall oblige and take you to the fortress.'

The sun was close to the horizon when they came to the stone bridge that led to the fortress. The woman had spoken little along the journey yet when she did speak, her words were soft and soothing and reminded Caprion of Rosellene. And it seemed that the more Caprion looked upon the woman's attributes, the more like Rosellene she became.

It was as though he longed to see his love so much that Caprion's eyes had made it so. How the woman's hair was as long and dark as Rosellene's, with gentle curls that shone in the fading light. How the woman's hands were small and slender like Rosellene's. The woman's eyes were as blue and bright as sapphires, and the smell of fresh lilies lingered on her flawless, olive skin. In the end, Caprion was forced to walk in front of the horse, his back to the woman, so as to resist the urge to take her in his arms.

From the outside, the fortress appeared to gleam as if made of diamonds, cut and polished into large, rectangular stones then erected into a splendid monument of no fewer than nine towers, each with a decorative, arched window. But as Caprion tracked across the lowered drawbridge and entered through an unmanned gatehouse, he noticed that inside the fortress was quite unkept. He had little time to dwell on the state of the fortress however, and he quickly went in search of Rosellene.

Ten minutes passed and Caprion had merely scanned the lowest level. Bounding up the winding stairwell to the second level, he cried out Rosellene's name, hoping that she would hear his cries and come running. Alas, the second level was just as the first and all Caprion found were spiders and their elaborate webs cast from window frame to window frame.

Undeterred, Caprion surged on to the third and final level, where darkness hit him instantly. When his eyes adjusted to the change in light, he noticed a figure standing in the corner, a tall, slender figure that very much resembled Rosellene.

Caprion's heart raced and he seemed unable to move. It was just as the woman had said it to be and after all this time, he and Rosellene were reunited. But when the figure turned and approached him, the smile left Caprion's face. The joy vanished from his heart and he dropped to his knees in bitter disappointment.

'Are you certain this was the place and not another?' Caprion sighed.

'Quite certain. Have you doubts?'

'Clearly Rosellene is not here, nor be there signs of anyone having been here for quite some time.'

'Perhaps it was the journey that has clouded your vision.'

'Not so, my search was thorough. You claim to have seen her. Pray, tell me where?'

'Why, yes.'

'Yes, then make it that she appear so I may hold her in my arms once more.'

The woman smiled slyly. 'Dear Caprion, you are looking at her.' The woman stepped closer, her arms outreached. 'I am your long-lost love. Come, take me in your arms.'

In disgust, Caprion pushed the woman's arms away. 'You mock me when my heart is weak.'

'Look upon my hair. Is it not the same?'

Caprion paused, gazing upon the sleek black hair. So close was the hair to his face that he could smell the violets in the fillet around the woman's head.

'True, yet you are not the one I seek.'

A hand of soft ivory passed Caprion's eyes, coming to rest on his shoulder. 'And look to my skin.'

'Again you speak the truth yet you are not Rosellene.'

'And look into my eyes. Do they not remind you of Rosellene?'

Caprion swiftly turned away. The likeness was far too great for him to bear. 'Come now, rest awhile. The trip has made you weary.'

'Nay, I do not tire.' But no sooner had he spoken those words than his eyes became heavy. He tried to walk towards the stairwell but stumbled, falling hard on the stone floor. 'Perhaps I may close my eyes for a time.'

When next Caprion's eyes were open, it was dark. Thinking night had fallen, he made to stand but found himself half submerged in water and surrounded on all sides by a solid, stone wall. Getting to his feet, he realised he was no longer in the fortress.

The foul-smelling water and moss-covered walls indicated that he may be in a well, a well that was so deep it would be impossible to climb out of. With nothing more to do but think, Caprion thought back on the preceding days. And as he thought, the thin strip of light filtering through the grid at the top of the well widened then disappeared entirely as a figure came into view. A figure with devilish features.

'Hand over the ring, and in return, you shall have your freedom.'

Caprion put a hand to his chest. He knew not why a ring would be of importance to a sorceress, only that no good would come from handing it over.

So asked he, 'Why is it you seek this ring and not another?'

'That matters not,' the sorceress snapped.

'Yet you are a powerful sorceress,' taunted Caprion. 'Why not just take it for yourself?'

The bars shook. 'So you cannot.' Said he.

Grindella hissed through the bars, her expression snakelike.

'Sooner or later, I shall have that ring,' she threatened. 'You will curse yourself for not giving it up. I promise you that.'

With that, Grindella disappeared and Caprion drifted into a deep sleep.

Chapter Twenty-Three

Nicholas Cooper bolted upright, blinking in the dawning sun.

'Heavens no,' he pulled the parchment from his cheek and wiped his tired eyes. 'How could you sleep at a time like this? Old man, you are a fool.'

Heavy were his eyelids as he gazed upon the parchment, a map, now somewhat moistened after a sound sleep. 'Let us try this again, shall we.'

He held the amber pendulum above the map, his long slender fingers curled tight around the silver chain. Over forests, lakes and mountain ranges it was suspended. But movement, there was not.

'Neither will it move whilst ever the noise remains.' He shot a look of disgust at a bird on the window ledge. 'Be gone, I say!'

With a little convincing, the bird flew off.

'The highest room in the castle,' he tutted. 'And still no peace.' He moved back to the table, flattening the map with his hand.

But no sooner had he adjusted his spectacles than the pendulum was placed, rather forcefully, upon a book pile.

The contraptions in the room echoed loudly. Wheels spun. Cogs turned. Gears clicked. A location spell required absolute silence in order to work.

His moustache twitched.

His eyes narrowed.

His brow furrowed.

'This will never do!' He huffed and proceeded to wrap his lengthy beard around his head. He stared grimly at the contraptions and waited.

Alas, the ringing could still be heard through the layers of hair.

'How do you expect a man to cast a spell amidst this racket? Highly unlikely, I say, highly unlikely.'

He reached towards the book pile where he had rested the amber pendulum.

The pendulum was not there.

'You again.' His voice was gruff as he glared at the small, brown mouse atop of the book pile. 'I neither want nor need your assistance. Now go.'

The mouse sat back on its hind legs. It held something in its front paws.

'I say,' Nicholas gasped as the mouse took up the silver chain of the amber pendulum and scuttled across the table. 'I do not have time for your meddling.'

But meddle the mouse did. It scurried down the table leg and across the tapestry rug, the silver chain held tightly in its mouth.

Negotiating armillary spheres, telescope and a good many charts, Nicholas hastened after it, out of the astronomy tower and into the stairwell.

'Certainly not.' He watched the mouse bound down the winding stairwell. 'When I die, which at this rate will no doubt be timely, I shall return as a cat.'

And despite his pleading legs and grinding joints, he followed the mouse all the way to the granary. By this stage, he had missed breakfast and his lungs were screaming out for air.

'If I find no reason for this early morning venture you will find yourself on tonight's menu,' Nicholas puffed. He leant for a time against the mounds of grain, shaking his head. 'Could you not have taken us via the kitchens? I am famished.'

The mouse simply blinked.

'I know not who you are, yet I feel there is a reason for your foolhardiness.' Nicholas pushed himself off the mound. 'Lead the way, if you must.'

Leaving the pendent behind, the mouse scampered off.

'Let your speed not be a concern,' Nicholas called out sarcastically as he hurried to keep up with the mouse. 'I have youth on my side.'

It was not long before they had reached the lowest level of the castle, the cistern. Nicholas nodded.

'Perfect.' He took a moment to wipe clean his spectacles then allowed his eyes to take in the wonders of the space. 'Quiet, peaceful and no interruptions. Perhaps I will not return as a cat after all.'

Nicholas moved along the bridge to stand before the grand, marble pillars. Looking up at the elaborately decorated structures, of which there were four rows, he felt dwarfed by their scale. It was here, beside the water, so clear and undisturbed, that he could see his reflection. He sat and pondered.

At last, thought he, *my mind can be still.*

With serenity came movement. With movement came a location.

'So, Lord Bannock...you are headed to the enchanted castle. Interesting...' Nicholas returned the folded map to his pouch. 'I will make this known. Send forth a gyrfalcon.'

Nicholas's shoulders slumped. The mews were quite some distance from the cistern. 'I do not suppose you could shapeshift into a bird by any chance?'

Suddenly, at tremendous speed, the mouse raced towards Nicholas.

'It was merely a joke!' Nicholas screeched as the mouse launched itself onto his beard. 'You make a fine mouse!'

And despite having no energy left, Nicholas did the most splendid jig. His shoes shuffled, his knees knocked and his beard bounced. In fact, his movement was so erratic that it led him off the path and into one of the channels where he sat knee deep in water.

The mouse, having been catapulted from his beard and onto a small fountain, looked at Nicholas and appeared to smile.

'So it was more than serenity you wanted to share,' Nicholas's heart pounded with excitement as he surveyed the structure before him. 'Thank you, my friend. This find is truly remarkable.'

Chapter Twenty-Four

When Caprion awoke, the well and indeed the castle too, had vanished, and he found himself lying in the middle of a country lane being prodded, most unkindly, in the ribs. Opening his eyes, he caught sight of a peddler, dressed in a thick, deer-hide coat, a large crook in hand.

'Ah, he is alive!' The peddler said and instantly the prodding ceased. The crook came to rest upon the ground and he used it to shuffle forth to his rickety, horse drawn cart. 'Had to be certain, my lord.'

With a hand to his aching back, Caprion sat up on the cold road, covered almost entirely in a thick blanket of snow, and watched as the peddler climbed up upon the seat of his cart.

'Now, I am not a wise man, yet I do know that one is likely to get killed if one rests on a road, particularly this one as spring approaches.'

'I was not resting,' Caprion snapped irritably. 'I was in a well, a castle before that, yet now it seems both have vanished.'

The peddler tossed a large, hessian bag into the cart. The bag was filled with trinkets and made quite a loud clatter as it landed upon the thin layer of straw. 'Castles come and go when you drink, my lord.'

'I assure you I am not drunk,' said Caprion defensively. He put a hand to one of the wheels of the cart and pulled himself to his feet. A strange dizziness swept over him, and for a moment he believed he might well be drunk for all he saw was blackness. 'Pray tell me where the castle lies?'

'Castle, my lord?'

'Large dwelling,' said Caprion, sarcastically. 'With turrets and a moat.'

'There be no castle round these parts, my lord.' The peddler shook his head. 'None for miles.'

'Then have you, perchance, seen a witch?'

'Many, my lord.' The peddler paused to examine the work on Caprion's breastplate. 'Fine work that. Very fine indeed.'

Caprion tapped a finger against the pommel of his sword.

'Ah yes, a witch,' pondered the peddler. 'I have seen no witch on this day.'

Caprion searched the ground, only now aware that several pieces of his armour were missing. 'Have you lost something, my lord?'

'I had two arm guards,' said Caprion, circling the cart. 'Have you set eyes upon them?'

'Some beggar must have swiped them whilst you slept, my lord,' said the peddler, the crook resting now upon the large, hessian bag in the cart. 'Come, let us go.'

'Where is it we are headed?' Caprion asked.

'Palmirra. We will find lodging in the tavern there, unless you prefer to spend the evening here?' Caprion did not hesitate. He climbed into the seat and sat beside the peddler.

By nightfall, the village of Palmirra was reached, a dusty pink hue settling upon the horizon. The peddler pulled tight upon the reins and the cart came to a halt outside a small, stone tavern.

Caprion jumped from the front of the cart.

'Wait.' The old man leaned back into his cart, half burying his head in the straw. When he surfaced, a small, leather pouch appeared in his hand. The pouch, which was filled with ten silver coins, was thrown to Caprion. 'For the arm guards. I shall meet you inside.'

And with a tap on the hessian bag behind him, the peddler sped off.

With his hood drawn low upon his forehead, Caprion entered the tavern and moved to a table in the far corner, away from the hearth. Few raised their eyes as he took a seat and after placing a single coin from the peddler's pouch on the tabletop, he ordered a drink and enquired as to a room for the evening.

A busty woman with a turned-up nose took the coin, rolling it over once or twice in the palm of her hand before informing Caprion of several vacant rooms out back.

The tavern consisted of a large cellar with two adjoining rooms. It served not only wine, beer and ale, but food as well. While a fiddler played a brisk tune, pausing regularly to take a swig from a large silver pitcher, women danced arm in arm, careful to avoid the men passed out upon the stone floor.

Caprion sipped the tempered liquid as he scanned the room and when it was drained from the mug, he stood and walked towards the back door. But as he passed by the fiddler, who now played a more mellow tune, a bulky man with half his left ear missing stepped into his path.

'Excuse me, Sir,' said Caprion politely, and without lifting his head, he stepped around the man onwards to the door.

Moments later, the man again stood before him, two muscular arms folded across a vast belly.

'I mean to reach the back door and you, Sir, are impeding the way,' Caprion spoke calmly. 'So I say again, excuse me, Sir.'

Caprion took a step to the right. The man took a step to his left. By now, Caprion was tired and yearned for a bed to rest his head upon. A quarrel was the last thing on his mind.

'Should your quarrel be with me, Sir, let us take it outside so as not to disturb the festivities of the tavern.'

'Nay,' the bulky man bellowed as Caprion stepped past him. 'You shall be punished for your crime. Let the people of Palmirra see what becomes of those who steal.'

Caprion turned, only to see the glimmer of a sword hilt before it came down hard upon the side of his head, and he fell heavily upon a table that splintered in two.

Chapter Twenty-Five

The Ormans lived in a treacherous, mist-filled valley. The settlement they had created was cold and foreboding, choked by the smell of ever-burning fires. Littered with bubbling sulphur pits and surrounded by a fence of human bone, few peddlers ever strayed from the path.

The Ormans were primitive beings. Soulless men with just one purpose in life – to kill or die trying. Tall but stocky, they were hairy beasts with wild unruly beards who spoke little, communicating instead with hand signals and strange grunting noises. Their skin was dark, black like the charcoal from the fires, and covered in battle scars. Left untreated, these scars were highly valued, a sign of honour amongst their fellow tribesmen.

Grindella feared not these devilish creatures nor the noxious wasteland that they called home. When she rode into the foul-smelling settlement, she felt at ease, comforted rather than threatened by their unwelcoming presence.

Along the rocky path she rode, past leafless trees and crumbling fortress, until she came to the base of a stone stairwell, which led to the Black Hall. Here she dismounted and began the steep ascent, calling out to the leader of the Orman army.

'I have come to claim my debt.'

When the top was reached, two duty guards appeared before her, a shield and seven-foot spear in hand. To most this would be an adequate deterrent, yet to a sorceress it was merely an opportunity for amusement. With two flicks of her hand, first right then left, both guards were raised off their feet then sent across the hard, stone floor.

From the shadows of the Black Hall, alarmed by the sudden scraping of metal outside, a man of great size and strength stepped forth. His chunky hands came to rest on his hips and he glared down upon Grindella through narrowing eyes.

'I am owed a debt,' said Grindella, her voice echoing against the stone pillars that surrounded her. 'I have come to claim it.'

Orlov merely grunted then gestured for her to enter the Black Hall. She was led across a black, stone floor to the far end, where she was asked to sit in one of three high-backed chairs, all of which were positioned upon a hide.

'We will take Rawdendale Castle,' said Grindella, sounding like the task was simple. 'How long before your men are ready?'

Orlov's bristly eyebrows rose high on his forehead. Surely, he had misheard her. So, leaning forward on the edge of his seat, he questioned, 'Castle?'

Mirroring his movements, Grindella, too, slipped forward on her chair. 'Yes, castle. Rawdendale Castle.'

Orlov slumped back in his chair, his hands gripped tightly around the curved, wooden arms. They could not take on Rawdendale Castle, not alone.

'So, what say you?' Grindella asked, growing impatient. 'How long will battle preparations take?'

'Moons,' said Orlov, flatly. 'Many moons.'

Although, asking for his insight, Grindella already had a time frame in mind and *many moons* was far too long for her liking.

'You have one.' She stood and walked across the stone floor. 'I shall meet you then at the pass where the three rivers join.'

'It is not my decision to make.' Orlov called.

He was the leader of the king's army. Not the king.

Grindella whipped around. 'Ask your king then how much he values his daughter. The decision will not be difficult.'

The instant Grindella had left the hall, there was a loud crack and Orlov fell sideways in the chair, its shattered right arm laying now on the floor.

'My love!'

A woman, so beautiful that one's breath could be taken away, hastened into the hall and knelt beside Orlov. Her gentle gaze fell first on her husband then the broken chair.

She spoke softly through cherry red lips, plump upon her pale face. 'It can be mended.'

A hand, broad and calloused, came to rest upon her long, raven-coloured hair and she lay her head upon Orlov's shoulder.

'Return swiftly.' She pulled his hands onto her swollen belly. 'Our son needs his father.'

Now Orlov was a hardened man, yet upon hearing the news that his wife was with child, tears welled in his eyes. He now understood the timing of Grindella's visit. When it was discovered that his wife could not bear children, he had bargained with the sorceress.

At the time, he had thought not on his part but only on the positive outcome. His stomach now twisted into knots at the prospect of going off to war when there was so much in his life to celebrate. How he cursed the sorceress.

'Finally, the Gods have listened to our prayers. We are to be parents, my love.'

On the inside, Orlov was fighting a ferocious battle, suppressing the fury that was building in his stomach. Yet, on the outside, he appeared quite composed and taking his wife into his colossal arms, he told her, 'We have much to be thankful for. Tonight, we shall celebrate. Go and have the women make ready a feast.'

Andreas looked lovingly at her husband, nodded, then left the Black Hall. It had not always been this way, however. When her father, the Orman king, had arranged for her to marry Orlov, she had refused. But in time, her love for Orlov had grown. She had seen a gentler, softer side to the great leader, and he showed her much respect.

Already in a lather of sweat having heard the news from his daughter, the king stormed into the hall, some moments later, his dark, flowing robes trailing behind him.

'Is it true?' He said, grabbing Orlov with both hands, a slight tremble coming over his body. 'We are to take Rawdendale?'

Orlov's muscular hands came to rest upon the king's shoulders, but still the old man shook. 'Can it be done?'

'The time constraint is a concern.' The old man put a hand to his wiry beard and gave it a few tugs. 'Supplies are scarce. The mountain has much to offer, though. She will provide us with the metal we need to forge swords, shields and armour.'

For a time, the king strode back and forth across the black stone floor, thinking and gesturing much with his hands. Finally, with a loud clap of his hands, he agreed that if every man, woman and child had a task to complete, then yes, they would indeed be ready for battle within one moon.

Preparations began immediately.

Like the men who wore them, their armour was not at all attractive. Styled from single pieces of iron, the breastplates were flattened thinly then shaped, laced to the body with thick pieces of leather. The journey ahead was long and the lighter armour made for ease of movement. The shields that they carried were pointed at the ends, enabling them to push the tips into their enemy when in close combat or if wanting for another weapon.

Rocks broken from the mountain, by hammer and pick, were crushed into smaller, more manageable sizes before the ore was melted down and poured into a mould. Once stretched, folded and refined, the metal was transformed into fine blades. The blades forged were tough, with a hard yet sharp edge, light and well balanced.

And as day intertwined with night, the king looked upon his army and was pleased with what he saw. Having asked the blacksmiths to put up their anvils, the fletchers to put away their planes, an evening of festivities began. They danced, sang, ate and drank barrels a plenty, the thought of war drifting from their minds like a gentle melody. But when the moon, full and bright, sat high in the sky, there came a flicker in the distant mountains and Orlov came to attention, alarmed by what he saw.

'It appears our preparations may be tested sooner than expected.'

In polished armour, trimmed with gold, an army approached, flowing down the mountainside like a silver river. Riding five abreast, they sat tall in the saddle. Thin swords bounced against their knees while swallow-tailed flags waved high above them.

In front rode their leader, a man as tough as the hide on his shield. He was stodgy, yet a warrior, nonetheless. A king who let nothing stand in his way of glory. He had wealth beyond compare, but a vicious disease seeped through his veins, making him want more.

Riding now through the celebrations, King Tyrone's booming voice silenced the crowd. 'Good of you to welcome us like this,' he bellowed.

'Uninvited yet welcomed, nonetheless.' The Orman king took Tyrone's hand and shook it firmly. 'We are relieved to have your aid.'

Throwing a leg over his saddle then slipping from the leather onto the damp ground, King Tyrone stretched his tired legs. 'My friend, it has been some time.'

'You must be exhausted from your travels. Come, sit with us and join the festivities.'

'That we shall but we bring our own entertainment,' King Tyrone waved a hand and a skinny fellow dressed in woollen stockings, each leg being of a different colour, stepped forth. 'Sing for us, boy.'

And so while the minstrel sang songs of war and romance, they ate rich cheeses and dark, heavy bread, thick pottage and three types of meat, and swiftly through the spiced mead and cider they went, until the time came when the songs became too mellow for King Tyrone to tolerate and he commanded, after first throwing his half-eaten chicken thigh at the minstrel, that he play something more uplifting.

'Fine ale and good music,' said King Tyrone. With his mouth full of food, he drank from his horn cup, remnants of custard pie floating distastefully in the mead. 'Not enough pie though, for my liking.'

Hidden beneath the table, the Orman king grabbed the jerkins that he wore and twisted tightly with his hands. 'Had we known of your coming, we would surely have baked more pies.'

'It cannot be helped, I suppose,' said King Tyrone as he picked at his teeth with a knife. 'I shall simply have to eat more of the pork.'

Orlov grimaced as King Tyrone plunged his entire hand into the pork pudding and scooped a handful onto his trencher, the stale bread almost cracking under the weight. The king certainly had a splendid appetite, polishing off five dishes and still having room for dessert. His eating was apparently a virtue, for he proclaimed, 'A hungry man was not a warrior for he lacked the vitality and forcefulness of a well-fed man.'

By repute, he was a self-seeking man of deplorable actions. A tall, handsome man with shoulders as broad as an ox and the strength to match. However, the man sitting before Orlov contradicted these notions. He saw a man of slight stature. There appeared divots across both cheeks, like someone had dug parts of them out with a blunt spoon. His eyes were dark, chin square and he was missing an ear, sliced off when a poleaxe breached his helmet. Loud and booming was his voice as he chastised the dogs who barked as they begged for any unlikely scraps.

Afterwards, with bellies satisfied, celebrations continued, bathed in the light of lanterns. Many chose to dance, hand in hand in circles, accompanied by a minstrel who, through a hornpipe, played some lively tunes. Some competed at chess or gambled much at dice, an addiction for many, while others passed the time drinking and embellishing tales of their heroism.

Most entertaining, however, were the words told to a group of children by an old man, gifted in the art of storytelling. Around the crackling fire they huddled, mesmerised by the old man's tale, which began, like all good tales, with a knight and a ferocious dragon intent on burning the local village and gorging himself on the townsfolk.

Also taking in the words was Orlov, who, while hugging his wife, pulling her close to rest his forehead on hers, thought about their son and how one day he too, would be amongst the children listening with big, round eyes to the animated stories.

And all night not one of them had given a thought to Grindella, the woman who had brought them together. By the time the last Orman crashed onto a hard, straw-filled pillow and allowed his eyelids to block out the night, she was half way to the mountains of Tangaringy, with one final errand to run. The errand was not small. In fact, it was quite a large and fiery errand.

Chapter Twenty-Six

When next he woke, the moon was high in the sky and Caprion was being knocked this way and that in the back of the peddler's wagon. The blow to his head was taking its toll; the wound seemed to be broadening. As blood seeped through the cotton cloth that bound his wound, they came upon a hut in the woods.

Entering the hut, a candle was lit from the stoked-up ash in the fireplace, then the peddler set about gathering ointment and fresh bandages with which to treat Caprion's injuries. He directed Caprion to an uncomfortable-looking mattress then eased his way onto a wooden stool.

'Believe none of which the man speaks. A thief I am not,' Caprion sat upon the hard, straw mattress. 'I would like to take refuge in your humble abode for the night, if it pleases you.'

'My lord, you are most welcome.' The peddler looked down upon a face most pale and clammy. 'But nay, it may not be one night, but many.'

So it was that Caprion stayed with the peddler for three nights. While the knight fought off fever and sickness, the old man tended to his wounds with ointments made from bark and thistles. With food and water, Caprion's strength soon returned, and on the fourth day, after he had washed, dressed and was setting about to leave, he noticed the old man standing by the door, a bulging sack slung over one shoulder.

'Shall we go?' The old man asked.

Caprion raised an eyebrow. He could not recall inviting the peddler to join him.

The old man could sense Caprion's confusion. 'Make haste, my lord. The princess awaits.'

Now both eyebrows were raised. He watched the peddler rub the speckled feathers of a large female falcon which had landed upon his shoulder. It was offered a small rodent, which was seized in its hooked claws.

'Fever can make a man say and do many things.'

'You know of the princess?'

The old man nodded. 'You are lucky I am not the enemy, for I know much about Rawdendale too.'

'And I was just starting to like you,' Caprion stood and with a smile, lay a gentle hand on the old man's shoulder. 'It would be a shame to have to kill you.'

The old man shuffled down the steps of his hut and into the stable, returning with two horses, both of them saddled. 'Come, I will take you to her.'

'To whom?'

'The princess. She is not far from here.'

'I should ask how you came to have such knowledge,' Caprion took up the reins and jumped into the saddle. 'But my heart is now awakened and I am eager to leave.'

When they emerged from the forest of snow-covered trees sometime later, they came upon a splendid lake of blue, so vast that one could not see from one side to the other without turning one's head. In the middle of the blue lake stood a tall castle with a single spiral tower. Plated in bronze, decorative sections of the battlements reflected brightly the golden sun and upon the turrets that jutted from the defensive wall, sat pointed rooves.

Near the entrance of the castle, rising from the water, two angels stood. With wings unfurled, they held harps and wore on their bronzed bodies a flowing shift.

'Believe it or not, they do not float but rest upon a bridge,' said the old man and he stepped from his horse onto the cold earth below. 'We must wait therefore, until the tide recedes.'

But Caprion did not heed the old man's words and continued on to the edge of the lake, where in parts the water had frozen. Barely had his horse taken a few steps when bubbles of steam erupted from beneath the water's surface. Suddenly, the ice shattered. The heat from the bubbles was so intense that the horse on which Caprion rode doubled back to the shore, his fetlocks red and blistered.

'One must be patient,' said the old man and he sat down upon a fallen log to rest his tired bones for he knew that the lake was enchanted and could not be crossed at this time. 'The tide will soon recede.'

Still, Caprion would not listen and instead took next a boat that lay upon the sand and slid it into the water that had once again cooled. But each time he rowed nearer the castle, the waves returned him to the shore until, at last, he stepped exhausted from the boat and sat beside the old man.

Neither of them spoke until several hours hence, when the tide finally began to recede and Caprion led the second of the horses onto the bridge. But scarcely was he on the bridge than he heard a shuffling sound that was not of his horse's making.

He turned to see the old man madly trying to keep up and he asked, 'What is it you are doing?'

The old man stopped, straightened and drew in a deep breath. 'At this very moment, my lord, I am catching my breath. It would be most kind if you slowed your pace.'

'I mean to say, why is it that you stand here and not by the shore?'

Gracefully, the old man bowed. 'I am here to aid you, my lord.'

Caprion watched as the old man slowly straightened up, his aging bones clicking in several places. Half under his breath, he said, 'I fear it maybe I aiding you.'

'While you fight the dragon, I shall release the maiden from her bindings and assist her safely back to shore.'

Caprion smiled. The old man sounded convincing. 'Dragon?'

'Ghastly creature it is too. Incredible speed. The fire is most intense.'

'While your story is most entertaining, I do not believe in ancient myths.'

'This is no myth, my lord,' said the old man, his breathing now slowed.

Caprion pulled the reins a little tighter as the horse was spooked by something ahead. 'And I suppose you will break the chain that binds her hands with merely strength alone?'

Suddenly, the old man threw open his cloak to reveal three daggers and a bone handled knife. 'Strength and one of these should suffice.'

'I would say it shall.' Caprion agreed, his eyebrows raised. 'Very well, should I encounter a dragon…'

'Not *a* dragon,' the old man said, straightening his cloak. '*The dragon*, my lord. *The dragon*.'

'My mistake,' said Caprion. 'Should I encounter *the dragon* and be in need of assistance, you may rescue the maiden.'

And as Caprion scooped the old man and his cloak of knives up into the saddle behind him, there came a sound like thunder and an ugly looking beast with exceptionally long arms appeared at the castle gate.

'That is your dragon?' Caprion chuckled. 'In my mind's eye, it appears an ogre.'

The old man tightened his grip around Caprion's waist. 'Nay, my lord. That is not the dragon of which I speak.'

The foundations of the bridge shook as the ogre took a few ungainly strides towards the statues, the tips of his callused fingers nearly scraping across the ground.

'Leave,' the beast bellowed. 'You are not welcome here!'

As the old man's nails were pulled from his flesh, Caprion turned to the ogre and said, 'Come now, my friend. Where are your manners?'

'No visitors…not welcome!'

'We shall not stay long. Kindly give us what we want and you will not see us again.'

There came a stiffening to the ogre's limbs. His long fingers curled and he opened his drooling mouth to roar.

'My word,' said the old man, shaking. 'Perhaps we should do as he says. I am sure the princess is perfectly fine…ah, see. Here she comes now.'

And indeed she was, running through the gate tower. But before she could reach Caprion, the ogre seized Rosellene with one massive hand, set her high upon the gatehouse just above the portcullis and roared, 'Mine!'

The portcullis dropped. The windlass had not been used.

'You are mistaken,' said Caprion, quickly jumping from the saddle and drawing his sword. 'The princess is mine!'

Caprion, now on foot, charged towards the ogre. The great beast took with both hands a sword of his own, six feet in length and with a dragon-engraved hilt. The sword momentarily glimmered in the sun before erupting into flames, turning the sky a hellish orange. The ogre roared again and a wave of heat washed over Caprion, knocking him to the ground.

'That is *the dragon*!' cried the old man, cowering in the saddle, an arm raised to shield his eyes from the blinding light.

Feeling the hair on his face burn, Caprion hurried back towards the old man asking that his shield be thrown to him. Protected now by the shield, Caprion pressed on towards the ogre as the old man shuffled towards the gate tower, his aged eyes never leaving the foe.

The old man looked up, his face grim. Bristly, grey eyebrows descended towards his nose. 'That is a pity.'

Rosellene looked down upon the old man. 'What is a pity?'

'That I shall not be needing these.' And he held open his cloak so that the knives were exposed. 'Nor shall I receive a kiss from the fair maiden following my daring rescue.'

Rosellene's mouth laughed and her eyes smiled. 'No, those you shall not need it is true, yet in return for my daring rescue you shall indeed receive a kiss.'

The old man inspected the iron gate. He held tight the lattice grill and shook it. 'You shall have to jump.'

He held out his arms.

Rosellene stifled a laugh. The drop was almost forty feet.

'I shall find another way down,' she called. 'First, we must end this fight.'

'End?'

'The ogre is harmless,' added Rosellene.

As she spoke, the crackling of the ogre's fiery sword drowned out Rosellene's soft voice leaving the old man questioning. 'Harmless?'

Just then, the ogre caught sight of the old man and bounding across the bridge he swung his mighty sword.

'Excuse me, my lady,' the old man said politely. 'But it seems I am on fire.'

And quite calmly, he cast himself off the gate tower into the lake's icy waters, to his death, or so it would seem. But peering over the edge, Rosellene saw not a body burned but a body drenched, immersed in a barrel of wine.

The old man slowly hauled himself from the liquid, sipping firstly some of the fine mead. 'Harmless, you say?' Little more than skin and bones, the old man stood shivering. 'I would call that quite inhospitable.'

Rosellene's anxiety intensified. 'Please tell him to stop.'

'How, my lady?' The old man shrugged. 'I cannot even get near them.'

Helplessly, Rosellene watched the battle unfold. For a time, Caprion fought well, deflecting each and every one of the ogre's strikes. But the ogre was strong and he hit hard on the shield so that soon the thick metal weakened, warping from the heat. Depending thus upon his sword, Caprion swung both high and low striking the ogre many times.

But the ogre's skin was like the hide of a pig and where his sword would have oft sliced open a man, it merely scratched the ogre's thick, leathery skin, making his rage more intense. With each strike, Caprion's faith weakened. It would not be long before the ogre delivered a blow that would force him to the ground. He only hoped that he might continue his struggle just long enough to allow the old man and Rosellene safe passage back to the shore.

'You must try,' begged Rosellene.

The peddler paused. Looking at Rosellene's pleading eyes, the old man's heart dropped to his saturated feet. 'Perhaps you could do something, my lady.'

Rosellene looked towards the battle, her heart heavy. 'There is little I could do.'

'Physically, nay.' There was a glint in the peddler's eye as he trudged towards the gate tower. 'Yet there are other means to end the quarrel.'

Rosellene's lips tightened. 'It would never work.'

'Maybe not, yet how will one know if one does not try?'

Rosellene shook her head. 'I am weakened.'

'Have faith, my lady,' the peddler said reassuringly. 'You have strength enough.'

There was panic in her voice. 'But at length I know not how?'

'The ogre has the advantage.' The peddler's eyebrows were raised, the right somewhat more so than the left. 'Take away that advantage.'

'And if it does not work?'

'It will,' said the peddler, confidently. 'You will see.'

Chapter Twenty-Seven

Levitation was a difficult spell to master. It required a clear and focused mind. Rosellene had not practised such a spell for many years. There was much gathering, preparation and chanting to do if she was going to lift an object. But there was not the time.

Then, she had a thought. 'I will need some ale or cider.'

The peddler smiled. 'Certainly.'

'And a feather.'

The peddler blinked rapidly.

'Throw me the chicken if you need to.'

She hastened down the narrow, spiral staircase, brushing against the rough, whitewashed walls, and paused at the windlass. The chain had loosened from the winch. *Pray*, she thought, *that the postern be open.*

It was.

Rosellene met the peddler by the portcullis. She washed first her hands with ale from the peddler's flask, then drew strange symbols upon the ground. Some in the form of uncompleted shapes, others that swirled this way and that in unjoining lines. Next, she took up the feather and held it between her hands until heat radiated from her palms and her entire body shook.

The greatsword wavered.

The ogre struggled to maintain his hold on the hilt. His chunky fingers wrapped around the leather grip, straining as the blade was pulled from his grasp. He strangled the cross-guard with one hand, the pommel with the other. But it was to no avail.

The dragon soared through the air towards the gate tower, hovered for a time above the wine barrel, then dropped into the honey-coloured liquid. The fiery sword went out with a hiss.

The ogre's skin reddened. A fist was made. Raised.

'Hermes, no!' Rosellene screamed. 'He is a good man!'

Running towards the men, Rosellene threw up her hands. 'Stop, both of you!'
The ogre's arms dropped. They slapped against his sides.

Caprion lowered his shield, the tip of his sword scraping the ground.

Rosellene threw her arms around Caprion. She felt the links of his mail. The warmth of his breath. The beat of his heart. 'Long have I waited for this moment.'

Caprion quivered. The sword slipped from his fingers, the strap released from his shield and gently he pressed his lips upon hers. 'How my heart aches for thee.'

'Hold me.' Rosellene rested her head against Caprion's chest. Breathed deep the scent of leather. 'Forever. Do not let go.'

Beside one of the bronze statues, the peddler rested. He watched the ogre try to remain standing. Totter. Stumble. Then stagger dangerously close to the water's edge.

'Quickly,' he cried. 'Or he will surely burn!'

Without hesitation, Rosellene cast a spell upon the waters of the lake, and the ogre, when he plunged beneath the surface, did not burn. He did, however, continue to sink, quickly to the sandy bottom.

'Hermes!' Rosellene rushed forth to the water's edge. 'I fear he cannot swim.'

And before he could complain, question or otherwise, Rosellene thrust a thick rope anchored with stone into Caprion's hand and instructed him to cast it into the water so that the ogre could be saved. It took the strength of all three but finally the ogre's balding head surfaced and he sucked in several deep breaths.

Caprion stared at the water and then the ogre. He shook his head. 'How is he not dead?'

Rosellene hesitated. *Did he hear the incantation?*

'Perhaps,' said the peddler. 'the enchantment has ended.'

For a time, the ogre clung to the side of the bridge, bobbing up and down with each passing wave, before hauling his great frame from the water and collapsing onto the stones.

'Thank you.' he puffed, turning his tiny black eyes to Caprion.

'It is Rosellene you should be thanking. She felt you were worthy of the rescue.'

'And indeed, he was. I would have been a travelling companion for Lord Bannock had it not been for Hermes,' said Rosellene, an arm around his neck.

'He must come with us, Caprion. We cannot leave him here. The sorceress will surely kill him.'

Caprion looked the ogre over. There was little chance of them getting to Rawdendale unnoticed if he joined them. Nonetheless, a beast of his size could be a very useful ally.

Caprion nodded. 'The ogre may join us.'

'I help you,' said Hermes. He now stood; his vast shadow cast across them all. 'We win the war.'

'No, Hermes, you do not need to help,' said Rosellene. 'Your debt has been paid. When it is safe, you can return home to be with your family.'

'We will help.'

'Take a seat, big man,' said Caprion as he led Rosellene away. 'I shall not be pulling you out again.'

The ground shook as Hermes did just that, narrowly missing the peddler with his colossal frame.

'An army of ogres would aid our cause,' Caprion spoke quietly to Rosellene. 'Do you deny that we could use their support?'

'I do not deny it, but I do not condone it either.'

'Then what is to be done?' Caprion wondered. 'Sheer size may be tactic enough.'

'Let us be gone from this wretched place and think of it anon.'

Caprion smiled. 'Indeed. Let us be gone.'

And he whisked her away behind the fortress wall.

'We shall leave, but not before I ingest every aspect of your beauty.' He traced her jawline with the back of a finger, moved across to her lips. 'I never knew I could desire something so much until you were gone. Nay, *desire* is not the word.' Caprion ran his fingertips through her hair, staring deep into her eyes. 'Rosellene, I *need* you.'

Rosellene could barely breathe. Hoping it was not a dream, she reached out for Caprion's body. Held tight his arming doublet. 'And I you.'

A dilemma then met them as they reached the shore, for the snow had not quite cooled the horse's blistered fetlock enough to support a rider, and the peddler's horse surely could not support three. So Caprion told the old man to step up into the saddle to join Rosellene and that he should walk the distance. Hermes, however, had a different idea, and soon Caprion's armoured legs were thrown around the ogre's neck and he was carried into the forest.

They were not long into their journey back to Rawdendale when Caprion caught sight of something in the distance and he stopped Hermes abruptly, sliding silently to the ground. Scanning the forest of conifers, tall, slender trunks gently touched by the moonlight, he watched as shadow after shadow broke the filter of light.

Two by two, almost in complete unison, an army of men marched at a steady pace. Their armour was thin, made from a single piece of iron, and on both shield and breastplate, Caprion could just make out the faint outline of a gateway.

The Ormans symbol of protection.

With hand held to his lips, he led the horses backwards until the three were completely enveloped in darkness, all the time watching the procession of men. Armed with pikes, halberds and axes, the Ormans came in their hundreds. For a time, the only sound in the forest was that of boots as they trudged through the snow and the screech from a lonely owl perched in the topmost branch of a tree. But then the softest of sighs was heard and Caprion turned just quick enough to catch Rosellene as she fell from the horse.

Caprion knew he could not linger and after laying a tender kiss upon Rosellene's pale and clammy face, he took up his sword and moved towards the rear of the army to where a small group of five men rode on horseback. With blood rushing to his extremities, Caprion struck the first rider from behind. A quick twist and his neck was broken.

Caprion moved forth to his next victim, slicing through his jugular as if the skin were parchment. A puncture to the chest left his third victim gasping for air as he slid from the saddle. The fourth and fifth men were little trouble. They were left on the furrowed track, a mess of sprawling innards, deep maroon stains in the pure white snow.

When next Rosellene looked upon Caprion, she saw a pained man and knew that he planned to leave.

'Bring as many reinforcements as you can muster, my friend,' said Caprion and the ogre dropped his head in acknowledgment. 'We shall meet again at the castle as soon as you are able.'

The reins of several Orman horses looped around his hand Caprion turned next to Rosellene. 'Can you ride?'

Rosellene nodded. 'Where will you go?'

'To seek mercenary forces.' He looked into Rosellene's fearful eyes as he lifted her into an Orman saddle, and taking her by the hand, said, 'And you will go?'

Rosellene knew where he wanted her to go. He wanted her to be safe, away from the battle that was to come. But how was she to help the women and children who took refuge beneath the castle? She would not leave them defenceless.

She might be a princess, yet she was skilled in weaponry too. She could manoeuvre both the cross and longbow as well as any man and was talented with a blade.

'To grandmother's hut, as far from Rawdendale as is possible,' Rosellene lied. *Let his heart rest easy thinking I am safe.*

'Take this,' Caprion took the ring from around his neck. 'I feel it may be more valuable than you believe.'

And slipping the ring back onto her finger, Caprion disappeared into the darkness.

Chapter Twenty-Eight

The secrets of The Red Valley were not obvious. Built into the mountainside, the population was densely packed into grand, terraced buildings, tall and slender, that reached towards the clouds. Layer upon layer of stone and marble, these structures looked out upon the winding river and fertile, green lands below, divided evenly into small, rectangular paddocks by dry, stone walls.

A fortress stood at the very top of the highest mountain peak, accessible only by climbing the stairwell with one thousand steps. It was said that the view was uninterrupted and one could see for miles. That was, of course, if one were able to climb the stairwell that twisted and turned so completely.

With only one way in and one way out, The Red Valley was well protected by a mighty guard tower. The secrets had been safe for more than five hundred years and the Nogard tribe lived peacefully, rarely venturing beyond their borders. Tending to crops and livestock, they truly believed that no one knew what was hidden beneath the rock. That no one knew why the smoke billowed each day and the mountains shook. Why the earth tremored and the surface of the lake rippled.

No, the secrets were not obvious but they were there. Grindella had seen them.

For years, she had in her possession a mysterious stone which, having traded for it with a warlock some many moons ago, had remained in her care. Orange with flecks of gold that reflected in the sunlight, the stone was larger than a man's head, smooth to the touch yet durable. It was told that what lay inside was a beast mightier than any other that had walked on this land.

It could soar amongst the clouds with wings of leather and from its mouth came fire hot enough to burn. At once, Grindella made to crack open the stone, but not even the most powerful spell would release the fire-breathing dragon.

Once near extinct, these colossal winged creatures wreaked havoc on the nearby villages. With a thirst for human blood, they sought out their prey, taking one victim every seven days during the summer. So they were hunted by professional slayers, heroic knights in dazzling armour risking their life for fame, fortune and the chance of immortality. For it was said that the blood of a dragon was imbued with magical properties. But for many a daring knight, it came at a cost. Not all blood could be consumed. Some blood was toxic to human kind and the smallest drop upon a man's lips would freeze him to the very spot he stood.

These creatures were wise to the tricks of men, but although they fought well, defending themselves with claws, wings, tail and flames, charring, maiming and torturing many knights, in time the dragon numbers were depleted.

It was told, however, amongst the silent whispers of peddlers, that while many species had been made extinct, there were some breeds that survived, retreating to a valley shrouded in mist and intrigue. It was here that they bred, growing to great masses, protected by a tribe most caring.

Eager to find such a valley, Grindella rode forth towards the mighty gate house with its stained, wooden door and decorative, metal plates. What an army she could create with the assistance of dragons.

'Can I help you?' the Nogard man asked cheerfully as he stepped down from the gate house.

His pants were fuller than most, with cuffs of emerald green and stitching of gold. Upon his leather tunic, a woollen cloak was thrown, thin and tattered at the ends. Tattoos covered his cleanly shaven head. Patterns stained with dark blue ink. There was a darkness to his complexion like water mixed with mud and the features that protruded from his face were sharp.

'Yes,' said Grindella, looking beyond the man's shoulder to the paddocks filled with stock. 'I believe you can.'

'Is it a purchase you are after, my lady?' The man moved towards the enclosures. 'We have some prime goats on offer and some good-quality lambs.'

Grindella was not one for conversation and she wondered how much longer the man would persist. 'I know what it is you hide and if you want it to remain hidden I suggest you give me what I desire.'

'Hidden, my lady?' The man questioned and he watched the colour rising in sorceress's cheeks.

'I have come for dragons you fool.' Grindella's lips tightened and her eyebrows converged.

The man was silent. His pock-scarred face twitched slightly and his dark eyes narrowed.

'There be no dragons here, my lady.'

'I have no time for games.' Grindella contemplated whether she would impale him on the fence or feed him to his own dragons, if he did not soon agree to her demands.

'Look around. Nothing but mountains, lake and valley here.'

The man screamed. Flames licked the soles of his boots.

'I will need them to fly, of course, a great distance, and have strength enough to pick up boulders. What breed would you recommend?' The leather of the man's knee high boots quickly burned through and the flames heated the soles of his feet. 'Would you suggest choosing one of the Sea Loch dragons or a Sierra?'

Having subdued the flames by standing in a pail of water, the man surrendered to the demands. 'When do you require the services?'

'I shall expect the dragons fit and ready before the next full moon.'

The man shook his head. 'I am afraid that is not possible.'

'Make it possible,' commanded Grindella. 'You are a dragon trainer, are you not? You will have the dragon of my choice ready before the next full moon.'

'Dragons hibernate, my lady. It is not wise to wake a sleeping dragon.'

'Nor is it wise to refuse a sorceress,' said Grindella. Nerves twitched below the surface of her skin. 'I know plenty of dragon hunters who would long to take advantage of a sleeping dragon. Blood. Tears. Scales. Highly profitable, I hear.'

The man stammered as Grindella set her unblinking eyes upon him. 'Take me to them. I wish to select the best.'

'My lady, winter is not yet over.'

'They are dragons. The absence of a little sleep should not be detrimental. Wake them! Get them prepared!'

'They will be weakened from their slumber,' said the man, trying to keep up with the wrathful sorceress.

'Then I suggest you wake them soon so that their strength is regained.'

'Their hunger too, will be most intense.'

'Perfect,' Grindella tittered. 'There will be a few thousand knights at Rawdendale for them to feast on.'

Grindella continued on. Suddenly, she stopped. No longer could she hear the scuffling of the man's scorched boots.

'What is it now?' She asked, turning. 'Blisters?'

'The dragons are reformed,' said the man meekly. 'No more do they thirst for human blood.'

A darkness crept upon them as the clouds above loomed, and like the singed, leather boots Grindella crackled.

'The enemy need not know. It shall not be a trial.' And she took the quivering man by the ear.

First the man led her to one of the houses on the mountainside, reaching not towards the handle of the door but to the lantern post beside it. Here, after pulling it firmly, the facade was moved aside and there before them lay a field of spindly grass, dappled here and there with huge, bubbling mud pools. The door quickly closed behind them and they moved forth to the entrance of a cave, its mouth drooling with moss.

'These are our wingless dragons, my lady.' The man lit up the cave with a lantern. 'They might be small but they have a highly flexible skeleton and their sense of smell is strong…look at their enlarged nasal passage.'

Grindella looked upon the dragons with their spear-shaped tails and leathery black skin. These would never suffice. She shook her head. 'What else do you have?'

Hidden beneath the icy waters, the Sea Loch dragons slept in a lair littered with jewels. Lined with spikes, their tails curled gently around their scaly, green bodies as they nestled amongst the thick bed of gold, silver and pearls. Peacefully did they slumber in the depths of the loch, bubbles ascending from their nostrils.

'Mighty powerful dragons they be, those from the loch.' The man tapped a foot against the frozen surface. 'That is, if you can convince them to leave their treasure for long enough. Very possessive.'

Water and fire, thought Grindella. *What good is a dragon that cannot breathe fire?*

'Tell me you have the dragons for me.'

Sunlight bounced off the man's tattooed head as he nodded. 'I think you will be pleased with what I show you next.'

They climbed the misty mountains; pointed peaks that rose and fell sharply like the spikes on the tail of a dragon. Across the jagged stones, they trekked. Noses cold. Feet wet. Breath short. Until, at last, they reached the summit.

Grindella cursed. Snowflakes danced about her face.

Part hidden by the thick, swirly mist, a dragon rested on the mountaintop. Its tail, the lightest of blues, jerked suddenly, knocking over a small cairn.

The man threw his hands on his hips. The air was thin.

'These are the largest of all the dragons we have on offer here,' he began. 'The tails of the Sierra are long and barbed, used for striking. They have bones that are hollow and light, making them perfect for flying, and their wingspan is extraordinary. Their flames travel a great distance and their scales are tough, almost impenetrable.'

Although her face did not show it, Grindella was indeed pleased with the dragons before her. She needed strength and ammunition. Sierra's would be perfect for the task.

'I will send word when and where the dragons are to come.'

'And payment, my lady?' The man questioned.

One sharp twist, thought Grindella, *and I could break your neck.*

'Payment?' she repeated.

'What shall it be?'

'Your payment,' said Grindella, a smirk just visible beneath the hood that had been pulled over her fair hair. 'Is that you shall not be killed.'

Chapter Twenty-Nine

He was lost. In both mind and direction, he had lost his way.

Head clouded with concern over leaving Rosellene, Caprion had strayed from the path and found himself in a section of the forest where it was not wise to be.

Nothing grew in the Dead Forest. The trees were rotten wood, bent and curved into strange shapes with knots that looked like faces and branches that stabbed and poked at your skin. The air had cooled and not a sound could be heard apart from the shuffling of his horse's hooves as it reared backward, throwing him to the ground then retreating from whence they had come.

As he lay on the bare earth, contemplating which direction to take, his eyes were suddenly blinded by a light, most intense. Shielding his eyes with his arm, Caprion tried to determine the source of the light as it came closer and closer until it was upon him.

Then a hand reached out, soft and delicate, pulling him to his feet, and he marvelled at the beautiful woman standing before him.

She had not changed. Pale, flawless skin and the bluest of eyes that seemed to draw you in as though under a spell. Her tall, slender body was dressed in a loose-fitting robe, green like the leaves that shot miraculously from the branches of the trees close by. Pulled into a braid, her long, curly locks fell down the centre of her back ending just shy of her knees. Upon her head rested a wreath of fresh flowers and when she spoke that familiar angelic voice was heard.

'My darling, you will never be lost.'

The gentle hands then touched his cheeks, taking away the redness that had been caused by the biting winds. He felt the warmth of a tear cascade down his cheek and onto his mother's hands. She dried away the tear with a kiss and an overwhelming sense of love trickled over his body. Like being wrapped in a blanket, Caprion was no longer cold.

'You are still here.'

He spoke like a child, stammering on every word. Mouth dry, yet his lips were drenched with tears.

'I never left. I am here always, yet you may see me only at this time.' He followed his mother's gesturing hand, surprised to see a forest now very much alive. 'When night becomes day, our worlds collide, if only for a fleeting moment.'

Again, he was lost. It had been near twenty years since Caprion last saw his mother. And although, there was much to say, he was unable to speak. At that very moment, words eluded him and all he could do was stare in amazement as flowers began to bud on the surrounding shrubs, animals scurrying through them.

'Trust that the outcome will be positive.' A smile crossed his mother's tender lips and a rustling was heard behind her. 'And that we will be there to support you in every way possible.'

Behind her, upon mighty, white steeds, an army of faeries rode forth into the light.

'We may be few in number but we are fine warriors who will stand beside you as you defend Rawdendale Castle.'

Caprion scanned the line of soldiers before him. Two hundred or more men dressed in light, leather armour, their translucent wings protruding just below their shoulder blades. While they had speed and accuracy on their side, they were not immortal and could still be killed like any other man on the battle ground.

This was not their war, thought Caprion.

He would not let such beauty be involved in such ugliness.

'You do not have to do this,' his voice was raised so that all would hear what he had to say. 'This is not your war. Why risk your lives for some mortal realm that means nothing to you?'

Then came a voice from behind the rows of soldiers. A deep, familiar voice.

A voice from his past.

'We are not as malicious as you think, Caprion.'

The soldiers parted, making way for the High Faery, who, at six feet tall, nearly equalled the height of the riders. Caprion could feel his body stiffen at the sight of him. His heart raced. His hands curled into fists and he swallowed more than usual. The hate he felt for this man was intense.

You took my mother from me, thought Caprion, *and for that I wanted to slit your throat.*

'I understand how you must feel. Had my mother been taken from me, I too, would want to slit the throat of the man responsible.'

His hands uncurled and he could feel the eyes of two hundred soldiers boring into his skin. How many of them knew? Could they all read minds?

'You were fourteen at the time and too young to know the truth.'

'Truth?' The word escaped his mouth before it could be stopped. 'About what? How you kidnapped my mother before my very eyes leaving me with no kin, alone in this world?'

'We should not have waited so long to tell him,' his mother sighed. 'The damage is done. Engraved upon his heart.'

His mother looked up at him and he could no longer see the brightness in her eyes. They were grey, clouded with tears that rested on her lower lids.

'What I am about to tell you may cause you surprise. I am sorry that it has taken this long to share with you. Perhaps, had I done so sooner, your life may not have been so tainted by fear.'

Caprion held his mother's gentle hands in his. 'Say what must be said. I am listening.'

'Before I met your father, I was betrothed to marry a man I barely knew. Being young and foolish, I fled. That is how I met your father. We fell in love and had fifteen wonderful years together. But then I was called back home. The betrothal had to be honoured.'

Caprion's mother watched his reaction carefully. It took some time for the information to be absorbed, but when his eyes enlarged and grip tightened, she nodded and said, 'It is true. I am of the faery realm, as are you.'

The shock was instant. Caprion fell backwards, body numb.

He hated the fey. There was no denying it. Ever since his mother's departure, he had done his best not to offend them. Rowan and thorn trees were avoided, sacred to the fey, and always was he neat, tidy and obedient. But today, his beliefs were tested by the beautiful creatures that stood before him.

Their beauty seemed not to be a facade as stories told made it sound and their complexion, which was said to be black, white or blue, was not hidden by a mask. Strangest of all, they were not repelled by iron nor salt nor bread, all of which were contained in a small, drawstring bag in the pocket of his trousers.

As if reading his very thoughts, his mother smiled. 'We are spirits of nature. We work with the four elements and wield their powers, using them to our advantage. We are bestowers of favours. Healers of the sick. Breakers of spells.

It may be best if you cast aside all previous thoughts on our race until such time as you know us better.'

Nails, long and gently rounded, brushed through his hair, which had now formed tight curls. His limbs tingled and there came a heaviness upon his eyelids.

'Come, rest your mind for a time. You must certainly be tired and famished. Share some food with us, my son.'

Caprion hesitated, his belief still strong. 'If I do, will I, perchance, not be able to return?'

His mother gently smiled. 'We have no power over you, Caprion. You may come and go at your will. You are, after all, one of us.'

Power. With that one word, he was captivated and petrified at the same time. What did it mean having the queen of the fey as your mother? Did it bring advantages? Protection?

'All in good time,' his mother said reading his mind. She stood proud, the soft, green fibres of her dress falling back around her ankles. 'Do not worry yourself with such things now. There are greater challenges that demand our attention. Come, let us return to Birch Glades.'

With merely a gesture, the riders parted and there before them was a most glorious sight. Lush, green meadows filled with vibrant flowers. Slow, flowing streams brimming with fish. Tall buildings, topped with rooves of gold and doors of pure silver.

A feeling of complete tranquillity leeched into every pore of his body.

'I still know not why you wish to join the battle,' Caprion said, his breath captured momentarily by the wonder before him. 'Why leave such beauty?'

Slowly, they traversed across a bridge from one cobble stone path to another.

'We are in union with all living things, and as such, seek to protect them as best we can. In recent times, however, destruction has come to our lands. Hills just beyond the castle.'

Caprion knew the place. Great holes had been cut into the rolling hills, mined for their ore. A once pristine place, now a wasteland.

'While our intentions are always pure, it is not wise to be digging in those hills. King Tyrone's behaviour has offended our race and for that he must be punished by faery law.'

King Tyrone's behaviour offends many, thought Caprion.

What of the harsh conditions? The fey were from a climate of warmth. Why expose themselves to such unpleasantness.

'The environment can be extreme. Winters are especially harsh.'

'We can adapt,' his mother said. 'You need our aid.'

Under his breath, a faery nearby muttered, 'And much more.'

'What is it you have seen?' Caprion snapped. 'Are we fighting a losing battle?'

He gave his mother a curious look and she answered in her gentle tone.

'Grindella seeks aid from a most powerful source. A source found in The Red Valley, not seen for many years.'

Caprion paced for a time, hands interlaced behind his neck. *Could it be true? Could they still exist in the mountains?*

'You mean to say the stories of my youth are true?'

'Myths and legends are no more.' His mother's tone was gentle, yet he could hear a subtle anxiousness sing. 'She aims to use them at her discretion.'

'The walls of Rawdendale are already weakened. They may withstand an ordinary siege but add the strength of dragons.' Caprion paused. The task was overwhelming. 'We cannot defend against a dragon.'

'No, you alone cannot.' Thereupon, his mother paused, then said, 'Yet there are those in the forest who can. The ancient knowledge they possess could prove useful against such an attack.'

Chapter Thirty

The rivalry with the Ormans had existed long before Rosellene's birth. So long was the feud that few recalled the reason for its existence. Some claimed that the Ormans had blocked the stone-cut conduit, the only water source to the castle, forcing the nobles to move outside the castle wall, where they were set upon.

The Ormans, of course, recorded things differently. Nonetheless, Orman raids were a regular occurrence amongst the farming villages outside the castle. During the night, village after village would be plundered.

The peddler knew all too well of the raids and Orlov, leader of the Orman Army. Years before, Orlov had come to Rawdendale as a teenage boy, accompanying his merchant mother and father, trading fine, silk fabric and perfume. During their travels, Viktor, Orlov's father, had become severely ill and too weak to continue.

For six days, he had laid in a confined chamber of the castle, suffering from fever associated convulsions and dehydration. Water contamination had been suspected, but when on the seventh day, he had claimed he was being burned alive and his skin had become red and blistered, thoughts turned to a different evil.

When his wife left his bedside to seek council with the physician, the poor man, his mind overcome with hallucinations, ripped off his bed gown and dived out the chamber window, believing he was diving into a deep pool of water. Shortly after, he had been pulled from the castle moat, his neck snapped in two.

So it came to be that a lord, pitying Viktor's wife, had taken them both in, having the boy of fourteen serve as his squire. Orlov had been a loyal squire, caring for the horse and armour of Sir Theoderic. And when the time had come to join his lord in battle, many years later, he fought honourably until being taken prisoner by the Ormans.

A rescue party set out the following morning but had ridden not more than a few miles when Orlov met them on foot. He nursed a badly injured shoulder, and bruises to the face and neck, but seemed in relatively good spirits. Relieved to see him alive, no one questioned his gallant escape until years later when a castle gate had been left unguarded and a small party of Orman men had ridden in setting fire to the timber keep. When the Ormans left, Orlov, now a trained knight, rode at the head of the party.

Long had the Ormans king desired the fighting techniques of the men of Rawdendale. Their skills and art of dodging had made his men appear weak. The Ormans tactic of killing their opponent with one brutal blow was made useless and they could not withstand the stamina of these men.

And when a young knight became his prisoner, he had seized the opportunity, making allegiances with him and promising that he would be given wealth beyond his imagination and be regarded amongst the king's men as his son, riding as the army's leader against the neighbouring villages. In return for this, Orlov was to spy on the combat ways of the Rawdendale company, learning their techniques so that in battle the king's men would no longer tire but compete equally.

Still today, the peddler had not forgiven himself for taking the young boy in, and he had sworn never to return to Rawdendale, too ashamed of his mistake.

Sometimes promises had to be broken.

Rosellene left her horse with an attendant at the livery stable and made to leave. 'You must meet father.'

Home once again, Rosellene's spirits were high and she longed to see her parents.

The peddler stroked the nose of his dapple grey. 'I shall tend to the horses first, my lady.'

Rosellene paused a moment, drinking in the features of the old man.

How familiar he looked now that the fever had broken.

'The horses can wait.' Rosellene took the reins from his hand and tied them loosely to a rail. 'He will want to thank you.'

'I will come anon, my lady,' the peddler stammered. He looked at the thatching on the stable roof. It was in desperate need of repair. 'You go ahead.'

Rosellene took the old man's hands. 'You have done a great service. I will be most pleased to present you to our king.'

Reluctantly, the peddler allowed himself to be led through the courtyard and into the great hall, where they were greeted by the king and queen.

Tears long withheld flowed from Rosellene's blue eyes onto her father's tunic. She wondered what his reaction would be to see her home. She should not be here. She had lied to Caprion and disobeyed her grandmother.

The king's glassy eyes revealed the answer.

'You have never been one to do as you were asked.' The king smiled. 'You are well? Not mistreated?'

'I am safe, Father, and that is all that matters. Much thanks to this dear man here.' Rosellene paused. How terrible she felt. They had spent days together and she had been too ill to ask the peddler his name. 'Forgive me. I do not even know your name.'

The peddler bowed. 'Your grace.'

The king's face beamed. He recognised the old man instantly, despite a beard that longed for a trim.

'Sir Theoderic,' said the king. 'Welcome home, old man.'

Theoderic's voice shook. 'Thank you, your grace.'

'Come, rest yourself.' The king ushered them over to one of the larger trestle tables. 'It was known, you could be entrusted with such an errand.'

Theoderic did not move. 'I am at a loss, your grace.'

'To what cause?' The king asked.

'Why you should want me on your grounds? Entrust me with such an errand?'

The king's eyes softened. 'That was a long time ago. You are not to blame for the outcome.'

Theoderic felt tension in his throat. 'I thought it best to leave.'

'And now it is time you returned,' the king's voice echoed around the room. 'We will need men with your talent to guide us through this battle.'

Theoderic bowed. 'It would be an honour, your grace.'

Wine was poured into several fluted goblets and trays of food set upon the table.

'Please,' the king waved an open palm across the table. 'You must eat. I am sure you are hungry.'

Hands reached out for bread, lavished with butter and sage, cheese of the richest kind and roasted meat.

Leaning back against the padded red velvet of his throne, the king looked towards his daughter. 'Sir Caprion, he is where?'

'Gathering men.' Rosellene set down her goblet. She had known the merriment would be short lived. 'The Ormans have left the valley. They are coming, Father. They are coming.'

The king pushed aside his plate. 'How many men?'

Sir Theoderic made to reply, but before a single word was uttered, the hall's mighty doors were thrust open and there stood an old man, looking quite dishevelled.

'I found it!'

Beard trailing behind him, Nicholas hastened into the great hall. Lightened in parts by what appeared to be fragments of stone, his dark robes skimmed across the floor. Just below his chin, nestled amongst his wiry whiskers, the nose of a little, brown mouse could be seen.

'Forgive me, your grace,' Nicholas came to an abrupt halt in the middle of the room. 'I should have knocked.'

He turned to leave then caught a glimpse of Sir Theoderic.

Suddenly, Nicholas was jumping. Jumping as best a man of seventy-two years could do in no shoes on a hard, stone floor.

'Brother,' he cried and took Sir Theoderic into his arms, squeezing him tightly with his frail arms. 'You are well, I trust?'

Theoderic nodded. 'I am, dear Brother, I am.'

Brother? Rosellene thought and she nodded at the resemblance.

'And my dear, Rosellene,' Nicolas turned and threw his arms around Rosellene. 'How good it is to see you.'

'And you,' Rosellene smiled. Nicholas still moved with excitement. 'What is it that you have found?'

Nicholas looked to the king. He had not meant to interrupt. The king nodded.

'For many years, it has been lost,' said Nicholas, his face aglow. 'A mystery now solved. Solved, I tell you!'

'Nicholas, pray tell me, I beseech you,' said Rosellene. 'Whatever have you found?'

'The door!' Nicholas cried. 'I have uncovered the door.'

Still with no inkling as to the door of which he spoke, Rosellene turned to her father for guidance. 'Is he not stranger than before?'

'Indeed.' Wrinkles formed near the corners of the king's mouth. 'What door do you speak of, Nicholas?'

'The very door we have been searching for all these centuries!'

The king's eyes widened. With trembling hands, he moved to the edge of the throne and stood. 'It cannot be.'

Nicholas felt as though he were twenty years younger. 'Beneath this very room in fact.'

Feeling light-headed, the king fell suddenly and uncontrollably onto the throne. *Could this be the door we've longed for? Might Rawdendale finally be free from depression?*

The thought was difficult to fathom.

The king spoke to Rosellene. Beads of sweat were forming around his neck, staining his tunic. 'You must see it with your own eyes.'

'Father?'

'Take your grandmother with you. She will be able to recognise whether it is real or false.'

Rosellene beamed. 'She has recovered then?'

'She has. Her ankle is mending well.'

Rosellene swallowed. She longed to hear of her dear friend Isabelle but her absence was enough to make her fearful. Still, she asked. 'And Isabelle?'

Eyes were cast to the floor.

'Her heart would not again start.' Sabine entered the great hall. A plaster made from linen cloth and wax had been applied to her foot and she walked with the use of a cane. 'I am sorry child.'

Rosellene could not speak as she embraced her grandmother. She looked to her father for instruction.

'Go now.' the king nodded. 'We have much to discuss here.'

So they followed Nicholas to the ground level of the keep, his long, white beard thrown carelessly across one shoulder as they passed through the granary and the great boxes filled with wheat, malt, barley and oats. And still farther did they trudge, across floors of dirt, until they arrived at the cistern, where Rosellene's mouth near hit the floor. She had quite forgotten the beauty of this place.

Cool and dark, pools of water gathered around huge, marble pillars, shaped and curved upwards like fingers on a hand. Patches of mould grew on the roof, furry and green, and a small beam of sunlight streamed through a grate into a circular basin made of marble. The reflection cast onto the water's surface was magical.

'Such a long way down.' Rosellene felt slightly out of breath, as the air had become cool and dense. 'What brought you to the cistern?'

'The water,' said Nicholas bluntly, skipping down the dampened stairwell. 'It clears my mind. Helps me think. Very good for the creative mind. Very good indeed.'

They walked across a worn section of limestone and into a dark cavern. 'Ahh, here it is.'

In front of them stood a heavy, wooden door. The thick pieces of wood had been nailed together and hung on iron pintles set into the stone. Reinforced with both iron bands and studs, it appeared that whatever lay beyond the door was something highly valued that demanded protection.

'This I have not seen before,' said Sabine, eyes focused upon the door. She nudged the pile of crushed limestone at the foot of the door. 'Nor do I think we were meant to find it.'

Rosellene closer inspected the door. Intricate patterns were burned into the wood. 'Has it been opened?'

Nicholas ran his wrinkled hands across the surface of the door. 'There is no handle nor key to the lock.'

A paleness passed across Sabine's face. She fell silent and remained so for some time.

'You cannot open the door?' Rosellene asked.

Nicholas sat cross-legged on the cold ground, his bare feet now visible beneath his robes. 'If we had a key, then yes, the door could be opened.'

'There is a key,' said Sabine, quietly, as though she did not want anyone to hear. 'But I fear what may be unleashed if it is used.'

A stone fell through the well's metal grid above, and plummeted into the water. Eyes grew wide in the darkness. Muscles jerked.

'How do I explain?' Sabine said, head in her hands. 'Do you recall the stories from your childhood, the one about The Insatiable King?'

Rosellene nodded. 'But I know not why it is important at this point in time.'

Sabine touched the ring upon Rosellene's finger. 'May I?'

Pulled from her finger, Rosellene handed the ring to her grandmother. With a thick, gold band and a heart-shaped ruby imbedded between a number of small carnelian pieces, it was not at all elegant. Nonetheless, it was a family heirloom and greatly treasured by Rosellene.

Save to bathe, and the day she had bestowed it upon Caprion, she had not taken the ring off since receiving it from her grandmother at the age of eight.

She watched her grandmother take a hairpin from her bun and press the two points into the top of the ring. As if by magic, the heart-shaped crystal sprung open to reveal a ruby-encrusted key.

Rosellene was in awe. 'But what does such a small key unlock?'

'Treasure beyond your wildest imagination,' said Sabine. 'Gold. Silver. Precious stones. Rubies that belonged to The Insatiable King himself.'

'Such a small key,' said Rosellene sceptically. 'Could it really unlock treasures as rich as the ones you speak of?'

Sabine nodded.

'Why was it not given to father then?'

'It was, yet he did not trust himself with its possession. Concerned that the same greed may run in his own veins, he gave up the key,' Sabine looked from Nicholas to Rosellene. 'You have seen how he handles finances. To his own detriment, he is far too giving.'

'I still do not understand the danger,' said Rosellene. 'I knew not of the key, so why should anyone else?'

'Alone, this key will not unlock the door.' Perspiration formed around Sabine's hairline. 'There is another key, however, identical to the one you hold now in your hand. The chamber can only be opened when the two keys are turned in unison.'

A second key, identical to this one. It must be close, thought Rosellene, *to warrant such a response from my grandmother.*

'Where is the second key?'

'For years, it lay hidden, in a nunnery far from the castle. Seven years ago, it was stolen. Perchance, the thief knows not what they hold.' Sabine held her hand to her heart. 'My fear is that they discover the secret and seek to find the second key.'

Chapter Thirty-One

In the early hours of the morn, Rosellene climbed the narrow staircase in the keep and stood out on the ledge. A light mist of snow had fallen during the night, making the ledge slippery to the feet.

Moving cautiously, she made her way to the east wall and peered upon the twin peaks of Grimore, just beyond the castle grounds. But again, as it had been yesterday and the day before that, no sign of Caprion could be seen.

So stared she at the spindly trees, their branches naked. How like the trees she felt. Without Caprion, she felt bare. Cold. Alone. These feelings she was subject to could not last forever. If he did not return soon, she would not make it through the winter. Her hunger dwindled. Thoughts wandered.

If she continued doing nothing, she would become nothing.

She wrapped the mantle tighter around her body. No longer would she wait. As she made to return along the ledge to the keep, something caught her eye.

Swiftly, yet not so as to fall, Rosellene hastened down the keep and into the outer courtyard, barely avoiding the guard's trumpet as he announced the start of the day. Taking refuge beneath one of the chapel's grand arches, she waited for the influx of men to pass her by.

They came in their hundreds, confident mercenary soldiers as strong on a horse as they were on foot. Carrying lance, poleaxe and sword, they rode through the castle gates, congregating with the rest of the infantry in the courtyard.

Close by sat the archers, lightly padded in long-sleeved jerkins, their ash bows resting at their feet. With fingers bent from years of drawing back the string, they trimmed, bound and attached feathers to the shafts of their arrows or spliced the well-seasoned wood to make two or three-point footings. In battle, once the selection was made, it would take but a few seconds to load and shoot an arrow.

The smallest band were the men at arms. Consisting of less than one thousand men, these knights, lords and squires would be clad head to toe in armour.

Presently, they wore only a thin gambeson as they quietly walked through both offensive and defensive techniques, interchanging weapons from lance to sword.

Those not fit to fight were either sent out to gather the livestock, housing them in the keep along with other provisions such as corn, grain and beans, or put to work, dropping large stones into barrels filled with tar that later would be set alight then cast over the castle wall.

Then she saw him.

Soft curls that fell around a chiselled jawline. Tired yet pensive eyes that sat above a straight nose. Momentarily, her heart skipped towards her throat, and Rosellene hastened through the thick crowd to Caprion, her soul once again whole.

Bounding from the saddle, his eyes met Rosellene's, and for a moment Caprion was transfixed, watching as she approached in a long, blue gown, that same strange feeling growing in his stomach. Her forehead pressed against his, Rosellene breathed deeply, taking in the scent of the man she loved. She brushed the hair from his grimy face and tried to smile as she fought back tears, her arms now tightly around his mail-covered body.

She felt safe in his arms, protected. But he too, needed protection, and that would come not only from the sword nor armour that he wore. She could protect him. She could keep him safe. And thinking of surrounding him in a veil of white, she gently and discreetly etched some symbols onto his back with her finger.

'How I missed thee,' whispered Caprion.

For the first time in months, he felt stripped of all his armour, his sword replaced with a wooden stick, thrust onto the battlefield, asked to take on the Ormans alone. His thoughts returned to his time as a page, when at night the queen of Beaumont would read to him tales of knights, the boldest, most courageous knights imaginable, who had become weak and distracted by love.

He smiled recalling how, back then, he had told the queen he would never suffer the same fate. He would be more daring and more resilient then any real or fictitious knight. Yet as his knees buckled beneath his powerless body, he thought how wrong he had been. He had succumbed to love and was happy to do so.

'You are not disappointed,' Rosellene's voice temporarily broke the trance Caprion had found himself in. 'that my word was not kept?'

Gently, Caprion tilted her chin and stared into her glassy eyes. 'How am I to protect that which I love, if I know not where she is?'

He wiped the tears from her cheek with the back of his hand, the moisture mixed with the grime from his hand leaving a light smear.

'Let us not be parted again.'

Caprion drew her in once more. 'I want always to have you close.'

'And I you.' Her cheek against his doublet, she squeezed tight the soft leather.

'Father is soon to make his address.' Rosellene took Caprion by the hand. 'You have time to wash and eat before you are summonsed.'

A while later in a small but comfortable cabinet, seven men gathered around a large, oak table, awaiting the king's address. Some sat on the heavy, high-backed chairs while others stood, gazing through the windows upon the courtyard below or inspecting one of the thirty paintings that hung harmoniously in the room.

Amongst those admiring the finer details of a painting was Lord Elliot, a highly structured man, whose day was regimented from the moment he woke to the time he retired. It was routine for him to train both morning and night, and there were few men that could beat him on foot in combat. Having fought in his first battle at the age of fifteen, he knew much about the art of war. The king trusted his military tactics.

The brothers Casper and Constantine sat with their backs towards the hearth, hoping that the wait would not be much longer. They had brought with them two hundred well-conditioned and highly trained men. Renowned for their brutal training sessions, these men climbed mountains in full armour, battled the elements for weeks on end with rations barely enough for a day, and held stones above their head for hours at a time until the muscles in their arms twitched with fatigue.

It was not enough that the men be skilled with the sword in one hand, but both, and not only a sword but lance and dagger as well. Their balance was honed by standing bare foot on a galloping horse and their marksmanship sharpened by hunting wild boar. Needless to say, these men were physically fit and emotionally stable. There was little to nothing in battle that would challenge them.

At the back of the room, nearest to the king's chair, sat a man in his fifties, a long, cylindrical tube held under his arm. He was dressed differently from the other men, wearing a woollen over-gown and pointed leather shoes that came up to his ankle. Not only did he look different, he also held an entirely different skill.

Gabrielle Perini was an artist. He was a painter, designer and architect. He had first come to Rawdendale as a young man to finish the reconstruction of the chapel, which had been destroyed by fire. Many had thought that he would not see the reconstruction through however, and had frowned upon him when the original chapel designs were discarded and a new style envisaged.

Despite the exorbitant price of materials and labour, the king had agreed to the pointed arches, vaulted ceiling, towering spires and features of green marble. This influential new style had soon crept into the castle. Wide, circular windows with elaborate petal designs appeared, and on the roof sat hideous stone creatures (man, animal and beast), water spilling from their mouths when it rained.

But during a siege, when several of the chapel's spirals had been damaged from a stone projectile launched from a trebuchet, Gabrielle's talent had shifted from art to defence. Pained by the destruction of his work, he had studied the castle designs seeking ways to better defend not just his king and queen but his precious creations too. Over time, modifications had been made to the castle walls, sloping them with white limestone to keep invaders from scaling them.

A series of secret passages had also been designed. Entered through a trapdoor in the king's own chamber, the first passage led out of the castle grounds for escape or to collect water and more supplies if under siege. Another, cleverly concealed behind his own painting of a winged knight, led down to a secret chamber where the elderly, women and children would be kept safe during a siege.

His life was now dedicated to castle defence and he took great pride in the fact that, of the thirty-two castles in the island basin, Rawdendale had not been compromised. Presently, every one of the holes in the parapets had a well-stocked barrel of stones nearby, ready to drop upon the enemy if defence was broken.

Monthly checks ensured that the pulleys responsible for raising and lowering the portcullises (of which there were two for each gatehouse) were in good repair and the drawbridge had been reinforced with thick, iron bars. Of course, the castle had been battered and bruised by past siege attempts, but every effort had been made to fix the problems.

Money was tight however, so repairs were oft done using wooden supports rather than stone. Windows too, were absent of mullions and entire sections of wall walk were missing. Nonetheless, the defences were still tight.

Let the Ormans come, he thought.

Then, came a man truly revered by all, the epitome of a knight. He was, as the code requested him to be, always courteous and never boastful, always generous and never greedy. He would defend a lady, the church, his lord and would honour that which he had sworn to do.

Working first as a page, then as a squire for the next seven years, he had mastered both weaponry and horsemanship as well as having an understanding of blazonry, language, art and music. Having proved his bravery that fateful day when he had protected his queen from imminent danger, he was then found ready to be accepted into the brotherhood. He had moved from boy to man, and his father, had he been alive, would have been proud.

At the age of fourteen, with his body cleansed, Caprion had dressed in first a tunic of white, red robes upon this, before spending the night in the castle chapel in quiet vigil. In the early morning, he had attended mass, where he had confessed his sins and taken an oath to honour his king and his faith and to abide by the laws of chivalry. Once blessed by the bishop, the king had pronounced Caprion a knight, taking a sword and tapping it gently on both shoulders. Arising from his knees, Caprion had accepted a pair of golden spurs and been girded with belt and sword.

Now, in the quiet cabinet, Caprion ran his fingers along the forged piece of metal strapped to his side. With thirty-inch blade, the sword was light and well balanced. It had endured many battles, yet despite the number of lives taken and saved, the crescent-shaped pommel and decorative cross-guard at the base of the hilt were still intact. As he looked upon the pointed tip, he silently prayed that the loss of life would be minimal.

And lastly, a man who had thought his aged eyes would never again see the beauty of the great hall, with its finely decorated poles and woven tapestries. Quietly sat Sir Theoderic, casting a glance at those seated beside him, comparing the contrasting mannerisms.

Lord Elliot was yet to be seated. Still viewing the paintings, or pretending to do so, he rocked from one leg to another, his prominent jaw clenched. With a forehead of deeply set wrinkles, Sir Theoderic could tell he was feeling the tension.

Gabrielle, on the other hand, was calm and confident. His posture was straight, and he sat head held high. Appearing a little more anxious then his brother, Casper sat stiffly in his chair, arms folded tightly across his chest.

'Gentlemen.' The king strode across the room and took his seat at the oak table. 'Yesterday, the Ormans were offered a settlement. If not accepted by midday on the seventh day, we will go under siege.'

Constantine shifted forward in his seat, his forehead creased with lines.

'Regardless of the settlement's appeal, we will be at war,' he stated. 'This is not an ordinary siege. The Ormans fight for entertainment.'

A few of the men nodded in agreeance.

'Nonetheless, we are to wait until word comes that our settlement has been denied. In the meantime,' the king looked towards Gabrielle. 'Let us ensure we are properly defended.'

Taking the cylindrical tube from beneath his arm, Gabrielle uncapped the leather top and carefully pulled from it a large piece of parchment, which he uncurled and spread across the table, covering it almost in its entirety. The king laid weights upon the corners then drew the men's attention to the markings in the centre.

'The tower, keep and gatehouses need to be well protected. I will require a large supply of archers stationed here; more are to position themselves around the curtain walls. I should think about one hundred, one hundred and fifty in total. What say you, Gabrielle?'

'Indeed, your grace. The gatehouses alone will need the presence of thirty to forty men.'

The king then went on to outline the plans should a siege take place. He stated that Lord Elliot should send half the archers, armed with spears, to be firstly positioned on the eastern hill. 'After positioning the spears in a line, let the horses of the Ormans be impaled as your men take refuge beyond the line of spears.'

Further, the king's speech went on to say that should a knight from the enemy be captured, he should be stripped of horse and armour. Any man of worthy rank should be taken prisoner and held for ransom. If lost in battle, they should seek to find their way back to their own banner or that of another.

Finally, with heartfelt passion, he concluded the meeting by saying, 'Control your men. Let there not be unruly behaviour. Be true to your lord. Be true to your faith. Be brave and act out of loyalty.'

Chapter Thirty-Two

A cool mist was settling over the castle grounds when Caprion arrived for the evening watch. As he made his way to the watchtower's third floor, he bid the previous guard a good night, stoked the fire then continued his ascent up the spiral stairwell to the fifth platform, where he lit the many firesticks affixed to the merlons.

Caprion watched as the grounds beyond the castle began to ignite with the glow from a multitude of small torches. 'Still the numbers continue to grow.'

At first, there had been no more than a few hundred men, foot soldiers and infantry, who had waited quietly for reinforcement that came several days later in the form of five hundred crossbowmen, one hundred and fifty longbowmen and one thousand additional men at arms. After fighting a small battle in Glebe, these men had moved south. They dressed in full plate armour and fought in close formation, making them a formidable opponent. They had won the battle in Glebe and were keen to win a second. Divided evenly into units of twenty men, each unit being led by an experienced leader, they marched in complete unison, stopping not until they had reached Grindella's grand pavilion.

While the increasing numbers disturbed Caprion, the sight of something smaller made his heart race.

'That is most strange.' He leaned against a merlon, eyes squinting in the fading light. 'Are you friend or foe?'

He watched a lone rider approach the mainland bridge, coming to a halt in the centre, a large, yellow flag billowing behind him. The markings on the flag were unmistakable. 'Foe. Definitely, foe!'

In a matter of moments, five men on horseback were at the gatehouse, Caprion among them, ready to ride out and meet their guest. Apprehensive of the awaiting decision, they moved through the gatehouse and onto the crest of the bridge, where, alone, Caprion rode out to speak to the dark-skinned man.

'What news do you herald?' He asked.

'Settlement has been denied,' said the dark-skinned man, the corners of his mouth gently curving upwards. 'Of course, an honourable surrender could be arranged.'

'So be it,' said Caprion, calmly accepting the decision.

And with a simple shake of the head once inside the walls of the castle, battle preparations intensified. Movement quickened as armour was donned, weapons collected and provisions checked. Then, as quickly as the movement began it halted, as father Michael stepped onto the balcony, hand raised.

'Bow your heads for a blessing,' said he, and in unison over six thousand men got down on bended knee, the clang of armour like that of chiming bells. They listened, some with eyes closed, as the priest spoke of defending the church, remembering their chivalric virtues and upholding justice.

Using the branch from an olive tree, father Michael dipped the leaves into a bowl of holy water then splashed this upon their heads, saying, 'Be thou valiant and brave as thou face thy enemy. Be true to thy king and to thy God, and trust that with the help of all the angels and saints thou shall be protected in battle.'

While the blessing was received, the men going forth knowing that, should they fall in battle, their sins had been forgiven, the lone rider returned to Grindella at great speed.

'It is done, my lady.'

With the point of a finger, Grindella dismissed the guard and retreated to her pavilion, closing behind her the heavy entrance drapes. Moving forth to a standing cage that housed her falcon, its talons tightly curled around the perch, she took from a drawer concealed in the bottom of the cage, a key. A ruby-encrusted key.

'You brought this upon yourself.'

And for the first time in years, Grindella smiled.

'So, my love,' Grindella's words were gentle as she took the bird upon her wrist and stroked the soft plumage on its chest. 'Finally, after all these years, we will regain what is rightfully ours. Come, let us check upon our army.'

Icy were the winds that bowed at her feet as she stepped from the pavilion and mounted her mighty steed. High in the saddle she rode, past flickering fires and hordes of tradesmen, fletchers and armourers, sword smiths and surgeons, working together to make ready the camp.

The king's stocky horses were rugged, their deep chests and broad backs hugged by thick, woollen arms. So too was the king's army. Clad in tights and thick-padded jerkins, hurriedly, they worked to erect tents across the frozen wasteland, providing temporary relief from the elements as well as a splash of colour, albeit brief before the next dusting of snow.

Men cursed. Barked. Frowned.

Frustration set in as fingers became pinched, ropes broke and stakes refused to hold in the snow. But above all else, the sound of King Tyrone's voice boomed.

'Faster, men…I wish not to freeze before the battle even begins!'

The falcon puffed up its feathers, the air entrapped. The movement caused the two small bells attached to the bird's leg to ring, the tone short and crisp.

'The air is cool.' Grindella pulled the bird closer to her chest. 'We shall shelter for a time here with Lord Bannock. I do not care for that man's voice. It is most unpleasant.'

Lines of worry on his forehead, Bannock laid his armour upon the trestle table within his pavilion and inspected the decorative helm with his numbing fingers. Tracing the golden swirls on both body and comb, there came a pounding upon his temples, an endless thump within his veins. The pain was so much that he fell into a chair and cradled his head, driving his chubby thumbs into the skin.

How did this come to be? Why was he here preparing for battle when he should be at home in front of a warm hearth, his stomach full of roasted vegetable and rich venison? He was not physically fit nor was he highly skilled. His training had been minimal, his food intake high and his armour, merely for show.

And, as such, that was the dilemma facing him.

His body would be covered first in a padded jerkin, the straps pulling on his oversized stomach. Providing freedom of movement, a layer of chain mail would next be thrown upon the jerkin. But would this stop the point of a lance or the tip of a sword? He was beginning to doubt.

Although the breast plate emphasised his body shape, it was made of thick steel. But again, he doubted his protection. What if he were dismounted and had to fight on foot? Would he weaken under the weight and become an easy target? How he wished he had trained more. Listened more.

'And eaten less.'

Startled, Bannock turned his pale face towards the pavilion's entrance.

'Come now,' said Grindella, irritated by Bannock's weak mind. 'There are more important matters to attend to.'

'I cannot agree.' Bannock ran his fingers through moistened hair. 'At this time, I cannot think on anything more pressing.'

'There will be no battle if all goes to plan,' said Grindella, and she picked up the leg guards from the table. 'You think I wish to see you squeezed into these?'

Bannock sat up. His head no longer throbbed. 'No battle? Could this be true?'

'Our army is in every way impressive. Why, they should be running from the castle.'

Bannock's breathing eased, the colour restored to his face. 'I should like to know your plan. Pray tell me more.'

'And you shall,' said Grindella, and she made to leave. 'We meet now to discuss the details.'

After Bannock, King Tyrone was next to enter Grindella's pavilion. Foul was his mood and the expression on his face clearly showed this unhappiness, his wrinkles deepening with each step he took. Not one for waiting, he stormed across the plush hide, throwing himself into the chair at the very end of the table, where he sat shaking off the snow that dusted his beard.

'Let us begin,' his voice boomed. 'War is calling.'

'Keen to shed some blood,' said the Orman king. He slapped hard his hand on King Tyrone's back. Flakes of snow fell to the table. 'Unlike others who are only here for the food.'

Bannock slid his hand away from the dried figs that lay in a golden bowl upon the table.

'I too, am keen for the battle to begin,' said Bannock, squeezing his rear into the narrow chair.

The Orman king leaned nearer King Tyrone. 'He fears that if we do not go to war soon, there may not be sufficient food to satisfy his hunger.'

Before finding a seat beside his king, Orlov glanced longingly at a large, polished stone neatly positioned on a satin cloth. The surface looked so smooth that he had to reach out to touch it, but no sooner had his fingers lain upon the orange surface than a pain, sharp and most intense, shot up his arm and in his ear came a whispered warning.

'Dragons can breathe fire from the moment they hatch,' the whisper continued. 'It would be wise not to stand too close. That is the egg of a Sierra, a dragon of the sky. Terrifying beast.'

Orlov backed away, yet the voice followed him. 'I recall a story of a young knight who, having stumbled upon a dragon's lair, stole from it a single piece of treasure. Forever was he cursed, not dead nor living but drifting in between.'

Grindella laughed. 'It may be one thousand years before it hatches, yet, in the meantime, I shall tap into its magical powers.' She tossed back the voluptuous cape she wore and lay upon the chaise lounge, a hand propped under her delicate chin. 'Gentleman, shall we begin?'

And so, around a large wooden table they sat, the finer details of battle discussed. Draped across the tabletop between the flask of red wine and platter of figs, battle plans were viewed. Challenged. Changed. Then finally agreed upon.

'The siege engines will take time to assemble,' said King Tyrone. 'Could take several days. We should begin, therefore, following the construction.'

Grindella rolled onto her back, a plump cushion beneath her blonde locks. 'If we are ready.'

'In these conditions, we will need to be, my lady,' stated King Tyrone. 'If the wait is much lengthier, we may freeze before we get the chance to shed any blood.'

Grindella turned her eyes to the candles that flickered in the chandelier above her. 'The men can wait.'

His arms folded across his chest, King Tyrone leaned forward on the table. 'For how long?'

'The men are already exhausted from the journey alone,' Orlov said, his eyes wide. 'If we must go to war, then it would not be wise to wait.'

'Perhaps we are not needed at all,' King Tyrone stood. With his hands clenched behind his back, he strolled around the table. 'A powerful sorceress like yourself could easily penetrate the castle of Rawdendale, could you not?'

'Easily,' admitted Grindella. The tone of sarcasm was high. 'It could be a sleeping spell I use, cast upon the guards so that we slip past them on their watch and storm the castle through the gatehouse, or maybe we send dragons with stones in their claws to break down the great stone walls. What say you, King Tyrone?'

King Tyrone was silent. His feet dangled in the air, a golden curtain sash around his neck. Grindella threw open her arms. 'Anyone else wish to question our plan of attack?'

There came no answer.

'Someone cut him loose, before his face turns blue.'

A dagger, double-edged with a leather hilt, was pulled from Orlov's belt. Its sharp blade sliced through the curtain sash and King Tyrone dropped onto the plush hide.

'You may think twice before questioning me again, King Tyrone.'

Scornful was the look thrown across the room, as King Tyrone retreated to his chair, the broken blood vessels around his neck gently massaged.

For a time, the men fell silent. Then Orlov asked, 'Why now?' He tapped a finger upon his pursed lips. 'A winter battle is unheard of and indeed a risky venture.'

The dragon egg upon her lap, Grindella took to stroking the smooth, polished surface. 'Perhaps I have had no reason.'

'Until now.' Orlov leaned forward in his chair. 'What is it that entices you to Rawdendale that previously did not? What can you gain from the castle?'

The stone was stroked again. Over and over in the one direction. 'No one mentioned a castle.'

'So what you seek is not protection or strength of men?'

'Look around you,' Grindella mocked. 'Do I not have both protection and strength of men?'

Orlov sat back in his chair, twisting the hair upon his chin. 'There is something else within the borders, is there not?'

The men shifted restlessly. Frowns passed over their faces.

'I have heard it said that a river of gold flows beneath Rawdendale,' Bannock's eyes seemed to twinkle at the thought.

King Tyrone scoffed. 'Would not the state of Rawdendale be better were there a river of gold beneath it?'

'Not just gold, nay. The mountains are teaming with jewels of every kind and the tunnels are lined with silver.'

King Tyrone turned to Bannock. 'Do you think a sorceress wants for gold, you fool?'

'Who knows what else there may be…'

Blood splattered across the table. A tooth embedded in a fig.

King Tyrone sneered. 'Keep talking and you will have more than a thick lip, my friend.'

While Bannock stemmed the flow of blood and arguments continued over the so-called riches of Rawdendale, Orlov's attention shifted elsewhere, his gaze now upon the dragon egg.

A ripple moved beneath the surface.

'Another treasure lies hidden,' Orlov's words were slow, cautious. 'It may be best if we leave it thus.'

The arguing stopped. Questioning eyes turned to Orlov.

'You are wiser than you seem,' said Grindella. She cradled the dragon egg in her slender arms. 'Your task is to take the castle and no more. You will get what you are owed. I have no need for a castle.' She turned to Bannock. 'Nor for treasures, should they exist.'

But Bannock made no comment, his pupils dilated. He too, had seen the egg move.

'Our entry to Rawdendale should not be difficult,' continued Grindella. 'The castles protection has been weakened, and as Orlov stated, I have strength of men and much, much more.'

The dragon egg came to rest on the table, upon the silken cloth thrown across the worn top. Parts of the polished stone protruded and a tiny crack formed. Chests rose and fell quickly as they watched the stone break apart and out tumbled a small, blue creature.

Its leathery skin was covered in a sticky membrane and a red glow appeared within its jaws. It clawed at the silk and unfurled its delicate wings. Two large nostrils sniffed at the air and it opened its yellow eyes, blinking in the light.

Bannock cupped his hands over his ears as it let out a shriek most frightening. 'I would have called it sweet until it opened its mouth.'

Orlov looked troubled.

King Tyrone looked intrigued. 'Are there more?'

'Many.' Grindella lowered her arm before the dragon and it crawled upon her shoulder. 'Sea Loch dragons, Sierras, drakes and worms. Impressive beasts.'

The dragon seemed to hiccup and several puffs of smoke drifted into the air. Bannock watched as the dragon nuzzled its narrow nose into Grindella's neck.

'I should like to see them,' he said.

'And you shall,' Grindella smiled. 'You shall see them soon enough.'

Chapter Thirty-Three

'So, my friend.' Angus sat his whetstone on the stool beside Caprion, one eyebrow cocked. 'Tell us what is on your mind so that your face may finally be free of that frown.'

Caprion shot Angus a look of disdain. He continued to sharpen the edge of his blade.

They sat in the armoury. The room was pinched, dark and smelt strongly of oil. Neatly assembled in rows around the brick walls stood suits of armour, pikes, swords and all manner of helmets, from basinets to great helm.

'We have been friends a long time,' Angus leaned a little closer, the sharpened blade resting on his knee. 'I know when you have something to say.'

Caprion took a hand to his brow and rubbed hard at the furrows growing ever deeper. 'There is much to say, dear Angus, but how I shall say it, I know not.'

By the open window, Sir Theoderic got to his feet. 'If it is quiet council you seek, I shall take my leave, lord?'

'Nay.' Caprion waved a hand at Theoderic. 'Stay. You may be one of few whom understand my words. Pray close the shutters though, so that what is spoken is heard only by those in this room.'

Sir Theoderic was a tall man, yet still he needed to stand on his toes in order to reach the high windows. When the shutters were closed, he sat on the bench beside Marcus, who had been attending to Caprion's mail.

'We will hear what it is you need to say and no judgement or ill words shall be made.'

'We shall see,' said Caprion quietly, and for a time his eyes lifted not from the earthen floor. 'This will be a battle like none we have faced before.'

Angus reeled back, a hand thrust upon his hip. 'Throw a sorceress in the melee and I say we will have more than a battle, my friend.'

'There will be others too, at the battle.' Caprion still searched the ground with his eyes. 'Others come to aid the people of Rawdendale.'

Angus squeezed his lower lip between his fingers. 'Others?'

A fine needle was being drawn through the cotton fibres of Caprion's aketon. The horsehair padding had been replaced by a thicker layer of wool and now Rosellene used a running stitch to bind the ends.

The queen would be proud, she thought.

Rosellene knotted the thread then snapped the needle free from the garment. 'By others, you speak of the men readying themselves for battle within these castle walls and the ogres come from the mountains. Do you not?'

Caprion swallowed several times. 'They are not the others I speak of.' Rosellene shifted on the wooden trunk, fingers interlaced.

'Man, woman or beast,' Angus shrugged. 'It matters not. If they stand with us, I say they are most welcome.'

'What if I added the fey to the list.' Caprion's dark eyes were heavy as they stared directly at Angus. 'What say you then? Would you be so welcoming?'

'The fey?' Angus scratched a little at his beard. 'Never seen one myself but I hear they have superior skills, which may be to our advantage.'

Caprion turned to Theoderic. His face had changed little at the mention of the forest folk. 'And you, Sir Theoderic. Have you had dealings with the fey?'

'When I was a child, we would gather kindling from the edge of the forest,' Sir Theoderic began. 'One morning I wandered a little deeper into the forest and became snared in a rabbit trap. My screams for help went unanswered. I could feel myself slipping away but, just as my eyes closed, a light appeared in the distance. They claimed it was merely a hallucination. My pain so intense that I believed I saw a man release the trap, setting free my foot. A man with translucent wings protruding from his back.'

'It was not a hallucination,' said Caprion. 'I too, have seen them with my own eyes.' Breaths were drawn. Eyes wide and questioning.

'You saw them?' Marcus could not decide if he was excited that the fey existed or terrified. 'When? Where?'

'The Dead Forest.'

'You went where?' Marcus suddenly stood. 'On what cause did you venture there?'

Caprion held up his hands. 'It was not my intention.'

The squire resumed his seat. 'Why is it they fight for us?'

'They wish to support their queen's son,' said Caprion.

Sir Theoderic near but fell off his chair. 'He is here?'

Caprion nodded. 'He fights under the Rawdendale banner.'

'Translucent wings and a suit of armour?' Angus tutted. 'It cannot be.'

Marcus leaned forward and stared at his boots. Sir Theoderic adjusted his position on the bench. Rosellene stole across the room to rest a gentle hand upon Caprion's shoulder. 'But it is.'

Angus jumped to his feet. The sword hit the ground with a clang. 'You? No. I would have known. It would have been obvious.'

'The revelation is new to me also,' Caprion mused.

Angus scratched again at his beard, a little harder than before. 'So all this time I have been in the presence of a prince?'

'Do not think differently of me,' said Caprion. 'Nothing has changed. I do not consider myself a prince. I am Caprion of Green Mere, a knight like any other, who will defend my king and stand beside his men.'

Angus huffed. 'So your skill with a blade was…?'

'Talent,' smiled Caprion.

'Your horsemanship?'

'Talent.'

Angus narrowed his eyes. 'And nothing has changed?'

'Nothing.'

Angus smirked. 'Then I shall continue to whip your arse whenever it is necessary.' The room suddenly became brighter.

'I would not have it any other way.'

'What do they look like, the fey?' Marcus strolled across the room. 'Are they like you and I?'

'Ugly, you mean?' injected Angus.

A boot was cast through the air.

Caprion turned the worn, copper ring on his forefinger. It, like the others, had loosened in the cooler weather. 'Beautiful. Very beautiful and there is a calmness when you are in their presence that washes over you like a lullaby.'

'We could use that to our advantage,' suggested Angus. 'Put the bastards to sleep.'

'Tell me, why have they come to Rawdendale's aid?' Sir Theoderic asked. 'What shall be owed in return?'

'Nothing,' said Caprion. 'King Tyrone has done them an injustice. Their lands have been destroyed. They merely want him to know they are displeased.'

'And you, Caprion. How fare thee?' Rosellene asked, a hand upon his knee. Gentle were her words. 'The shock must have been great.'

'I cannot say how I feel as yet. Too much invades my head at this time, so little have I thought about the situation. I do fear their involvement. I am only just reunited with my mother. If she were to be taken from me again…'

'Let us not think such thoughts.'

'I am concerned too, as to my reputation. Should people question my abilities. My stature. My loyalty. What then? Shall I keep my heritage a secret, even for a time?'

'We cannot act for anyone but ourselves. These actions that we take, that is what people will remember. It shall make no difference where we came from nor from whom. It is whether or not our actions are honourable. Just. Fair. That is where the importance lies. We all have our secrets.'

Chapter Thirty-Four

She had broken her promise.

There were many things in life that she could control. Love was not one of them.

She had vowed never again to fall in love. Never again to allow her heart to be broken. But how could one's heart break when it was so content?

He came to her that night, to the warmth of the chamber, a gentleman dressed in clean cotton shirt, doublet and a robe of rich velvet. And she, having arranged the meeting, had washed with scented water, dressed in a tight-fitting gown and laced her hair with strings of pearls. But her heart would not be still, already in a flutter. When there came a knock upon the door, her heart all but flew away.

'Please, come in.'

She returned a smile as Caprion entered the room. Slowly, she pushed closed the door, rubbing a finger across her teeth, hoping that none of the reddened beeswax smeared upon her lips had stained the enamel.

'Can I offer you a drink?'

Rosellene hurried across to the bulbous pitcher and poured wine from its narrow neck into two silver chalices. Seemingly, something was wrong with her voice. It was not normally so high-pitched. So, gently, coughed she to clear her throat then carried the chalices across to Caprion, standing now by the glazed window.

'Have you any word on reinforcements?' Rosellene asked.

There appeared a glow to Caprion's cheeks as he took the chalice in his trembling hands.

She is perfect, he thought.

Eyes that sparkled. Skin that glowed. Lips, sweet enough to eat. So captivated by her beauty was he that Rosellene's question had to be repeated several times before an answer was finally given.

'We have indeed.' Caprion took a long sip from the chalice. Mellow with a fruity tone. 'Just now word was received. The fey are but a day away.'

Rosellene felt much relieved. She knew little of the faery folk that resided in the woodland realm apart from the knowledge that they had been of great assistance to the witches of old, sheltering them when they were being hunted.

'I am reminded of something.' Setting his chalice on the window ledge, Caprion pulled from his doublet a small item wrapped in silken cloth. 'Would you mind if I left this here? I fear it may break if left unattended.'

Eager to discover what was concealed beneath the silk wrapping Rosellene too set down her chalice.

'Of course,' she said. 'But what is it?'

'It was given to me by the fey. It appears to be a mirror, yet the reflection is quite distorted.'

The emerald cloth fell open and revealed a hand mirror, most beautiful, with ebony handle and frame of gold.

But a mirror it was not. And Caprion was right to have it covered and conceal it in the chamber.

'Most distorted,' said Rosellene when the mirror was received. She turned away and looked at the curved tin. A shiver traced her spine. 'Perhaps all it needs is a good polish? I shall put it away here in this drawer for safe keeping.'

And pray, thought she, *that no one find it for fear that the devil may be watching from the other side.*

But it was a woman, not the devil, that was seen when she stared into the reflective tin. A woman with flawless skin and the bluest of eyes.

His chalice near drained, Caprion sat uncomfortably upon the window ledge. All of a sudden, the room was stifling.

'Do you mind if I take this off?' Caprion tugged at his doublet. 'The fire is making me warm.'

Rosellene did not mind at all. 'Of course not.'

She smiled, knowing that his sudden rise in body temperature was not due to the fire. So tried she to calm his nerves, pulling him from the cushion.

'Dance with me, Sir Caprion.'

So they danced. Her full skirts swished the reeds on the floor as they glided, spun and twirled, until dizziness took them over and both tumbled onto the bed's soft, feather down mattress.

Silently, they stared at each other, chests rising and falling, breath heavy. 'More wine?' Rosellene asked.

She made to leave but Caprion caught her hand. She swallowed. Then it happened. Quite unexpectedly.

'May I kiss you?'

So sincere, so genuine was it spoken that her body all but melted.

Need you ask? My lips are yours. Take them.

In an instant, their lips pressed together. Soft, so soft. He kissed next her long neck then travelled behind her ear, breathing in the sweet citrus perfume she had dabbed on her neck. Her eyes closed.

'You are most beautiful,' she heard him whisper before he took her hand, interlocking his fingers with hers.

His palm was moist. Again, he leaned in close so that now their noses touched and their breath was one. Gently, he touched her cheek with the back of his hand.

'I devote my life to thee and promise to protect you always.'

And while others shook in the bitter conditions, they were warm in each other's arms, neither one afraid of the love they now shared. Until such time as the air was still and the movement of the mattress woke Rosellene.

'Must you go?' She wrapped her arms around Caprion's shoulders 'I should like you to stay.'

Kissing her hands, Caprion whispered. 'I should like that also, but while the enemy sleeps, we must make haste.'

'Make haste?' Her slender arms slipped from his shoulders 'How? Where and for how long shall I worry about you making haste?' A quilted dress was dropped onto her narrow shoulders, a cape thrown upon this.

'Rosellene, it is early. You should stay beneath the warmth of the duvet.'

Twisted then formed into a bun, her hair was fastened with a metal clasp. Then she moved to the trunk at the base of the bed and foraged through the field of clothes for a small, hide bag. The journey might be long and she wondered how much she should pack.

Dressed now himself, Caprion moved towards Rosellene. Gently, he spoke. 'Rosellene.'

'If you must away, then I am going with you.' Without even glancing up, she hastily shoved possessions into the bag, many of which would not be suitable for the journey ahead. Only when two strong arms reached out and held her did she stop. The tears, however, continued to flow down her cheeks until her focus was lost. 'I will not lose you too.'

Caprion held tight her trembling body. 'I do not plan on getting lost.'

Rosellene could feel small sections of her heart tearing away. 'How long must I wait?'

'A day.' Gently, with his thumbs, Caprion tried to dry the tears from her cheeks. 'Perhaps two.' Although, not pleased by the decision, Rosellene nodded.

'I shall give you two days, no more. Then I shall come searching for you.'

Caprion pulled her into an embrace. 'I would not have it another way.'

There came a soft knock upon the door and Rosellene was surprised to see Oliver standing in the doorway when it opened.

Caprion started out the door, sword in hand. 'Oliver will keep you safe in my absence.'

'You are heading out the northern gate, are you not?' Rosellene called, several paces behind him. But as they descended the stairs, there came no answer.

So Rosellene repeated, 'Pray tell me that you are heading out the northern gate.'

Caprion held Rosellene's hand as they made their way along the corridor. 'It is far too dangerous to exit via the northern gate, even under the cover of night.'

Rosellene pulled suddenly on Caprion's hand and he jolted to a stop. 'Which way then are you leaving?'

She knew the answer. There was only one way they would not be seen nor followed by the enemy.

'It is our only option,' said Caprion softly. 'We total fifty men. You have nothing to fear.'

'There is much to fear in that forest,' said Rosellene. 'We both know that.'

But despite the danger, that evening, while the enemy slept, Caprion and a band of fifty men, the majority of them archers, crept from the castle in the shadow of darkness.

'Have faith, my lady.' Oliver brushed back Rosellene's wind-swept hair as they stood in the courtyard. 'He will return soon enough.'

And, momentarily, Oliver's words were comforting.

Chapter Thirty-Five

The men were on edge as they entered the forest, a mass of creaking bones. The moon was full, but still it was dark, little light filtering through the tall, creepy trees. The darkness made the forest even more forlorn.

Not wanting to light lanterns for fear it might draw attention from beasts and shademen alike, they stumbled much on the slippery undergrowth, moving cautiously so as to escape the creatures that lurked in the darkness.

Unfortunately, even without the light, their presence was soon apparent.

Little was known about the population of shademen that infested the forest. Some said that they were half man, half beast, and ran on all fours. Others claimed that their faces were gnarled like the trees that surrounded them. They certainly existed, since strange noises could be heard coming from the forest and the occasional light flickered in the darkness. Despite knowing this fact, the men were taken by surprise when, all of a sudden, some were snared in thick nets, Caprion included, and sent flying up through the air, coming to rest amongst the tree branches.

'Try hacking at the net with your knives,' Caprion spoke in hushed tones, his gaze darting backwards and forwards across the trees. 'Make haste, men. They could soon be upon us.'

The men who had not become trapped huddled together below, hands on bows, their fingers twitching. But barely could they see the archer beside him, so aiming at an opponent would be difficult.

'I think I see something. Yes, there in the distance.' But although Marcus pointed, no one knew where it was he pointed. 'Do you see them?'

'I can see no better than were my eyes shut,' Angus grumbled.

Marcus grabbed Angus around the shoulders and pulled him closer. He pointed again. 'There, see them? Huge, white eyes that glisten.'

'You need not point either.' Angus pulled away. 'It will do you no good.'

'I too, see them,' said another, whose voice shook almost as much as his hands. 'They shine like stars in the sky. Yet why so high?'

'Men cannot fly,' said Angus. 'So I suggest you aim that bow nearer to the ground.'

'And stars cannot move either,' huffed Marcus. 'So I guess what we are seeing is neither star nor man.'

'Hush now.' Angus threw an arm across Marcus's chest. His head turned from side to side, ears alert. 'I fear they are upon us.'

It was true. They were not alone.

From the darkness, a voice spoke. 'And have been for some time.'

A timber torch was lit. The hessian burned quickly, spilling light into the forest and onto the shademen, thick as the trees. Dirty faces framed with beards. Bare feet with curled nails. Stocky bodies dressed in fur.

'What is your reason for passing through our forest?'

One of the shademen, older, with a thick greying beard, stepped forward. A dagger hung from the taut belt around his waist, a quiver was strung over his shoulder and a string of bear claws hung around his neck. Known as Bear, he was the leader of the men.

Marcus raised his eyebrows. 'Your forest? I did not know one could claim a forest as one's own.'

'I do not think we are in a position to question the ownership of the forest or anything else for that matter,' whispered Angus. Then he turned to the shademen and said, 'The castle has been threatened and we wish to seek reinforcements.'

'Reinforcements? From the very men you excluded?' Bear spoke gruffly. 'You have guile, I will give you that.'

'You will be rewarded for your aid,' said Caprion. 'The king has agreed to relinquish the forest to you.'

Bear tugged at his grimy lips but no answer was given.

The ground shook.

Then, for no apparent reason at all, the trees began to fall.

Oak and pine. Beech and spruce. One after another they gracefully bowed, dispatching leaves and branches as they bounced against the hard earth.

Neither star nor man, thought Caprion. 'Good timing.'

Trekking over the fallen limbs, Hermes appeared, a band of no fewer than twenty ogres behind him. Slow and cumbersome, the mighty beasts clambered towards them, the top of their balding heads tickled by the uppermost branches.

'Good?' Angus chimed. 'I would call that perfect timing!'

With the heel of his high boots upon the cotton net (frayed in several places), Caprion jostled with the other men as he tried to stand. 'Never before have I been so pleased to see an ogre. Up here, Hermes!'

'Hermes?' Marcus queried. 'Ogres have names?'

'This one does, yet I know not why he would want to rescue me,' Caprion paused. 'I did try to kill him, after all.'

'Perfect, so truth be known their intent is probably to fry us up for supper, drop us, net and all, into a boiler.'

Small, beady eyes hidden amongst a leathery face appeared next in front of the net. 'Rosellene…safe?'

Caprion could see compassion in those eyes. 'At the moment, yes, Rosellene is safe, but the battle is yet to begin.'

Hermes steadied the net with a hand, his fingers like sausages. 'Rosellene safe with Hermes.'

'You might have another fight on your hands,' said Marcus quietly. 'The big lump wants to take Rosellene for himself.'

'And that big lump may also save our skins,' said Caprion. 'Might I suggest you use his name in future.'

The men were released and fell uncomfortably from their net bindings onto the ground.

'We thank you for your aid,' Caprion addressed the ogres. 'King Ivanhoe will be indebted to you all.'

'Grindella's enemy.' Hermes tapped a hand to his solid chest. 'Our friend.'

Several of the shademen exchanged glances then one of them asked, 'Grindella?'

'The witch who seeks the throne,' Caprion explained. 'The reason we go to battle.'

The shademen were quiet. They looked to the ground as if they had lost something. 'A witch, you say?' Bear asked.

'You know of whom we speak?'

Bear locked eyes with another member of his tribe, a taller man, Birch, his dark hair laced back with leather tie. 'There is a woman who frequents the forest from time to time, but she be no witch. Her magic is much more powerful than the simple spells of a witch. No, I say she be a sorceress.'

'In this very forest, you say?' Caprion asked.

Angus grabbed Caprion's arm and tried to hold him in his place. 'Do not be getting any ideas, my friend. A sorceress should be left alone.'

'Indeed,' answered the tall man. 'Her hut is not far from where we sit.'

Despite the resistance, Caprion pushed forward. 'Shall we see for ourselves then? It may be to our good fortune that the sorceress is home. What if the battle could be over before it begins?'

Murmurs and mumbles erupted amongst both sides of men. Caprion cursed.

'What brave men you are that you would fight an army with sword and spear but cannot contemplate the mere thought of entering a sorceress's home.'

Murmurs erupted once more, only louder. Accusations of cowardice were not taken well. 'Calm down, men.' Bear threw his hands in the air, silencing the noisy crowd. 'You will be pleased to know the witch is not at home.'

Caprion tapped a finger upon his sword hilt. 'We make our visit swift then. To be safe.'

'Safe and witch.' Angus pulled at his twisted beard. 'Those two words do not belong together.'

'It is indeed risky, yet there may be a way to bargain with her.' Caprion ignored Angus's loud protest and continued speaking. 'Suddenly, she seeks Rawdendale for her own. Strange, is it not? What is it that she seeks and why now does she seek it, in the middle of winter?'

'Let us set your mind at ease then,' said Angus and he moved forth into the darkness.

So onwards to the sorceress's hut they went. It was not long before the ground grabbed at their boots, sucking them deeper and deeper into the boggy mud. The trees too, were denser and the air that touched the exposed skin on face and hands was cool. Icy cool.

The sound of bells drifted through the air.

'We are close,' said Bear. 'Keep alert.'

Marcus stopped.

'Why would someone leave a perfectly good money pouch in the brush.'

A small, blue pouch was affixed to a branch. He went to loosen the string that bound it to the spiky wood but a hand, swift and sharp, slapped it away.

'What are you playing at?' Marcus growled.

'They be prayer ties, my friend.' Birch shone the torch along the brush, revealing an array of trinkets. Bells, ribbons and food items were tied or nailed to the branches. 'Offerings made to the spirits. I would leave them be.'

Marcus narrowed his eyes. He did not fear the spirits. Again, he reached for the pouch.

Birch angled the blade deftly under Marcus's chin. 'I said, leave them be. You would be wise to heed the warnings. I have not seen a more powerful woman.'

'You are but fools,' Marcus huffed. 'She is merely an outcast who dislikes visitors.'

'Hold your tongue before I cut if off,' Angus took hold of Marcus's shirt collar. 'You are lucky Birch got to you first.'

'Is that fear I sense?' Marcus pulled away. 'And I thought you were stronger than that, my friend.'

'My sword and ability to wield it are my strength,' Angus lowered his voice as they came upon a circle of green conifers. 'You cannot fight a sorceress with weapons and expect to win.'

Marcus laughed. 'There is nothing to fear. Come, I will prove it to you.'

'Wait!' Angus tried to stop him but Marcus continued on towards the hut.

The shademen hung back, seeking the tree's protection. Drawn were their arrows, fingers twitching near the woven hemp. Too often had they been caught by traps and snares.

'Let us tread carefully,' warned Caprion as he and Angus moved along the earthen track. 'I do not wish to dangle in a net for the second time.'

The hut stood raised upon four mushroom-like stones. It had a wooden exterior and the top of its pointed thatched roof was hidden by trees.

'Like I said,' Marcus reached for the doorknob. 'Nothing to fear.'

There was a sudden crack and the wooden door seemed to splinter. Caprion flinched.

An arrowhead, curved like a leaf, protruded from Marcus's leather jerkin.

Angus swallowed hard at the pools of saliva layering his throat. 'You damn fool!' Blood trickled from the corner of Marcus' mouth.

He spoke in short bursts. 'I thought...you said sorceresses...do not use weapons.'

'My words were true,' Angus said. He supported Marcus's weight, thrusting a shoulder beneath his armpit. 'This is not a weapon but a carefully concealed trap. Pray there are no more.'

'You are in luck, my friend.' Caprion tore off a section of his shirt and used it to absorb the blood pooling around the wound. 'The arrow has gone right through.'

'Then you must snap the head off.'

Marcus let out a wail. The arrow head now rested in Angus's hand. 'You could not have warned me?' He grimaced.

'Where be the pleasure in that?' Angus winked. 'Now, let us get you off this door, shall we?' Supporting his shoulders, the men gently pulled Marcus backwards, sliding his body off the thick, yew arrow.

'Tall and thin to your advantage,' said Angus and he took to ruffling Marcus's damp hair. 'Let that be a lesson to you, laddie.'

On the doorstep, partly buried by the twisting ivy, a large, metal bowl lay. Slashing at the vines with his knife, Caprion took up the bowl and held it forth as a shield.

'You still intend to enter the hut?' Angus raised an eyebrow. 'Are you mad?'

Caprion winked. 'We both must be.'

And although he shook his head, Angus too, took up a makeshift shield and entered the darkened hut.

Angus put a gloved hand across his nose. 'What is that smell?'

'Here.' Giles entered the hut, a torch in his hand. 'Let us shed some light on the scene.'

Angus jolted backwards. Something slithered across his boots. 'Looks as though the animals have free range while she is away.'

Giles cast the light across one of the shelves lined with bottles. 'Those that are not contained.'

Angus pressed his nose against the bottles. 'I have a mind to release them.'

'For some, it may be too late.'

Angus nodded then pointed to a feature in the corner of the room. 'What is that?'

Caprion turned his head. 'I see nothing more than a bed.'

'Indeed' Angus took a rough glove to scratch his beard. 'Do they even sleep? Do they not transform into animals and roam the world at night?'

Moving nearer the hearth, Caprion reached beneath the cauldron and pulled some parchment from the ashes.

An owl shrieked.

Angus tottered.

Bottles shattered.

'That may indeed be a warning,' Giles said, every muscle in his body tense. 'Caprion, let us linger not.'

'I shall not be long.' Caprion viewed the sketch on the parchment. Lengthy tail. Sharp claws. A large, stone wall. 'Wait outside if your nerves cannot be held.'

Giles edged nearer the door but did not exit. 'I fear her return. If we are found in her hut, she will skin us alive and use our sinew for bow strings!'

'Maybe yours,' said Angus with a grin. 'I am merely skin and bone as it is.'

For a time, Giles stood quietly, waiting while Caprion looked over every scrap of parchment, checked every floorboard and opened every box, jar and trunk within the room.

But then…

'What means this?'

Caprion turned and watched Giles untie the leather drawstring of a small, deerskin pouch and onto his palm tipped a number of stones. Red, brown, yellow and one the brightest of blues.

Giles curled his fingers around the leather pouch. 'Nay, let it not be so.'

Caprion moved nearer. 'What troubles you?'

Giles looked up, heat in his eyes. 'The bag belonged to Saxon.'

At the name, the other Rawdendale men in the room turned and stared at the stones. 'Saxon?' Caprion questioned. 'I know the name not.'

'He was betrothed to Rosellene.'

Caprion's eyebrows fell. 'He died many moons ago.'

'Murdered he was!' A voice came from the back of the hut and a warrior swung at a bunch of herbs hanging from the rafters. 'Traces of aconite were found. Tell me that is not sinister.'

'You suspect sorcery?' Caprion asked. Giles rolled the stones over in his palm.

'No.' Giles looked up. The heat in his eyes now a raging fire. 'Now we are certain.'

'Where did this take place?'

'The king received word that a scout had spotted the Ormans breaching our borders. So he sent a small band of men along the road to Marburg Court, Saxon being one of them.'

Caprion glanced towards the rafters momentarily. 'How many moons ago was this?'

'Would have to be twelve at best, my lord.'

'Twelve, you say,' nodded Caprion.

'Yes, my lord.'

'On the road to Marburg Court?' Caprion questioned. 'Perchance, was it near the old ruins?'

Giles slowly nodded. 'Indeed, it was, my lord.'

'None of the men survived.'

Giles paused, his back stiffened. 'I commented not on the survival of the men.'

'You did not need to,' Caprion confessed.

'What is it that you know?'

'If it be sorcery that took Saxon's life, than I say it be by his own doing.'

Giles' fist tightened around the stones. 'That is a mighty high claim to make, my friend. You will need some substance behind it. How is it that you come to have such knowledge?'

Caprion paused. 'It was I who found the carnage.'

Chapter Thirty-Six

'Father has agreed to return the forest to the shademen.'

Evening was well upon them when Caprion returned from his journey. Now, in Rosellene's chamber, the fire had been stoked and a large helping of pottage was being ladled into two crockery bowls.

Rosellene returned the ladle to the steaming pot. 'I thought this news would please you?' She carried the bowls across the room, her thoughts turning briefly to the absence of her dear Isabelle.

'I am sorry.' Caprion's distant eyes focused on her once more. 'This is good news.'

The bowls were set upon the table. Supper would have to wait.

'There are more pressing matters, I fear,' said Rosellene softly. 'I know the battle draws nigh, but should we not celebrate the small successes along the way?'

The coat around Caprion's shoulders was withdrawn. Folded. Unfolded then folded once more. 'Indeed, we should. I am glad relationships have been restored. Payment is just.'

Rosellene took the coat from his hands and lay it upon the table.

'What troubles you?' Her voice was soft and melodic. She dove deeply into his eyes, searching for a clue. 'Do not say it is the battle, for I know that not to be true. Something has rained upon your soul and dampened it so.'

The thick, green drapes of the window were pushed back and Caprion led Rosellene towards the hard, stone seat. 'Come, sit with me awhile.'

'I am beginning to fear what may escape your lips next.' Rosellene sat. Caprion paused.

'I harbour some news.'

'News?' Rosellene pouted. 'Of what kind?'

'I would like to say comforting, for, in time, that is what it shall be, yet initially such news will be difficult to hear.'

'You cannot stop there,' begged Rosellene. 'I am anxious enough. Pray tell me quickly. Let it be done.'

Caprion's heart thumped. 'It concerns Saxon.'

Rosellene's body stiffened. She had not thought of her lost love for some time. There was a tremor in her voice. 'What of him?'

'Upon our journey into the forest, we came across a hut. It belonged to the sorceress. Finding no one home, we entered the dwelling, hoping to discover something with which to end the war before it begins.'

'The sorceress. Why would you even contemplate entering such a place?' Rosellene sat back, folded her arms. 'Did you find such a thing?'

Caprion shook his head. 'Nay, we did not.'

'What then did you come across?' Rosellene asked. 'Creatures. Potions. Herbs. Pray tell me.'

Into his pocket a hand was slipped and from it drawn a small, leather pouch. Rosellene reached for her heart. It tried to escape.

'This belonged to Saxon,' she whispered, taking it gently in her hands. The bag was untied, the stones tumbling into an open palm. 'It was a gift. Protection. The stones were to keep him safe in my absence. How did they fail?'

The stones shifted in her hand as she turned them over, one by one. 'There can be no other explanation. My worst fear has come to light. Saxon was murdered.'

'It may appear so, but nay.'

'Nay?' Rosellene's voice echoed through the room. Getting to her feet, she paced across the floor, the hem of her dress unsettling the dust. 'Why say you this? The bag is a catalyst. Taken by Lord Bannock to the sorceress so as to perform a ritual.'

'Please, Rosellene, sit down,' Caprion took her soft hands and led her back to the seat. 'Saxon was dying.'

'Of course, he was,' she snapped. 'I am not a fool.'

'No, my lady, you are not.'

'Had a sword been thrust into my stomach, I too, would be dying.'

There came a sigh. 'He had taken ill. He wanted not to burden you with his sickness.'

Her head turned sharply, teeth ground.

'Whom is it that you spoke to? Who has poisoned your mind with such thoughts?'

'No one.' He shook his head. 'The words came from Saxon himself.'

Rosellene pulled her hands from Caprion's.

'Nay. I do not believe you.' She rubbed her temples. 'He was not sick. I would have known. He would have told me so.'

'He loved you, Rosellene.' Caprion laid a hand upon her bouncing knee. 'He wanted you not to see him weakened by sickness.'

'You think he took his own life? Discarded his protection? Gave it to the sorceress freely in exchange for a swift and seemingly honourable death?' Rosellene shook her head. 'He could not. The church would never condone such a sin.'

She ran her fingers across her brow. It was burning. *Why are you treating me this way?* Her mind wandered. *I thought you cared for me.*

'On the morning of the slaying, I was delivering a message to Lord Marburg and came upon the men. Saxon was alive, but barely. He refused all aid. He asked that I pray for his sins so that he might enter heaven's gate and finally be free of the pain that had invaded his body. So I knelt beside him and prayed with him until he slipped from this world into the next.'

Tears formed in Rosellene's eyes and spilled onto her cheeks as if someone had poured wine into a glass and it had overflowed. 'Why are you doing this to me?'

Her body rattled. It was difficult to swallow.

'Am I not tortured enough that you poke and prod at my heart as if I were a beast on its way to market?' She pushed him away. 'You should have prayed harder.'

She pushed again.

'Why did you not try harder? You could have saved him!'

Caprion reached for her arms as they swung, punched and struck him most violently.

'Do not touch me!' She screamed. 'Come near me not!'

Caprion listened not to her demands. He reached again for her arms. Pinned them to the sides of her body. Held her tightly as she swayed.

'I must pray to God.' She wriggled free, and hauling up her heavy skirt, bent down to kneel in front of the window seat. 'We must pray before it is too late.'

But will he listen? she wondered.

She had been cruel to God and perhaps he had not forgotten. Not forgiven. 'He must not deny Saxon a place in heaven. He was a kind man.'

Yet he lied.

'He swore an oath not to lie. How could he betray his God? His king?'

Prayers were ended abruptly. She was sorry she had not learned earlier of Saxon's fate. Was it wrong to have kept her magical abilities a secret? Had he trusted her with his illness, surely, she could have saved him or at the very least eased his suffering. A tonic of wormwood and mint. Perhaps the addition of dried toad. She wondered as to the length of his sickness. How long had it invaded his body?

'Do not fear your enemy,' Rosellene choked. It was difficult to speak when one's lips were covered in tears. 'Do not fear them! Is that not a commandment of a knight?'

Caprion only nodded.

'Then he was no knight. Had he faced the sickness, battled it like any enemy, he would still be here today.'

But you would not.

Rosellene felt cold. *If Saxon were alive, would Caprion have come to Rawdendale at all? Would the king have required his services? Would I have fallen in love?*

'I feel I did not know the man.'

'Do not torment yourself,' Caprion whispered. 'Allow yourself to grieve, but no more.'

Have I not grieved enough? Will I ever know what transpired that fateful day?

'I have many questions.'

'That will remain unanswered.'

'It pains me to have these thoughts. Forgive me for what I am about to say.' Rosellene paused. 'With every breath of my being, I loved Saxon.'

Caprion lowered his eyes. Rosellene took his hand.

'Yet, had he not died, we would not have been united. That, I cannot imagine.' She took his hands to her lips. Pressed them together. 'You give me strength. Of mind, body, soul. I fear nothing with you at my side.'

She crept upon his lap and snuggled against his gambeson.

And when there were no more tears to cry, Caprion carried her to the bed, laid her beneath the covers and held her until she fell asleep. Ended was the torment.

Chapter Thirty-Seven

It was upon them. A time of paranormal activity. A coldness like no other.

The witching hour.

When death claimed the elderly, shutters dared not be opened and women stayed inside. Protected by merels, scratched and burned into the wooden frames or shoes coveted away under floorboards, most remained in the safety of their homes.

But not at Rawdendale.

Death and destruction were coming no matter the time.

As night became day, trepidation clung to them like shadows in the darkness. Hearts raced. Stomachs tightened. Pupils dilated. Into the bailey they marched, shoulder to shoulder, a wall of tower shields, listening to orders barked by Lord Elliot.

'Wars are won not by the strongest, yet by those that can hold their nerve. Have patience. Have courage. We will break through their formation. Let them scatter. Let them flee. See how far they get.'

Angus grunted. His men were ready. The unit tight. They knew how to form, maintain and fight within the wall. Every man knew his position and they followed orders. His orders.

Yet Angus knew the approach would be drawn out. They were only as strong as their weakest warrior and already a chink in his armour was showing.

In the front rank, Oliver faltered.

'Make it be over. Pray make it be over soon.' He had meant to whisper but his lips were near frozen and the words simply escaped them.

'Shift from this rank and it will be over soon enough.' Beside him, Angus turned and shook him most forcefully. 'Do we not look intimidating: a wooden wall, hidden and safely protected?' The young man just allowed his teeth to chatter. He could not agree.

'Harden up, son. We stand beside you.' He glared at the young soldier through the slit in his bascinet. Breaths cut into the curved visor allowed the warm air from his lips to filter through, fusing with that of the cool morning. 'Your sword's hunger will soon be satisfied.'

Oliver turned his reddened eyes to Angus. 'There is but one man I wish to skewer with my blade.'

'Just one?' Angus queried. 'I pray you claim many more.'

Oliver's face twitched. 'Just one.'

Angus nodded. The boy was not in the mood to talk.

'The castle is well defended, laddie,' Angus went on, looking above him to the archers that waited beside the arrow loops. 'The obstacles are great. Hidden marshes. Unstable moat. Not one but two portcullises to pass through.' He grimaced, spying the three-legged cauldrons on the wall walk. Fires burned below, thick flames eating hungrily away at the wood. 'Should they survive the onslaught of boiling water, heated sand and arrows, then, by all means, they can bite into our swords.'

A few of the men chuckled. Oliver did not.

'Soon the enemy will be woken from their slumber as we attack their food supplies and set fire to their tents,' Angus continued. 'The shock will force them out, unarmed into the open field where a cloud, thick with arrows, will rain upon them.'

Bascinets nodded.

'We must, therefore, be ready for their counter attack,' Angus walked purposefully in front of his men. 'Do not lower your shield. Do not break formation. Do not stop to scratch your balls.'

'If we had any.' Sniggering was heard amongst the men. 'In this weather, I fear they may have frozen and abandoned their post.'

Angus chewed on the side of his lip.

'I suggest you find some balls.' Angus strolled closer to the man who made the remark. 'You will be needing them.'

'Will we be needing our feet and arms as well?'

Angus turned to a man on his left.

'Should you want to live,' he answered. 'I would make use of your limbs.'

'We are freezing our arses off out here.' The man pointed to the castle with his chin. 'There is a perfectly good castle behind us. Let us wait inside. Warm our bones. It will better prepare us for the fight.'

Angus huffed. 'At least, now I know you will be awake when the fighting starts.'

'It could be days before they attack. Months even.'

'When the enemy realises they have no food, horses, nor bedding, they will either fight or flee.'

'How will we know if the raid was a success?'

'You will see soon enough,' smiled Angus and he looked to the ridge beyond the castle. Sometime later, he pointed to the same ridge. Flames from the beacon danced in the dark. 'Well done, lads. Well done indeed.'

Before the first rays of sunlight had hit the castle walls, Marcus had climbed the uneven precipice, torch in hand. Upon reaching the top, he had taken from his coat some strong-smelling oil, drizzled it onto the dry grass mound that formed the beacon and taken to it a flame.

When at once it had ignited into a raging fire, Marcus had scaled backwards down the precipice and looked towards the castle, waiting. He had not to wait long before the castle burst into an orange hue, the contrast of colour strong against the dimness of morning.

From the flanking tower, an archer hastened down the stairwell. He slipped, stood then whispered something in Angus' ear.

Angus narrowed his eyes and grunted.

'Our friends have company.' He strode across the courtyard and barked at the men who manned the gate tower. 'Open the gates!'

One of the men spat at Angus through his chipped teeth.

'What in God's name are you doing? Open the gates? This is madness!' Angus stepped nearer. Fists clenched.

'Open the gates, my friend, or I will open your skull.'

The winch shifted. The portcullis rose.

'For the king!' Lord Elliot cried and as one they moved, the frozen earth crunching beneath their tapered sabatons.

Angus slapped his hand across Oliver's back. His helmet rattled. 'May your sword sing, laddie.'

They smelt them before they saw them.

Dark, hairy beasts in stained leather aketons, feebly laced to their stocky bodies.

A few paces more and they saw a thicket of weapons in their way. Pikes, halberds, axes, silhouetted against the raging fires.

For a time, apart from shivering in the bitter conditions, neither side moved. Jeers were made. Taunts were thrown. Insults were cast and caught. Then they advanced.

'Shield wall!'

'Hold strong!'

'Lock!'

'Advance!'

They aimed to kill.

Angus was pleased. There was little joy in killing a man who did not fight.

There were no drummers on this day, not from either side. Instead, the sound of twanging swords, cracking bones and splitting wood filled the winter air. The Ormans were strong and it took all their strength to hold their ground.

Grunting like wild boars, the Ormans came at them, hurling weapons and crushing shields. One hairy beast tried to reach beyond the tower shields, chopping at the Rawdendale men with his axe. But that only made Angus angry, and with two hands he swung his sword, hacking off the beast's arm. The beast spun wildly, spraying a half-dozen men with the bright red liquid that squirted from his severed arm.

Slowly, they pushed their way through the mass of ugly men. A dagger to the neck of one, the flesh hacked from the thigh of another. An Orman's shield fell to the ground. Another tottered sideway. Intestines spilled from his sliced belly.

No longer able to hear the whizzing of the arrows, Oliver raised his visor, only to have it slammed firmly upon his head.

'Keep your visor down!'

'But I see nothing through this slit.'

'Maybe that is a good thing.' Angus closed the gap in their formation once again. 'They will reload soon enough, and believe it or not, an arrow through the head will kill you. So I say again, keep that visor down.'

The snow had darkened with Orman blood. Husbands. Fathers. Sons. Brothers. Dead or dying on the frozen earth. The carnage soon became a mountain, one that was difficult to climb. The Rawdendale men were dominating.

'Push through the bastards!' Angus cried, adrenaline racing through his veins. 'Victory is upon us.'

They pushed forth and it seemed the men of Rawdendale were winning the skirmish. Then Lord Elliot shrieked, 'Look to the east men! To the east!'

And there upon the ridge, King Tyrone stood.

Chapter Thirty-Eight

Bannock awoke to the sound of screams, his mind as confused as the men on the ground. Fumbling in the darkness, he pulled on some mail and his helmet then cautiously moved outside the pavilion.

Crouched on the hillside the enemy sat, two wings of archers, their bows raised towards the heavens. The arrows were thick as they were loosed into the air, raining down on the unsuspecting enemy. With heavy helmets removed, Bannock's men dropped dead on the field, arrows striking exposed flesh.

As the snow-covered ground reddened, the archers sent forth one last spray of arrows before mounting and retreating up the mountainside.

'God's teeth!'

Bannock's pavilion was alight. Scattered by enemy poleaxes, glowing, hot embers from the campfire had been thrust upon the fibres. The cotton burned quickly, the smell of dry leaves in the air. Pavilions were not the only thing burning. Cordage had been set alight, so, too, the food supplies. Wagons filled with sacks of oats and grain roasted in the crisp morning air. The field was now a place of panic and unrest.

It was no place for Bannock.

'Horses!' He demanded, struggling to pull on his tight-fitting boots as he made his way past Grindella's pavilion. 'Get the goddam horses!'

He would flee when it was safe to do so. For now, he would play his part.

'Take your men and a unit of two more to the eastern hillside,' he yelled. 'Eric, form the western rank and await further command.'

No longer could he drive his men towards the gatehouse. Soaked with oil, the hickory was now ablaze just beyond the outer curtain. There was little option but to send his men east and west.

On hearing the plans, Grindella was not impressed. It seemed their mission was being abandoned, moving away from the castle instead of towards it.

'You are sending them in the wrong direction!' She screeched.

'You would have us burn instead?' Bannock questioned, his boots now on.

'That measly fire? It would surely fade should I spit on it.' The whites of Grindella's eyes enlarged. 'Send forth another unit.'

Bannock shook his head. 'I will not allow my men to perish.'

'Have they not armour to protect their precious flesh?' The sorceress threw a cape upon her shoulders. Slid a knife into her belt. 'Lead your men as I have commanded.'

Except for his chest, which heaved most heavily, Bannock moved not.

When will I be returning home? he wondered.

'If you do not leave,' Grindella cut open Bannock's leather tunic with a knife. 'I will slice open your chest and pull out your innards whilst you are still alive.'

Heart faltering, Bannock turned and ran.

Rank was made and the three closely formed packs marched east, west and towards the castle through the ankle-deep snow. Bannock, however, had instructed his men not to scale the rock inferno but wait, shield in hand, until the flames subsided.

And so the battle was joined. The flurry horrific.

There were no rules. No hostages. No chivalry. No escape.

Men, half blinded in their armour, hacked at their opponents with bills, spears and axes, some so blunt that men were left with limbs dangling at their side. Bones were scored or completely sawn off. Muscles ached and hearts pounded louder than those of the horses fast approaching.

The riders were skilled in battle, manoeuvring their horses in a dancing motion forwards and backwards amidst the screams that surrounded them. Outside of their enemies' reach, they stabbed and jabbed with their arming swords, the double-edged blades dripping with the brightest of blood after multiple withdrawals.

At times, the sky was foreboding, stained by a barrage of arrows. Cast into the air, they fell heavily upon their unsuspecting victims, plunging pointed tip into flesh, mail and wood. Struck in the neck, a rider toppled from his horse, swimming with the mass of dead bodies. Close by, another reeled in pain as he tried to pull a bodkin from his forearm.

Bannock sat in the saddle. A trail of blood traced his bearded jawline. The poleaxe felt heavy in his hand and his arm wavered. Innards slid from the blade. Stomach juices. Intestines. Veins.

Then it could not be helped. His stomach jerked and he felt the acid soar up his throat and erupt onto his chest armour.

He glanced left and then right. His men were being annihilated. One after the other they fell, screaming to God to save their souls. But on this day, God was not listening or the calls were too many to answer, for he did not come to those men.

Bannock dropped his head. He had seen enough. There was no escape from the onslaught. Or was there?

Turning his eyes towards the curtain wall, he watched as the last of the flames flickered amongst the moistened rocks and disappeared.

It may be our only hope, he thought.

'Get to the castle!' He screamed, his voice scratching at the back of his throat with sharpened nails. 'The castle!'

Bannock was out of breath.

He clung to the ladder rung, looking most scathingly at those below who tried to hurry him with the point of their spear. 'Let me catch my breath, damn you!'

Eric removed the spear but not the loathing look from his face. He did not like Bannock. He found him lazy and incompetent. 'If you had not noticed, we are at war. Make haste or we all die!'

Bannocks chest expanded as he breathed the cool air deep into his lungs. 'Do you think this is easy?'

Of course, Eric knew it was not. Scaling a ladder apt to move whilst wearing a suit of armour and dodging a constant shower of arrows was definitely a challenge. Still, had Bannock been a few pounds lighter, he might not have been breathless.

Angled against the wall, seven ladders were at present being climbed by ugly, hairy men in their single pieces of armour. Long poles, forked at the bottom, had successfully pushed one ladder over, but still they came like flies upon a rotten carcass.

King Tyrone led the eastern wing. In the front ranks were the men at arms, some mounted and some on foot. Behind them marched the mercenaries. They wielded pikes and long spears, many needing two hands or two men to use the weapons.

Lastly came the archers, dressed in aketon and single piece breastplate. Nervously, they marched towards the siege weapons, eyes and ears now awake. Alert.

The trebuchets were positioned on the ridge, north-east of the castle, until they could be pushed closer to enemy defences. He could not move them closer yet. They were precious. Vulnerable. He did not want such expensive toys to be destroyed by fire before they could be used.

They were powerful and effective. Just like King Tyrone.

It had taken several weeks, from sunup to sunset, to build the three trebuchets. Much quicker than any had anticipated. Built on wooden frames, they had a horizontal beam which held, on the shorter end, a counterweight, and on the other, a sling, in which the stone projectile would be nestled. The stones, numbering in their thousands, were heavy, requiring two men, sometimes three, to carry them.

Although time consuming to reload, these weapons were capable of clearing men from walls, destroying towers and inflicting great injury upon any that stood in their path.

Aloft in his saddle, King Tyrone slumped, annoyed that the start had been early. He had not yet eaten nor was he sufficiently dressed, his belt unfastened and his head of fiery red curls unprotected. As he took the painted helmet from the hands of Thomas, his assistant, a spray of warmth covered the king's face.

'Hell, no!'

Thomas was dead.

A bodkin arrow was lodged deep into the soft fibres of his brain, the heavy shaft protruding through the back of his head. With blood drooling from the sides of his mouth, the young man lurched forward into the unsuspecting arms of the king and the king's eyes gazed upon the arrow, long and straight with a fletching of three swan feathers.

A rush of panic crept over him. Then he bellowed. 'They are mine, damn you! Mine, you hear me!'

A horn sounded on the eastern ridge. Crisp and clear through the still morning air.

The blood wiped from his eyes, King Tyrone looked upon the ridge. And there, in light leather armour, translucent wings billowing behind them like a battle flag, the silver army stood.

'To the ridge, men,' he roared. 'Let them not take what is ours.'

'Or use them upon us,' suggested Henry, the king's advisor.

'We shall reach the weapons before they have the chance to lift one stone.'

Densely packed units of fifty men were formed. They trudged through the ice and snow. Had it been summer, the shallower sections of the marsh would have been filled with reeds. But now the stalks had browned, their bulbous tops heavy with snow that glistened in the sun's first rays.

And whilst they had considered the marsh the most direct route to the ridge, they had failed to think on the repercussions of wearing plate armour in bitter conditions for such a lengthy time. Soon the skin numbed and confusion set in. The men in heavy armour sunk deeper and deeper into the marsh and therein appeared for many a trained knight a metal coffin.

The king struggled to breathe. Knee-deep in snow, he knew that if he fell, he would not again stand.

'Pull back!' He bellowed. 'Take cover!'

Henry turned to the king. Never had they heard such an order. Quietly, he asked, 'My lord, what are your orders?'

The king's face was pale.

'We shall be trapped,' he screeched.

'My lord?' Henry swallowed the huge lump that had formed in the back of his throat. 'What are you suggesting?'

Violently, the king seized Henry's tunic, and for the first time on the battlefield, King Tyrone felt terror.

'Flee, for Christ's sake!' He screamed.

Panic was instantaneous. Men reached for their holy medals and kissed them whilst getting to their knees to pray. Others fumbled in their pockets for the pieces of stale bread they had stashed there, protection or so they hoped, from the fey.

Henry feared for the lives of his men. Darkened by arrows, the sky looked ominous. Arrows struck chain mail, bursting apart the rings and finding exposed flesh on thighs, shins and necks. The king's men were being slaughtered but the king thought only of himself and his safety.

'Find you courage, men,' yelled Henry. 'Fight!'

Still they came. Wave after wave, splashing the men with arrows.

Yet they had to fight, or else flee and become caught in the Ormans melee. Then Henry froze.

His stomach tightened.

His limbs seized.

'When a man becomes weak, he dies.'

King Tyrone turned.

'You have weakened.' Grindella raised a bloody sword. 'Now you shall die.' It happened quickly. Henry could do nothing. One blow and it was done.

Grindella rode towards the men. Blood stained her cape.

'Fight or lose your head,' Grindella smirked. 'It is quite simple.' And she raised the severed head of fiery red curls.

Chapter Thirty-Nine

The solar was on the keep's upper level. Resting on a sloping plinth, the square tower was topped with four decorative turrets and supported by a solid, rock foundation. There was strength in its thick, stone walls. It would not be undermined.

There were adequate chairs. No one sat.

Large, airy windows. No one took in the view.

A raging fire. No one warmed their hands.

It was here that king and queen sought refuge, along with Sabine and several defenders, including a forlorn looking Caprion, whose eyes had not moved from the huge barred door that led to the spiral staircase.

Rosellene watched him pace across the flagstone, a finger tapping restlessly against his sword hilt.

The door is locked and that is how it shall remain, thought Rosellene. *I wish you not to fight. I will bind you to a chair if I must.*

'It is difficult, I know.'

Caprion turned his knotted brow towards the king. 'Your grace?'

'The wait,' the king continued. 'It is difficult to wait while your men battle without you.'

Caprion nodded, understanding in his eyes. 'My mind wanders. My stomach contorts. My sword arm flinches as though it were on the field.'

'Your feelings are shared,' said the king. He ran his hands down his close fitting doublet, moistening the velvet cloth. 'Your time will come soon enough.'

And as Caprion returned to his pacing, the king to his thinking, there came a knock upon the door. A soldier entered the room. His chest rose and fell quickly beneath his plate armour.

He bowed. 'Your grace.'

'What news?'

'The outer curtain has been breached. The northern tower too, is compromised.'

'The other towers?'

'They hold, yet I cannot say for how much longer.'

The king acknowledged the message with a nod then gazed for a moment out the large window. Rosellene held her breath.

'Your time is nigh,' he said to Caprion, his brown eyes glassy. 'Rebuild the defences. Allow them not into the inner wall.'

Something squeezed unpleasantly at Rosellene's chest. The muscles in her body filled with blood and she tensed, unable to move. It was as though her legs were in armour, plated with heavy guards.

'No.' She clung tightly to Caprion's armoured body, her head pressed against his sleeveless tabard. 'You must not leave.'

Fingers ran through dark locks. Eyes closed, barring the tears. Caprion turned to speak to Sir Theoderic but the words caught on the wire that lined his throat.

'With my life, my lord.' Sir Theoderic put a hand to Caprion's shoulder. 'With my life.' Caprion left through the barred doors. He could not look back.

The king had turned once around the room when he saw Rosellene had a hand to the door. His head shook. 'I will not allow it.'

'How shall we defend ourselves?' She picked up a candle arbour. 'The likes of this? A corset is no match for a blade.'

'And you are no match for the warriors outside.'

'Perhaps not, but I would rather die trying to defend myself than not try at all.'

The king's shoulders dropped. He wanted not to think of the enemy breaching the solar yet if they did, his daughter should be able to defend herself. Reluctantly, he let her go. 'Be swift.'

Rosellene did not hesitate.

With Sir Theoderic in close pursuit, she moved to her chamber, pulling from a trunk a petite suit of armour and a singled-edged messer, light enough to be used with one hand.

Sir Theoderic stood by the window. His skin appeared to match the colour of the freshly fallen snow. 'I trust you know how to wield that, my lady.'

'I do,' said Rosellene. She had tossed her long plait to the side while she tightened the leather shoulder straps of her cuirass. 'What is it? What do you see?'

'I would don that armour, my lady, and quickly.' Sir Theoderic swallowed as he looked down upon the wall walk, to the crenels crawling with hairy beasts. 'Our blades will soon be dripping with Orman blood.'

Rosellene took up her sword, watching the light covering of oil drip down the sharpened blade. She wanted its protection for her family. But first, she had to return to them.

'Aim for the back,' Sir Theoderic yelled. He pulled his sword from Orman flesh, then swung to strike another. 'There is little protection.'

But Rosellene was having trouble just keeping the enemy's sword at bay. Barely able to look upon his face, skin tight and leathery, teeth (what few there were) stained yellow, she parried each and every blow.

'If only he would turn around,' she groaned.

Finally, with a two-handed blow, she lunged forward to strike at the knee before stabbing the off balanced beast through the chest.

The blade was wiped clean on the Orman's jerkin then, 'Behind you!'

Another attacked Sir Theoderic from behind. He let out a roar then cut through the air with his blade. But the steel in Sir Theoderic's grasp was sharp and it sliced the man's head clean off his shoulders. It landed heavily on the ground then rolled; a dark red trail smeared behind. Clearly, the man was dead, but still Sir Theoderic took to the twitching body with his boot.

From beyond the castle wall, a pike appeared. Then another and another. These belonged not to the Ormans, though, for their bodies were covered in both plate and mail. They wore sleeveless surcoats, red like the blood that dripped from their visors, and upon the blood-red field, white boars squealed.

Rosellene recoiled. These men would not be so easily killed. 'Make for the keep!'

She watched Sir Theoderic disappear up the stairwell. She meant to follow but her sword had been thrust into the fleshy neck of a bearded Orman and now, no matter how she twisted, pulled and cursed, it would not come free.

'That is a pity.'

Rosellene stopped, her breath short and sharp. She tugged harder at the sword, a gurgling sound erupting from the man's throat, then looked for something else with which to defend herself.

There was nothing.

'Whatever will you do?'

She knew that voice. Wincing, she turned and set eyes upon his face.

Even a pair of carved, wooden spoons would do some damage, she thought.

His footsteps loud and heavy, Bannock walked towards her. There was hatred in his eyes, a look she had not seen before. It suddenly became cold and she was afraid.

'You are to blame for this destruction!' In an instant, Bannock had hold of her ankles. 'No guilt will be felt when I throw you from this tower.'

Her palms were shredded as she was dragged across the jagged stone and onto a crenel. His hand gripping the top of her cuirass, she was hauled to her feet and pushed towards the edge.

'Look at what you have done!' Bannock scolded. He grabbed her loosened hair and jolted her head forward. 'Does the carnage please you?'

Rosellene trembled. The drop was immense. If she fell onto the mound of snow at the base of the wall, there might be a chance of survival, but fall into the moat, its surface covered with a layer of ice, and death was imminent.

Bannock now looked into her weeping eyes. 'It was a foolish decision to reject me. One that will cost you your life.' He brushed a few strands of hair from her moistened face, drawing them behind her ear. 'It is a shame though, to discard such beauty.'

Her hands ached as they pushed against the stone. Although her chest rattled, Rosellene was determined not to show Bannock any fear.

'No words, my lady?' Bannock's voice was raised. 'Do you wish to yield?'

He shook her violently. It angered him that she refused to speak.

Rosellene smiled. 'It is true. I am to blame. You are right to end my life.'

'Yet it was not a life I wanted to end. A life shared was my intention,' Bannock paused. 'Would it have been so hard to love me? Even for a time. Did you think on your father and the heartache it has caused him? However will he recover? A king without a kingdom is no king at all.'

An icy wind hugged Rosellene's body, yet she felt not cool but warm. Burning was the blood that pumped through her veins.

'My father is a mighty king. A far better man than you could ever hope to be. As for love, it is not a case of trying. Love is magic. A powerful potion. Like the code of the knight, it cannot be tried for a time. Not for a day, a month, a year, but lived each and every moment.' Rosellene leaned closer to Bannock, the stench of leather and sweat slapping her in the face. She turned away.

When she turned back to Bannock, she smiled. 'When you love someone, you would do anything for them. Risk your life to protect them. Rescue them when they are in imminent danger, standing on the crenel of a castle amidst a mighty battle.'

The dilated response of Bannock's pupils showed Rosellene that he was processing the information. But the understanding was delayed, and she wondered whether he felt much pain when the arrow pierced the flesh beneath his arm.

'You should be thankful,' said Caprion, a leather quiver strung across his armoured back. He watched as Bannock drew in a series of short, sharp breaths. 'I was aiming for your skull.'

Bannock was white. His body trembled like falling leaves in winter. An arrow, short with a spearhead, had buried itself deep into his ribs. His right arm ached. It could not be lowered.

'Perhaps you should not have missed.'

Caprion did not miss. His skill with a bow almost matched that with his sword.

It hurt to breathe. His stomach muscles contracted and excess saliva pooled in his mouth. Bannock was about to vomit.

'Best to push the arrow through, they say, rather than pull it out.' Caprion put the slightest pressure on the arrow shaft. Bannock let out a howl. 'Shall I?'

'You have done enough.' His back against the stone wall, Bannock retreated.

Chapter Forty

It was mid-afternoon when the winged beast cast its huge shadow over the castle, the stone from its claws cascading down onto the gatehouse. As it circled around the tops of the crenelations, a screech came from the depths of its lengthy neck, so piercing that it sent archers cowering to the ground, hands cupped tightly to their ears. Through the air it soared, its muscular body rolling like ocean waves amongst the clouds.

Alarmed by the sudden darkening of the sky, Rosellene turned away from Caprion and moved along the wall walk, only to be knocked to the ground by the immense power of the dragon's wings. Her back against the hard, stone floor, she gazed at the leathery wings, blue like the scales that covered its body, wondering how such a mighty beast could maintain flight.

'Quickly, before it returns,' said Caprion, effortlessly picking her up and guiding her to shelter. 'Stay clear of the tail. The barb may well be poisonous.'

'Poisonous?'

Rosellene watched as the dragon scaled the main tower, its pointed tail thumping against one of the many decorative machicolations. She grimaced. Gabrielle would not be pleased.

There was a great flurry as men hurried to seek cover, colliding with each other, their eyes ever present on the sky, watching as the beast caught the jagged edge of the gatehouse with its thick, talon-like feet and proceeded to rock forwards and backwards, in an attempt to separate mortar and stone. The pit of their stomachs ached, burning more than hunger, as panic set upon them.

The beast circled again, this time a raging heat erupting from its mouth. The vicious flames reached the roof of the livery. Quickly, the snow did melt and the thatching caught alight.

Slipping in the now melting snow, the men of Rawdendale craned their necks towards the shadowy sky, watching the beast glide across the castle wall towards a pile of boulders on enemy ground.

They had to reach the safety of the stronghold and quickly.

'Take cover, men,' said Angus and he turned his tired eyes to Rosellene. 'And you, my lady. A dragon will surely seek out the royal bloodline.'

Too afraid to move, an archer remained in the courtyard. Down on his knees, he clasped his trembling hands and prayed, hoping that his soul would be saved on this day. Unfortunately, Angus did not have time for prayers.

'God is busy,' he said gruffly, one eye skyward.

But even with Angus prodding and probing him to get up, the archer continued to pray, talking to God about the existence of dragons. At this, Angus became enraged. His prodding, thus, intensified.

'Dragons are not real,' the man babbled. 'They guard treasure in lands far, far away.'

'Take a good look at the sky,' said Angus, crouched low as the dragon flew overhead. Had he stretched out his arm he would have been close enough to touch its scaly underbelly. 'That thing is real and if you do not get out of its reach, it will kill you.'

'It is but a myth,' said the archer, his eyes now firmly closed. 'It does not exist.'

There came a sound like thunder as a second boulder collided with the gatehouse. The shudder caused several men to topple over the side, the lucky ones clinging to an arrow loop. Angus looked up just in time to side step the falling debris that whipped past his ear and landed between him and the still praying archer. The archer's eyes opened. Liquid, pale and yellow, seeped from beneath his bent knees.

'Maybe God was trying to tell you something?' Angus huffed.

The archer, with thoughts now on his salvation, swiftly moved to shelter. 'Quickly, to the kitchens.'

Moving down the ramp, Caprion, Angus, Rosellene and ten other men retreated to the castle kitchens, the smell of burning trenchers strong. The cooks were gone. The bags in the cauldron left to boil. The meat on the rack left unturned. No one filled the pottery bowls in preparation for supper and the cockerel, supposed to be supper, was left roaming the floor.

'We need a plan of attack,' said Caprion and he looked around the room of frightened faces. It was fair to say that, despite having fought many battles, none had come up against a dragon before.

'Shields are no match for a dragon. They were forged in heat and would surely melt if exposed to the same element.'

'We must find the dragon's weakness,' said one of the men.

'Weakness?' scoffed another. 'A beast that size. Is there such a thing?'

A smaller man, humble and meek, spoke softly from the back of the room. 'We use poison to kill the wild pigs that threaten our sheep.' The man shrugged as all eyes bore down upon him. 'It is merely a suggestion.'

'And a good one at that,' said Caprion, a hand upon the man's leather tunic. 'Dragons are, however, slightly larger than pigs and I fear we may only make him drowsy. We need a different tactic if...'

Mid-sentence, Caprion stopped and looked into the courtyard. 'What in God's name!'

He hurried to the window, peering through the amber panes.

With no armour, shoes nor sense, Nicholas stood in the courtyard, a smile from one pointed ear to the other upon his face.

In awe, he looked to the sky. 'I knew they existed!'

The dragon flew overhead, the gust of wind parting Nicholas' beard.

'Such grace. Look at the way in which it moves. It combines the buoyancy of a bird with the flexibility of a serpent.' Nicholas clapped joyfully.

There came from the dragon's belly a rumble, most unnerving, and what followed next was an explosion of fiery flames, red, yellow and orange, that set alight the mews.

'The old fool,' said Angus, watching from the kitchen window as Caprion raced outside.

Caprion called to Nicholas, asking that he take shelter from the dragon. But Nicholas did not heed the warning.

'Nicholas, you must take shelter!' Caprion cried again. 'Alas, you will be killed by the dragon.'

'But the view from here is all the better.'

The dragon circled again.

Its neck arched. Its jaws widened. A fireball was expelled into the courtyard.

'Nonoo!' Caprion threw himself upon Nicholas just as the flames reached for his tunic. They hit the cobblestones and rolled.

Shaken yet unharmed, Nicholas inspected the singed ends of his beard. 'It was in need of a trim.' He shrugged.

The dragon soared over the kitchens, rafters rattling in its wake, then set fire to the gardens. Nicholas raised an eyebrow.

Dinner would take but moments if one had a dragon on staff, he thought.

The dragon flapped its mighty wings before doubling back over the kitchens, taking to several chimneys with a flick of its tail. As the bricks shattered before them, the men took up their bows and, through the narrow windows, aimed.

Nicholas laughed as the arrows left the nocking point, bounced against the blue scales then plummeted back to the courtyard. 'A dragon's hide is thick. You are merely giving him a tickle.'

A few of the men glared at Nicholas. They cursed his whittling remarks. In their lifetime, no one had ever seen a dragon. How was it then that he was an expert in their makeup?

'A net,' one suggested. 'Grab a net and we shall cast it over the beast.'

Nicholas chuckled. 'How much of the dragon do you think you will cover?'

Flustered, one of the men turned his reddened face to Nicholas.

'Clearly you know more then we on the subject of dragons,' said he. 'Pray tell us how we should bring the dragon down?'

Nicholas interlaced his fingers, then tapping his two thumbs together, said, 'A chain hangs from its hind leg.' He drew the men's attention to the rusted chain dangling from its ankle. 'Secure that and we have some chance of bringing the beast down.'

Angus patted the old man on the shoulder. 'I prefer the net idea myself.'

'The chain is your best chance,' Nicholas rested against a barrel of ale, the wood slightly charred. 'I never said it would be easy.'

'Chains it be then, but how are we to secure them?' Angus turned to Caprion but he was already half way towards the keep. 'Caprion?'

'Get ready some ropes,' Caprion yelled back over his shoulder. 'Wait for my call.'

Caprion bounded up the steps, mindful of the varied depths, and moved quickly through the disarming room then the guardroom and finally out into the great hall. Here he pushed open a series of wooden shutters before stepping though a mullion out onto a particularly worn gargoyle. Heights concerned him not, yet with only a grotesque beast at his feet, he felt his temperature rise.

He had walked only a few feet onto the roof of the chapel when a shadow crept overhead. Crouching low against the flagstone, he watched the beast circle, a great stone locked in his jaws.

While that is there, thought he, *the flames are not.*

Bow in hand, he laid his back upon the stone roof and waited for the beasts return.

Below him, voices were heard. He heard stress in those voices. Panic. There was but one chance to thread the rope through the chain.

But the rope was thick and the chain thin. Precision was everything.

Breathe. Your aim is good. Focus. Your mind is calm. Aim. Your sight is clear.

And as the beast swooped low, the talons brushing past either side of his head, Caprion let lose an arrow. Through a chain link it shot swiftly, the thick rope trailing from the arrows shaft.

Caprion held his breath.

Let us hope the rope is lengthy, he thought. *I do not wish to fly.*

The chain was speared and the dragon jolted backwards. He flapped in the air, unable to move save in a circle. And so, for a time, that is what he did. Round and round until a whirlwind did he make.

Then the beast crawled with its mighty claws to the top of the tower and perched there, letting out a squeal that sent shivers down the spines of the men who stood below. It heaved huge breaths of air, smoke billowing from its nostrils. Ropes, one by one, were lassoed around first its neck, tail and finally leg and using the strength of the ogres they pulled with much might, the dragon from its perch.

Ogres surrounded the frightened beast. Taut were the ropes gripped in their hands. Flesh bled and eyes watered as the fibres shred their fingers.

'We cannot hold the beast for long,' yelled Angus dodging a massive flame that licked the point of his boots. His face fell. The heat was intense. 'Let us seal that furnace too.'

Caprion (now returned to the courtyard) held a rope towards Angus. 'Do you wish to do the honours?'

Angus shook his head. 'The pleasure is all yours, laddie.'

Avoiding the three spikes on the end, Caprion launched onto the dragon's tail and moved forth along the body. The dragon's body was thick with muscles, the scales slippery to the foot. Its mighty wings tried to stretch but ropes looped around the barbs on the wing tips made it difficult.

Using the horns, curved like that of a ram, Caprion pulled himself onto the dragon's head. When his feet were securely wrapped around one of the horns, he lowered himself backward so that he lay against the dragon's head.

He now saw his reflection in the dragon's yellow eye.

Working quickly, the rope was looped around the nose and pulled tight. Heat erupted from the flared nostrils and he looped the rope again.

Enraged, the dragon thrashed his tail against the courtyard well. The stone base crumbled and parts of the thatched roof flew dangerously through the air.

'He weakens,' said Angus, and sure enough, the endless thrashing ceased. 'Watch the head, men!' The dragon's head dropped, thumping hard against the cobblestones, scales scratched and torn.

With its wings curled against its scaly body, it drew in a few heavy breaths. Finally, it was defeated.

Caprion leapt from its head into the courtyard.

'I will save the next one for you,' he said as he joined Angus and Rosellene.

'You are too kind.' Angus said.

Caprion gave Angus a nudge. 'He will not hold with ropes alone. We need chains.'

'The dungeon,' suggested Angus and Caprion nodded.

'Keep it safe and secure,' Caprion instructed Marcus. 'We shall not be long.'

'My lord?' Marcus swallowed, his voice raised. 'Pray, I hope not.'

No sooner had Caprion and Angus left the courtyard than the other men grew loud. In front of them lay a beast which many thought extinct or merely the essence of childhood stories. Killing the beast would be a great, great honour.

Eyes twitched. Shoulders barged.

'Let us slit the dragon's throat and drink its blood.'

Cheers erupted from the growing crowd. Capturing a dragon was truly a marvellous feat.

'You take the blood,' one man said, his dagger glinting in the fading light. 'I want for the heart.'

Imbued with magical powers, the heart had long been a talking point of warriors. Blood, drunk from the vein itself, was said to give men abnormal strength. Others claimed that the blood could kill, turning their victim to stone.

Lying on its side, the dragon seemed to cry, giant tears falling from its glassy eyes. Rosellene felt its pain. She knew what it was like to feel trapped.

'Step aside, my lady,' said one of the men as he lowered his dagger.

But Rosellene stood her ground. She would not have the beast slaughtered.

'You would die for a beast, my lady?'

Rosellene stepped nearer the dragon. A gentle hiss came from its head. 'If I must.'

Protecting Rosellene with his outstretched arms, Marcus faced the angry men.

'No one shall harm the dragon,' he said. 'Has not enough pain been thrust upon it?'

Feet shuffled. Weapons wavered. Marcus could see the contemplation of battle in the men's eyes. A mighty warrior was he. Strong with a blade and quick on his feet. Yet the dragon was immense. It filled the courtyard, its nose near the stables, the point of its tail knocking on the chapels iron door. He could not defend it on his own.

Rosellene looked to the sky. 'We are lucky there is but one.'

'My lady?'

'I fear if there is one, there may be many.'

Marcus too, craned his neck towards the wintery sky. The clouds were patchy and full of ripples. Could there be more dragons on their way?

The beast let out a cry. It seemed to echo in the sky above.

Marcus all but fell over backwards. 'Save our souls!'

Two colossal shadows engulfed the courtyard.

There was now not one dragon, but three.

Quickly, the men took cover. Into haystacks they dived and behind pillars and posts. The thought of dragon blood vanished from their minds.

Rosellene, however, did not move. She gazed into the dragon's eyes. Gently, she rubbed its damp snout and whispered something in its ear. Then, taking up her messer, she hacked at the ropes.

'Whatever you think you are doing, you are wrong,' Marcus spoke gently. 'These are wild beasts, my lady.'

'She does not want to harm us, she was instructed to,' said Rosellene as the ropes began to fray. 'If we restrain her any longer, her parents will destroy the castle. They are merely protecting their child like any human would do.'

And with a nod, Marcus withdrew his blade and sliced down on the ropes.

Chapter Forty-One

'The wait has been too long.'

The king pushed back the chair and stood, buckling the tapestry rug that covered the solar's wooden floor.

'She is in safe hands with Theoderic,' Sabine said reassuringly.

The queen huffed. 'He is an old man now. No more a knight than myself. There is little protection.'

The king moved past the mantle towards the door. 'I must go and find her.'

'And put your life in danger?' The queen's woollen shoes hurried across the floor. 'Your place is here.'

'My place is with my men,' the king said solemnly. 'What kind of king am I if I hide away? My men need encouragement to continue the cause. They will not fight for a ghost.'

A scowl passed over the queen's face. 'Then to your death you go.'

'Take care, my son,' Sabine said. 'Go swiftly to your men. We will follow.'

The king disagreed. 'You shall stay here where it is safe.'

Sabine let her eyes turn to the window.

'Shadows form in the sky,' she sighed. 'It is best we leave the tower.'

The queen rushed to the window. Dense layers of clouds drifted high in the sky. There appeared nothing ominous but the chance of snow. Her gaze fell next to the courtyard and its scattering of blue scales.

'Dear lord,' the queen blessed herself then toppled to her knees.

'See to the queen,' the king asked. 'Her fear is great. Do your best to keep her safe.'

Sabine nodded. She watched the king leave then pushed the door bolt across.

'I do not think your God can help you,' Sabine mocked after the king had gone.

'Do not talk to me of things you know nothing of.' The queen clutched the cross around her neck. The pendent hung from a golden chain, its links dripping with pearls. 'There will be an end to this suffering. Our prayers will be answered.'

Sabine laughed. 'Remember it is your daughter who has caused this unrest.' Cupboards were opened. Closed.

'What is it you are looking for?' The queen turned her head sharply. She watched Sabine pull items from the cupboards then carelessly turn them onto the table. The queen's chin dropped. 'No! I will not have it. Not in my home. Do your witchcraft elsewhere.'

Sabine stripped the leaves from a sprig of lavender, adding them and a few cloves of garlic to one of the goblets on the table. 'You think your God can hinder the power of your first-born?'

Moistened with lemon juice and several drops of oil, the ingredients were ground to a paste with the handle of a knife. 'Stop me if you wish but I do this for us all.'

'I wish you had stayed away entirely,' snapped the queen. 'Things were peaceful without your meddling.'

'My meddling is what has kept your family safe.' More leaves were added to the paste. 'We must fight magic with magic.'

Night had settled upon Rawdendale and the sky was black, lit up on occasion by sparks of fire. Valiantly they had fought that day and now, with heavy eyelids, they craned their necks, watching the monsters circle the castle.

In the darkness of the chapel, Father Michael got to his knees and prayed.

'Saint Michael, pray for us.'

'Saint George, pray for us.'

'Saint Florian, pray for us.'

Flames licked closer at his robes and his prayers became louder as if he worried God could not hear his plea above the dragon's mighty roars.

'Lord, we ask that you save us from these demonic forces. Take pity on us and grant us peace in our time of need.' He made the sign of the cross, paused to beat the flames from his woollen robes, then blessed himself once more. 'Be gone, I say! Be gone!'

Rosellene's fingers twitched. No longer could she do nothing. They could not win this battle with God alone.

It had to be done.

She glanced around the room at the twenty to thirty men who sought refuge within the chapel's holy walls.

So many witnesses, Rosellene thought. *How is it to be?*

She looked again at Father Michael. His faith was strong. He had given up all his possessions long ago in a vow of poverty and was always obedient to the church. She watched as he held close the wooden cross hung from his neck, a symbol of conformity.

There was her answer.

'Come.' She beckoned to the men. 'Let us join Father and pray.'

You shall have your miracle, thought Rosellene, *but I would have you know it is not heaven sent.*

They lowered their quivering knees to the hard, stone ground.

These men are too frightened to be concerned about magic, she thought. So close to death, most would kindly welcome any hope of salvation.

Rosellene closed her eyes. But it was not God she called upon.

Her manifestation was that they be joined by a powerful ally.

Strength to defend against the power of these mighty beasts. Armour to protect them from the heat. Ammunition to forge an attack.

A sigil was secretly drawn on the stones with the tip of her finger.

'Rosellene.'

Her eyes bolted open. She had been caught using magic, or so was her fear. A voice rang out. It called her name. Clearly. Softly. Calmly.

'I hear your plea,' said the voice. 'I am not far away.'

So quickly?

She scanned the men in the chapel. Their hands were clenched as tightly as their eyes. It was not they who spoke.

Where are you? Rosellene thought and the voice in her head answered.

'I am not like the others but I am with them.'

Rosellene got to her feet and rushed outside, the sleeve of her mail shirt catching on the door frame in her haste.

Seeking protection in the stables, Caprion stood amongst a large gathering of at least fifty men. They wore no armour, held no shields and their beards were wild and untamed.

A twinge of hope struck Rosellene as she crossed the courtyard.

'Christ,' Angus cried. 'What in God's name is that?'

A lizard-like creature loitered in the sky. Lengthy was its tail, long and muscular, ending in a blunt tip. Leathery wings grew from its back and from its stout body came four strong legs. Lion's feet at the front, eagle at the back with huge talons, each the size of a man's thigh.

The perfect ally, thought Rosellene.

'That is a zmey,' Bear explained, scanning the skies. 'Let us hope it is male. Be it female and we are all but dead.'

'It matters not whether it be male or female.' Angus breathed deeply. 'I say hand me a shovel and I shall dig my own grave.'

The beast emerged from the sporadic clouds. For its monstrous size, its movements were vast, its flexible body allowing it to bend, swoop and dive in all directions.

'Ah,' smiled Bear, his eyes squinting. 'We are in luck.'

Angus gave him a wrathful stare. Daggers in both hand and eyes.

'It be male, my friend.'

'That brings me great comfort,' huffed Angus and he tapped Bear on the shoulder. 'I shall still seek out that shovel.'

'Male zmeys are benevolent.'

Ears were cupped as a mighty roar escaped the serrated jaws of the zmey.

'I find it difficult to believe that a monster which possesses three heads, is benevolent.' Angus frowned. 'We cannot defeat that?'

'We will not have to,' Rosellene stood beside Bear. She placed a hand upon his wrist, felt the thickness of his fur coat. 'Our army has strengthened, has it not?'

'It has, my lady,' Bear agreed. 'It has indeed.'

'I have no knowledge of fighting dragons,' began Caprion. 'Yet I will follow any order you command of me, as will my men.'

Bear nodded. 'While we ourselves have never fought such reptiles, our ancestors have and hence, passed to us the skills needed to bring the beasts down.'

'How is it you will bring these dragons down?' Marcus raised an eyebrow. 'You carry no sword and wear no armour. You will be burnt and no more than a pile of ash will remain.'

'Believe it or not, the flesh will drip from your bones even in armour.'

Marcus was silenced. He did not like Bear, yet he liked less the thought of his flesh melting off his bones. It was most unpleasant.

'Dragons have speed, strength and sparks,' Bear continued. 'Armour will not protect you. Shields will not protect you. Swords will not protect you.'

'Such encouraging words,' Marcus whispered to Angus.

Angus took one of Marcus' hands and twisted it behind his back so that it now rested at the base of his neck. 'How is it we shall defeat the dragons?'

'First of all we need range.' Bear peered through the stable doorway out upon the courtyard. 'For our weapons to effectively pierce the dragon's thick hide, they need to be fired from a distance. Too close and they shall simply ricochet off the scales.'

The slightest of giggles left Nicholas's stomach and escaped his lips. 'A tickle. It will give them a tickle.'

His pointed boots swung carelessly beneath the barrel he sat upon.

'Let us next consider the distance of the flame and be well away from that,' continued Bear. 'As you may have noticed, the length of every third flame from a Sierra is considerably shorter than the others. We will time our strike then.'

Nicholas nodded modestly as he marked the parchment in his hands with a chunky piece of charcoal. 'Such is the characteristic of the Sierra.'

'Lastly, we shall look at the dragon's movement. If we can but bring the beasts down, then we have a chance of killing them.'

Caprion pressed a thumb deep into his tightened neck. 'One dragon is a challenge in itself. You believe we can bring down them all?'

Bear nodded. He stared at the zmey. Lightning bolts erupted from each head.

'With the aid of that, my friend, our chances increase. My men are prepared and wait for the order.'

Caprion rested his hand on Bear's shoulder. 'Then you shall have it.'

'We need to draw the first closer, confine it here in the courtyard. My men wait beyond the battlements. They will fire a series of arrows, thicker, with a fine-barbed point, designed such as to pierce then grip the tough hide. Attached to ropes, we shall have the ogres secure the ends to the wall. With the beast contained, we shall then penetrate the heart so that it bleeds out like a deer in the forest.'

'On your call,' said Caprion and he left with his men, headed for the castle wall. He would ready the ogres and set more archers in place. They would need them if they were to bring down the beasts.

Barely had the garrison moved beyond the towers to take their position along the wall walk when there came upon them a mighty gust of wind that brought the men crumpling to the ground.

The beasts were upon them once more.

With incredible speed, one swooped towards the eastern tower, a blood-red glow appearing from the depths of its stomach. Neck muscles contracted. Wings beat. The dragon opened its mouth.

'One,' whispered Caprion as he lay against the cold wall walk, peering through the crenel at the dancing embers.

The beast soared again.

'Protect the ropes!' Caprion cried, pushing himself up. 'Singed ropes will surely break.' Colossal ogre bellies fell quickly upon the ropes.

Screams rang out as the beast returned, lighting up the sky once more. Ogres reeled in pain, the smell of burning flesh strong.

A vile taste formed in the pit of Rosellene's stomach. She could not stand to watch her friends die, nor did she want the beasts to be harmed. If her fate was to die because of her secret, then die she must.

'Stop!' Caprion cried.

Rosellene did not stop.

'We need a distraction,' she called, running along the wall walk.

Caprion's body became rigid. 'Distraction?'

'We cannot bring them down without one,' Rosellene called over her shoulder.

'You are not to be the distraction,' Caprion spoke with authority. 'I will not allow it.'

Rosellene faltered. His voice was like that of her father.

'I am not asking for your permission. It is my decision.' Rosellene noticed a large shadow edge a little nearer. It was not that of a dragon. 'There shall be no more bloodshed.'

Her throat dry, Rosellene could speak no more. She swallowed hard, yet it made no difference. The nod was given and Caprion cried out, snared by two gigantic arms.

'Ready the men,' she cried. 'Aim for the courtyard.'

While Caprion thrashed against Hermes's massive body, she moved forth into the courtyard, the tears not ceasing until she stepped upon the uneven cobblestones and gazed at the sky's inferno.

Silently, she spoke, 'Come to the eastern postern.'

An answer came almost immediately.

'Guide me, child. What is it you desire?'

'The least amount of casualties. That is my desire. I shall endeavour to draw one into the courtyard. If you could deter the others, drive them from this place? Let this be the end to the bloodshed.'

'If that is your wish. I will do as you ask.'

'It is.' Rosellene pulled out a poniard and ran the blade across her palm.

Lured into the courtyard by the smell of royal blood, one of the dragons were trapped. Set upon by arrows, spears, pikes and anything else the men could lay their hands upon, the raging dragon beat its mighty wings until they could do so no more. Exhausted, they lay sprawled on the cobblestones, coughing weak, orange flames.

Rosellene had received her wish. She let down her protective shield. Breathed deeply.

The zmey had driven off the other dragons, spitting fire and hurling lightning bolts from its three heads. The winged creatures, maimed and tired, retreated to the distant mountains while the one in the courtyard was silenced.

All was well until…Nicholas came running towards them.

His words were hushed by the triumphant cries of the men but they could see him pointing to the ancillary room. See him frantically waving his arms. See his pained expression.

As he came closer, the muffled words became clearer. But how they wished they had not. 'Powder!'

The last thing they saw was Nicholas, airborne. Then everything went black.

Chapter Forty-Two

Long after the explosion was it when the dust settled on the castle. Only then could the damage truly be seen. Glass windows had been shattered, ceilings collapsed and entire walls demolished, the wattle and daub now exposed to the elements. Bodies, dead or dying, lay mangled amongst the rubble of stone and, for the longest time, all was quiet.

Then, slowly, a figure emerged, half-choking from the cloud that enveloped him. On unsteady feet, he staggered across the newly formed pathways, hands tight about his ringing ears. With his senses damaged from the explosion, Caprion could neither hear, feel nor smell. Undeterred, he pressed on with his search.

She had to be found.

He passed first by Gabrielle, who, with his shaken mind, was trying to catch the fragments of the chapel steeple, saving his precious artwork from further devastation. But even the strongest of men could not have borne the weight of this structure. Had not Caprion removed him from the path, he would have surely been crushed.

Next, came he upon an old man buried up to his waist in debris and so, after digging with his hands at the mound of fragmented stone and rock, he pulled finally the old man free. Then saw he a young boy who, having been crushed by a wooden door, reeled in pain. And while he struggled to lift the heavy door alone, two familiar men came to his aid, the second stronger than the first.

'Where is Rosellene?' Angus asked. To his surprise, there came not an answer. So asked he further. 'Pray tell me not that she has fallen?'

But again Caprion said nothing and, while the men pulled the young boy from beneath the door, he went on with his search until, at length, he found her.

Stranded on the barbican's single tower, the wall crumbling around her, Rosellene stood anchored to the roof. Hugging the flagstone, she dared not look down upon what was once a favoured garden. But standing on a narrow ledge with room barely enough for her tiptoes, she was slipping. Haste must be made, for it would not be long before the structure weakened and she fell, surely to her death.

Stairwell after stairwell Caprion climbed, but each was like the other, leading nowhere but to a dead end. Another route had to be found. A raised doorway could provide the answer. But when he stepped onto the wooden staircase, it crumbled beneath his weight, and once again, he was left feeling despondent.

Then a glimmer of hope. Part of the neck remained in-tact. If he had a way of getting from the neck across to the barbican's tower, a rescue would be credible. So found he a plank of wood, and sliding it across to her, Caprion stepped cautiously into the middle. A vastitude beneath him, he reached out to grab her moistened hand.

And in the half setting sun, she looked then upon his face and drew him nearer, his breath warm in the cool air. Her hands ran through his soft curls, and finally, after all these months, she declared her love for him.

But oh, how she fretted when she heard from him no reply.

Alas, she feared. *He loves me not.*

His hand slipped from hers and in an instant, he was gone.

For what seemed an eternity, she watched him fall, the whites of his eyes doubling in size as he neared the ground. Quickly and silently, a spell was spoken, her hands cupped towards the darkening sky. Over and over it was recited until her arms became heavy. But then they felt light, so like a feather.

Something was wrong. Something was terribly wrong.

So peered she over the castle wall, breath held, and there, hovering just above the moat, his aketon skimming the surface of the water, was Caprion. Her fingers gripped tighter the castle wall.

Someone else controlled the levitation spell.

Wild with rage, she sought the quickest route to the drawbridge.

How dare she take him from me, and now, after all that has come to pass?

She could feel the energy flowing through her veins, from fingertips to the very ends of her hair. There was a clamminess to her skin, and although it was winter, it felt like a summer's day.

'Rosellene.' A shallow voice caught her on the stairwell. 'Control your power.'

Rosellene stopped. A great many objects crashed to the ground behind her. Turning, she saw bowls, buckets, bricks and all manner of items broken, shattered or misplaced.

It was not the explosion that had caused the unrest.

Sabine wrapped her gnarled hands around Rosellene's wrists. 'Let it not come from anger. Let love be your guidance.'

'Anger infests my entire body,' Rosellene fumed. 'What is love but something that can be stolen?'

Sabine's face was pale and lathered in beads of perspiration. 'Anger will only feed her magic. You must harness your anger.'

Rosellene nodded. 'Let us away. This must come to an end.'

Sabine did not move.

'Grandmother, I cannot do this without you.'

But nothing more than a laboured breath escaped. 'My darling, I cannot.'

Rosellene grabbed her grandmother's hand. It was limp. Lifeless. 'Grandmother?'

'I am sorry.' Sabine dropped her gaze and Rosellene caught sight of her bloodstained cloak. 'I cannot.'

A dryness crept into Rosellene's throat as she gazed upon the metal spike protruding from her grandmother's stomach. Her legs weakened and she steadied herself against the stairwell.

Sabine's eyes were drowning in water. 'Away with you now.'

'I will not,' said Rosellene sternly and she kicked at the wall to which her grandmother was pinned.

Sabine let out a painful cry. 'Please, Rosellene, there is little time left.'

'There is time enough.'

'Look within the folds of my cloak.' A crumpled piece of parchment was pulled from Sabine's cloak. 'My power weakens, yet you are strong. Strong enough to overcome her.'

When the parchment was opened, Rosellene gazed upon what appeared to be an ancient spell, written entirely in the witches' alphabet. She recognised her grandmother's hand.

Rosellene's breath quickened. 'You believe it will work?'

'It must.' Sabine nodded as Rosellene opened a small bundle wrapped in white linen. 'You have everything you need to bring her down. Only doubt will make you falter.'

With the linen bundle concealed in her mantle, Rosellene looked over the spell once more. The writing was slanted. Swirling letters scrawled across the page with dark ink. Contained on the single piece of parchment, tainted brown with age, the secrets of banishment were held. If cast correctly, it would see Grindella banished from this world. Permanently.

'I shall free you.'

Though her body shook with pain, Sabine found the strength to smile. 'My darling, do this and you shall free us all.'

Rosellene hesitated.

'Go, child,' Sabine chided. 'Your father approaches. I shall be cared for. Away with you.'

And with a glance towards her father, who ran towards the stairwell, Rosellene marched out onto the battlefield.

Atop her mighty steed, its fetlocks buried deep in the snow, Grindella galloped before her army. Behind her, pulled along by a thick rope, Caprion's bruised and battered body was dragged.

Rosellene needed not to be taunted. The time to end this battle was nigh. 'Enough!' Rosellene yelled, her face pained.

Grindella slowed to a trot then pulled the reins tight. The horse stopped.

There came a murmur from Caprion's crushed body. He tried in vain to push himself up onto his elbows but alas, he could not. Far too weakened, his armoured hand skidded across the ground, his cheek coming to rest on the cool ice.

A sneer distorted Grindella's face. 'I am only just beginning.'

She directed a spell that saw Caprion cast into the air. Intense was the spell and draining. The muscles in Grindella's arm ached as she struggled to maintain the levitation.

Then it happened. A twinge. A tug. A snap.

If her heart was not already broken, she felt certain it would be soon.

Make it stop, Rosellene thought. *The ache is almost too much to bear.* So too, the crowd. *Make them stop*, she thought. The teasing. The taunting. How she wanted to silence the crowd. Make them swallow their swords. Sew their lips together with a fine tapestry needle.

'Here, take it,' said Rosellene. Her slender fingers unfurled and there lay the ruby key in the palm of her hand. 'If it will stop the pain in my heart…I want it not.'

A calmness seemed to wash over Grindella, the tension dissipating from her body.

'Is this not what you want?' Rosellene saw the whites of her sister's eyes broaden. 'We shall trade. Caprion for the key.'

Grindella reached out for the key but Rosellene closed her fingers to conceal it. 'Caprion first.'

'Very well.'

Grindella made two quick hand gestures which saw Caprion first plummet to the ground then slide across to Rosellene's feet.

Falling to her knees, Rosellene released the rope from around his neck and watched as Caprion drew in a long, laboured breath. Beads of sweat rolled down his face, his head a mass of curls.

'Are you not forgetting something?' Grindella asked, hand outstretched. Rosellene desisted. Her stance was wide. Her pouty lips flattened.

Grindella shook her head. Steely were her eyes. 'You cannot win.'

Rosellene threw back her mantel and there revealed the linen bundle.

'Mirium Conn, daughter of Ivanhoe. I bind thee to the ground upon which you stand.' The linen cloth fell open. Inside lay a smooth, oval stone no larger than Rosellene's palm.

Grindella's body twitched. 'You would be wise to leave well enough alone.'

A white cord was wrapped once around the stone.

'Mirium Conn, daughter of Ivanhoe. I bind thee to the ground upon which you stand.' Once more, the cord was wrapped around the smooth stone.

Grindella's body ached.

For a third time, the words of the binding spell were spoken as the cord was yet again wrapped around the stone.

'What have you done?' Grindella's knees buckled and she collapsed to the ground. 'You cannot defeat me!'

But as she was splashed with oil, an attempt to cleanse her of dark magic, she caught sight of the stone in Rosellene's hand. 'You know not what you are about to do.'

Rosellene smiled. She knew exactly what she was doing. In her hand, she held a stone, cursed by Grindella herself, hidden in their grandmother's hut. Should she burn it, which of course, was her intent, the hex placed upon the stone would rebound to Grindella threefold.

'Understand that her old ways were finished,' Grindella implored. 'It was time for a new wave of magic to take hold.'

Rosellene inched closer to her sister. Her fingertips rubbed together. Flames erupted. 'Please!' Grindella begged.

But it was to no avail. Rosellene bound her body in a rope of flames then went to ignite the parchment that she held.

With the flames scorching her body, Grindella threw back her head and laughed.

'You think death is something to laugh about?' Rosellene retorted.

'Not at all,' said Grindella confidently.

'Then why do you laugh?'

Grindella got to her feet. 'That key is but one piece of the puzzle. Should you want to complete it, you will need my aid.'

And there it was, the bargain. She had known it would come. So close to death, they all realised how valuable life could be.

Rosellene stepped a little nearer. 'You are in no position to bargain.'

'Kill me,' Grindella raised her hands to the heavens. 'and Rawdendale will continue to crumble.'

She would not show it but Rosellene was beginning to doubt herself. The dark magic was powerful, and although she held tight to the rope flames, she could feel the poison leeching into the tips of her fingers.

'Your tongue is forked. With you gone, Rawdendale will surely flourish.' Rosellene watched her sister wince in pain as she tightened the rope bindings. 'I may decide to keep you alive. Then you can see with your very eyes how fine Rawdendale has become.'

'Be it on your head then,' said Grindella. 'May you never know where lies the second key.' And with each passing breath, the ropes constricted.

Chapter Forty-Three

Slow was the death from a hanging cage. Frozen in winter, burned in summer. Murderers. Thieves. Prisoners alike were held in the small enclosure till their flesh did rot and dry bones gripped the bars.

Now, a sorceress it held, and in the icy winds she reeled through the iron bands.

'You know not what you do.' Slender fingers slipped through the spaces between the bands. They tightened. Shook. 'A power far greater than any of us has seen, lies beyond that door.'

Rosellene watched the cage swing over the moat, the water tainted still with blood. 'We shall be ready for it.'

'You?' Grindella laughed. 'You are not prepared for what is to come.'

The dark, velvet mantle was drawn across Rosellene's chest, secured on the shoulder with a pewter clasp. The wind bit. Its teeth sharp. How she wished she had something to warm her hands. They had reddened and all sensation had been lost.

'Your tactics will not work on me,' said Rosellene, confidently. 'I do not scare easily.'

Grindella sunk to her knees, a bulk of satin and linen. 'Fearful is what you should be.'

A guard moved onto the battlement. His armour creaked as he bowed. 'My lady.'

'Do not look upon her face,' chided Rosellene. 'There shall be no more spells cast on this night.' The guard nodded, turning side on to Grindella, who now hissed at him from her cell.

'Listen not to her words,' Rosellene added. 'Stand here and no closer.'

After securing the second ruby-encrusted key, she had bound Grindella to her cage and put a protection seal around the iron frame. Still, she had her doubts about the length of time it would hold. They had to hurry.

'I warn you,' Grindella sounded desperate. 'You cannot do this alone.'

'I shall not be alone.' said Rosellene shortly.

Grindella huffed then took to the bars with both hands, shaking them most violently so that the cage rocked from side to side.

Rosellene made to leave. 'My time here is wasted.'

'Has the old woman told you what lies hidden beneath the castle?'

Rosellene faltered. Turned. Stared at Grindella beneath the hood's lining.

'She has not,' Grindella smiled and got to her feet. 'Hidden away in that chamber so no one can use it. Such an injustice, would you not say?'

Rosellene stared at her sister. The wind pushed past her on the wall walk. It had no manners at this time. 'Whatever is hidden must be so for a reason.'

'Power. She had to be in control. Thousands of spells, yet no one could wield them.'

Rosellene bit her lower lip. She should not ask, yet she was curious. 'Spells?'

'Thousands of them.' Grindella pressed her face against the bars. 'Like the one you cast upon me this very day.'

A hand reached inside her mantle. The parchment crunched between her fingertips.

Does Grindella speak the truth? Does a spell book actually exist? Hidden beneath the castle?

'My words are true. Sheltered here in the castle, you have not witnessed the rise of our kind. Our numbers are many and our strength grows with each passing day. No longer will we fear exile. With that book, the people will bow to us.'

Rosellene turned away. 'Relish the view.'

'Take me with you,' Grindella pleaded. 'You will need my skills.'

Her sister could not be trusted. There was no danger. No threat. No dark magic to encounter. 'That would be foolish.'

Grindella sneered. 'It would be foolish not to.'

'So says you.'

With that, she left the battlement.

'This cage will not hold me!' Grindella screamed. 'My fate shall not be to rot in such an enclosure. Take the advantage while you can. I shall not be far behind you, sister.'

Beneath the castle, Caprion used a firestick to guide their way through tunnels dark and narrow. Although his hearing had returned, he was left with a continual ringing in his ears, a buzzing like bees around a hive.

'You believe she speaks the truth?'

'I cannot be certain,' said Rosellene. 'It may be her forked tongue, yet we will not know until the door is finally open.'

'Let us linger not.' Caprion held the torch towards a second tunnel. 'She may soon be free of that cage. We must be first to reach the door.'

So below the dungeons they crept, through narrowing tunnels, the walls thick with sickly green mould. Bats, startled by the light, flapped madly across their path while spiders perched high in the corners. The air soon become thin and stale. The path ended and their gaze fell upon huge marble pillars, almost three times their height.

Rosellene moved quickly across the stone bridge, tranquil waters below, over to the far wall. 'We are here.'

And there appeared before them a door, curved and wooden, with golden hinges that gleamed so that one could see one's reflection. Upon it, no doorknob could be found and the keyhole was at the very top, so high, in fact, that you would have to stand on your tiptoes to reach it. Silence fell upon them both and it seemed they were thinking the same thought. How could two keys be turned simultaneously if there was but one lock?

This, however, was an ancient door, forged hundreds of years ago. It held many secrets and would not be opened by common thieves.

Rosellene hesitated.

'Whatever lies beyond the door,' Caprion reached for Rosellene's hand, 'We will defeat it together.'

With a nod, Rosellene stood on her toes and carefully slid the key into the hole.

They had not long to wait before a second keyhole was revealed, parallel to the first. It was not only the hinges that gleamed but the entire door as it transformed from wood to solid gold before their eyes. Rosellene turned her illuminated face to Caprion and smiled.

But the smile quickly faded.

Rosellene jerked. Caprion unsheathed his sword. For there in the darkness, Grindella stood.

'My timing is precise, I see.' Grindella marched triumphantly towards the golden door. 'Come now, sister. Did you really think that amateur binding spell would hold? It was, after all, only a matter of time before I released myself.'

Rosellene's heart raced. She could not think on any spell with the thumping of her chest so loud.

'Shall I be the first to enter?'

Not a sound was made as the door opened in on itself and a light, brighter than the dawning sun, struck their eyes. For a time, they were blinded, squinting at the golden haze. Then, slowly, shapes began to form and they could see coins, thousands of them, towering above them and chalices, gold, silver and bronze, hidden amongst the towers and jewels: diamonds, sapphires and emeralds of every size and shape.

Without hesitation, Grindella moved through the doorway.

Rosellene, however, had not yet moved. Struck by the sheer magnitude of wealth that lay before her, she stood frozen in the doorway. How was it that this had laid hidden from so many, for so long? What a blessing it would be to return it to the people of Rawdendale, piece by piece, trinket after trinket. Rosellene sighed. Taxes had been high during the reign of King Simon. A very, very greedy king so it appeared.

Caprion too, waited. He stood by her side. But there was no glint in his eye nor hunger for such riches. A man of simple pleasures, he valued not materialistic things. If it could not be bundled upon his horse, in small, woven cloth, then it was not worth having.

He had seen greed before. Watched men turn savage, killing for something no larger than a thumb nail. And although, he had not seen a great many treasures, that which he had seen was nearly always guarded by someone or something.

'Darkness hides in that room.' Caprion raised his sword. 'Shadows not seen before.'

Rosellene's lips parted but no words escaped. A nervous wave crept over her body. Keeping Caprion close, she pressed on.

The room had an unusual odour, a mixture of dust, mould and antiquities. It reminded Rosellene of the trunk in her chamber which was filled with linen dresses, a lining of muslin and cloves between each garment. Along with the smell, the heat too, was most unbearable.

Caprion had a mind to take off the layers of armour he wore but visions of dragons entered his head and he thought better of it. But would a dragon confine itself to a room such as this? And what good would treasure be to a dragon?

Surely it would not be likely to trade at the local markets. Caprion shook his head. The heat was making him delusional.

Having lost complete control of her feet, Grindella ambled, nay, raced amongst the glistening towers, touching with her eyes, hands and bathing almost entirely in the loot.

'Father would faint at the sight, would he not? Imagine, all this wealth beneath his feet.' She cast her arms wide and spun. 'How angered he would feel.'

Rosellene was silent. The hairs on her arm stood to attention.

'Now.' Grindella thrust her hands on her hips. 'Where would one hide a spell book?'

Rosellene stopped.

A cool breeze circled.

She slipped her clammy hand into Caprion's.

They were not alone. The shadow had stepped into the light.

'So,' came a deep, booming voice that shook the entire room. 'You come into my home uninvited?'

A long, red vapour floated above the mounds of coins. It drifted. Danced.

'Uninvited, nonetheless, it has been some time since I had guests.' The vapour dove into the sea of coins. Next, a mighty throne surfaced, of golden curves and red velvet. It floated across the room, coming to rest beside a large, cedar table. 'Come, take a seat. You must drink with me.'

Three chairs were brought from the golden depths and positioned at the table.

'Just a small drink. I shall not keep you long.' A procession of chalices flew through the air and landed gracefully on the table. 'I have been here, all alone, for so many years. You cannot imagine my boredom.'

The throne on the far end slid backwards along the slate flooring. There came a sudden gust of wind, and before they knew it, all three of them had been scooped onto thrones and pushed into the table.

From the head of the table, the voice resounded. 'It would be rude to refuse your host.'

Breaths were drawn. Eyes broadened, as the vapour transformed into a man.

A man who wore a crown. A man who once was king. A very insatiable king.

'There is recognition in your face, my lady.' King Simon turned to Rosellene. 'You know who I am?'

Rosellene nodded. 'The hall is filled with your portraits, my lord, and stories, they are many.'

The Insatiable King sat upon his throne. He wore a full-length tunic, drawn together at the waist by a massive, gold belt, each chain link as large as a small plum. A fine, mink fur was affixed to the shoulders of his camel-hair coat and resting upon his grey hair sat a decorative crown.

'But of course there are,' he gloated. 'I was adored by the people.'

Either the stories are wrong, thought Rosellene, *or the king has rather an exaggerated version of his life.*

His people had loathed him. High had been their taxes and these were not only paid in coin but produce, clothing and livestock too. Faith had been important to the king and he had seen to it that every man, woman and child had attended weekly church services. For a price, of course. Forgiving sins was not done freely.

A fine, pewter jug was raised and from it poured a sour-smelling liquid.

Indeed, wine should improve with age, thought Rosellene, *but how long has the wine been resting?*

'So you approve of my wealth.' The king's lips were stained red. 'Come to steal it for yourself, perhaps?'

'No,' argued Rosellene and all three of them shook their heads.

'No?' The king wiped his mouth with the back of his hand. 'Then what is it that you seek?'

'A book,' said Grindella. 'That is all.'

'And might I ask as to the nature of this book and why, when it is in my possession, I should allow you to have it?'

'It is old, my lord,' Grindella claimed. 'You would want it not.'

A frown appeared on the king's leathery skin. 'Yet you would lay claim to it.'

'Merely for education, my lord.' Grindella shrugged. 'Nothing more.'

The king nodded. 'Your studies are of which domain?'

'Herbology,' said Grindella quickly. 'I wish to invest in the study of plants and their healing properties.'

The king smiled. 'You think me a fool, child, that I do not know what lies under my very nose. You think I have not inspected every page in that book. Studied every spell, ritual and chant that it contains.'

A sharp pain entered Rosellene's head.

Listen to my words.

The pain grew stronger.

I fear we are in great danger. Sister, together we must work.

Rosellene glanced across the table at Grindella, who gently nodded.

It was true. High was the danger placed upon them. With the knowledge gained from the spell book, the king was a powerful threat.

'Are you not tired, your grace?' Rosellene asked.

'Tired?'

'You have guarded your wealth well,' she continued. 'Would you not like to relinquish the duty to someone else?'

The shadows deepened on the king's face. His beady eyes were swallowed by his cheeks. 'You want me gone so you can steal what is mine?'

'No, your grace,' Rosellene threw her hands in the air. 'We wish only to set you free from the spell that binds you to this treasure. To this room. To this castle.'

A chuckle echoed through the grand room. Several coins trickled from their mounds. 'You know nothing of the spell that binds me here.'

'What if we did?' Grindella rose from the table and approached the king. 'What if there were a way of releasing you?'

'Lies,' said the king and a redness crept towards the roots of his grey hair. 'I cannot be released.'

'There is a way,' said Grindella. 'In fact, the secret lies within these very walls.'

'And I say again, lies!' A clenched fist pounded on the table. 'I am to remain in this realm until every piece of the shattered ruby is returned. Every…last…piece. That is my fate. It cannot be done.'

Rosellene stood. 'Let us find those shattered pieces and may you be free from your bonds.'

King Simon moved towards a large, golden chest.

'Two hundred years I have searched for the pieces.' The lid of the chest was lifted. 'Still, the ruby remains incomplete.'

'What if I told you we know where the last remaining pieces are?' Rosellene edged closer. 'What if they are closer than you think?'

The king hesitated. 'And in return?'

'In return, you shall leave Rawdendale your wealth.' Rosellene cast her gaze upon the treasures in the room. 'The castle you once ruled is not as it was.'

The king fell silent. 'My wealth should be shared.'

'The people would be most grateful, your grace.'

King Simon agreed.

'You are close, are you not?' The king looked up, one grey eyebrow cocked. Rosellene continued. 'Few rubies remain lost.'

'It is true,' the king sighed. 'I could be free from this burden. From these jewels. From this magnificent treasure.'

'Rest, your grace.' Rosellene took the king's hand. Many rings adorned his wispy fingers. 'Your task is now complete.'

Slowly, knuckle by knuckle, King Simon allowed his fingers to unfurl. Two ruby-encrusted keys rested in his palm.

'I have come to like this abode and all it possesses.' He grimaced. Snapped his fingers closed again. 'Perhaps I shall stay a while longer.'

Rosellene's breathing quickened. 'Your grace?'

The king's voice echoed through the room. 'I shall stay awhile longer.'

'But the rubies, your grace?'

King Simon extended his open palm. 'I shall not be needing them. They are yours.'

Rawdendale crumbles outside. The rubies have to be united. But how?

'Your grace, I beg you.' Tentatively, Rosellene approached the king and took the rubies from his hand. 'Rawdendale will crumble without aid. Is that what you wish? For your kingdom, your people, to suffer?'

'I will keep my treasure and you will leave.'

'What of Rawdendale?'

'Be silent, woman!' The king spat.

Rosellene stepped back. She could feel the king's rage. 'You must not do this, your grace, please.'

Jaws clenched. Fingers curled. There was tension in the king's body. 'You will be silent.'

'I will not.'

Creases formed in the corners of the king's eyes.

His hand raised.

His finger twitched.

His longsword unsheathed.

'I will keep my treasure and you will leave.' The king's voice was demanding. He pulled Grindella close. The blade brushed the nape of her neck.

Caprion too, unsheathed his sword, edging closer. But his weapon could not match that of King Simon. He did not become wealthy through being weak. There would be no doubt. If pushed, he would spill Grindella's blood.

'Do nothing,' begged Grindella.

Her hair clenched in the king's hand, she was dragged backwards across the endless hoard of glistening treasure, knocking over, amongst many other things, a small, wooden cabinet.

'Enough,' King Simon roared. He tightened his grip on Grindella's hair and shook his fist wildly. 'I tire of your company.'

And with her head thrust back so that the throbbing veins in Grindella's neck were exposed, King Simon brought closer the blade.

Chapter Forty-Four

'You always were greedy, Simon.' Ivanhoe appeared in the doorway.

King Simon turned. The blade came to rest upon pale skin. 'I hear your castle lies in tatters, your grace.' he jostled.

'And I hear you are refusing to leave.'

King Simon threw back his head. 'I have come to like the place.'

'But now it is time to leave.' Ivanhoe strode across the room. He held a ceremonial staff in his hand. 'Your debt is complete. You are free to go.'

'I will not. This is mine and you have no power to take it.'

'I have power enough.' Ivanhoe raised the staff. The crystal tip reflected the torch light.

King Simon scoffed. 'That is no match for me.'

Rosellene agreed. Her father was not a warrior. He held no sword nor cared to wield one. His words were his power, but now, would words alone be enough? They would not. She slunk away behind a particularly high mound of gold coins, careful not to let her mantle brush any from the pile and moved towards the eastern corner.

Her father would need her help. His distraction would last only so long.

'So says the king who has both his hands occupied.'

King Simon's breastplate rose and fell heavily upon his chest. 'One slip and I bleed her like a pig.'

'That is one option,' Ivanhoe agreed.

King Simon's response flouted him. 'There is not another.'

Ivanhoe tapped the staff with his ring.

King Simon laughed. 'You wish to beat me with a stick?'

Ivanhoe edged closer. 'I see no stick, your grace.'

'Make no mistake. It may be elaborate, but it is still a stick.'

Ivanhoe paused. Gaze cast upon the treasured-filled floor, he said, 'That may be so, yet this stick wields great power. Release her.'

'Great power, you say.' King Simon tutted. 'And you wish me to release this woman so that your powers are not bestowed upon me?'

Woman. A little more confidence radiated within Rosellene. King Simon did not know to whom his sword blade was held. Had he known Grindella's identity, the blade would have been wet long ago. A sorceress and the king's daughter. A bargaining chip for certain.

Ivanhoe nodded but did not raise his eyes. 'There will be no yield.'

'I do not wish to yield.'

Ivanhoe raised his eyes and set them upon King Simon. 'You will want to yield.'

King Simon's stance widened. 'You are in no position to threaten me.'

'Yield!'

'I have a mind to spill her blood and be done with it.' King Simon said.

There came a sudden din and a crack appeared in the gold-dipped staff. Then another and another until the gold foil had all but peeled away, leaving exposed a piece of ashen wood, carefully spiralled, its crystal tip caged by the mouth of a dragon.

King Simon all but choked. 'Who is this devil that stands before me?'

'I, King Ivanhoe, do hereby banish you from Rawdendale, never again to return.'

Ivanhoe dropped his chin and Rosellene added two keys to the trunk. The ruby was complete.

'That will cost you dearly.' King Simon's voice bounced from wall to wall. With that, King Simon was drawn into the trunk and the lid shut with a bang. For a time, it shook most violently, until Ivanhoe threw his body over the metal lid. The iron locks were closed. One. Two. Three.

Silence hung over the room. King Ivanhoe wept.

Rosellene threw her arms around her father's broad shoulders as he laid his head upon the trunk.

'It is done, Father.'

The king shook his head. 'It is not.'

'The king is no more.' Rosellene raised her tear-drenched cheek from her father's cloak. 'He is gone.'

A quiver passed the king's lips. 'Yet he did not go alone.'

Her eyes wide, Rosellene scanned the room. A fearful cry crept from her throat. Caprion hung his head.

Grindella could not be found.

The king took his hands from the trunk. No longer did it shake.

'Her power had strengthened and her intentions were malicious,' considered the king. 'Perhaps it is a blessing.'

'Where does she dwell?' Rosellene asked.

'Between heaven and hell, itself.' Tears slid from the king's tired eyes and meandered down the crevices of his face. 'Should my fate be the same for condemning a child to such a place?'

Rosellene's throat constricted as though thick hands held her neck and slowly squeezed. *Is this a deserving end to the sorceress? She is after all, my sister.*

The king paced the hall and its grandeur. He paused for a moment by a small, wooden cabinet. His face fell. 'Perhaps I am wrong. We should bring her back.'

Rosellene's head shook. 'Why would we willingly bring her back? She has been the cause of so much suffering. It would be a sin to do so.'

'I fear we must,' commanded the king.

'Why must we?' Rosellene's voice rang loudly. She had not meant to but she stomped across the floor. 'Only to bring her forth for a trial and her whereabouts sounds like trial enough.'

Tension in his face, the king looked upon his daughter.

'King Simon did not go alone.' He stepped aside, an empty cabinet before him. 'Nor did Mirium.'

The cabinet was small, no higher than the king's waist. Darkly stained, it possessed two large hinges attached to a single door, upon which an enigma was ornately etched.

'She spoke the truth,' Rosellene said, shocked. 'A spell book exists.'

The king nodded. 'But what is to become of it? There is no doubt. She will wield it to her own advantage.'

The king sat at the table. His hands quivered like an arrow in flight.

Grindella had longed for the book all along, yet for what purpose was it taken? Did she mean to study its contents or was it merely a means to return? And what of the spell book? Rosellene thought. What powers lay hidden between the pages?

'No harm will befall us if they remain trapped.'

'She shall not be trapped long.' The king blessed himself. 'One battle may be over, yet I fear a far greater one has begun.'

Rosellene looked at her father, at the pain in his eyes, the fear in his voice. He had said nothing of the staff nor the magic that he used to wield it. She had assumed her father did not possess the skill of magic, that it had indeed missed a generation, passed only to his daughters. That was a mistake. His talent was strong. Perfected. Was it humility that caused the disguise or fear of discovery? In a sense, perhaps the answer lay in both.

She looked next at Caprion, at the man she loved. The longing to hold him was strong and overpowering. She fought it back. For now, her father's need was greater than his. She took in his features, though. Absorbed them into her blood stream. Her heart. Her very breath.

His golden hair had lengthened over the months, his soft curls dropped so that they now rested upon his shoulders and the dented pauldrons that covered them. The chiselled jawline now supported a beard. It was not finely trimmed, nor was it washed. Presently it was held in callused hands, elbows propped against his legs. He had not eaten nor slept in days and exhaustion had finally attacked. Weakened, he could not defend himself. And what of his mother? The fey? Would they be acquainted once more? Would she, perchance, get to see this glorious land that they called home?

They would again need to call upon the men of Rawdendale. The shademen. Fey. Ogres too. Perhaps even seek aid from the Nogard tribe and their scaly beasts. The men had weakened, though. They would need to regain their strength. Yet the duration would be short, for in that time Grindella's strength too, would grow.

'Be the king I know and love. Greet your people. Give them hope. Confidence in their great leader. Show them not the worry in your mind nor let them see the fear in your eyes. Not yet, at least, until a time has come that we know how to fight this new war and win. But do share with them your glory. Tell them of the great riches which have been returned. They have much to be thankful for. Much to rejoice.'

In the months to come, the men would indeed grow strong. Their love for ʰr king strengthened. The king no longer weak.

ᴵn the months to come, Rawdendale Castle would be rebuilt. Stone by stone, ˙ by tower, little by little, it would be moulded into a place of strength, rity and power.

s they left the chamber and all its wealth, Rosellene thought on herself. The that she considered a burden, rendered painful and futile, was now looked upon as a more fruitful practice. It had served her well in the recent past and would need to do the same in the days to come.

Whilst many questions remained, with many more to be asked, she would for a time embrace the loves that surrounded her. Life was precious. It should not be taken for granted.

And she knew that whatever fate lay in front of her, she would walk towards it. Confidently. Proudly. For she was the daughter of a king. A princess.

Rosellene of Rawdendale.